PROMISED

PROPER ROMANCE

PROMISED

LEAH GARRIOTT

THORNDIKE PRESS
A part of Gale, a Cengage Company

LIBRARY OF CONGRESS CIP DATA ON FILE.
CATALOGUING IN PUBLICATION FOR THIS BOOK
IS AVAILABLE FROM THE LIBRARY OF CONGRESS

ISBN-13: 978-1-4328-7720-0 (hardcover alk. paper)

Published in 2020 by arrangement with Deseret Book Company/Shadow Mountain

Printed in Mexico
Print Number: 02   Print Year: 2020

To David —
You are my happily ever after.

ONE

Mrs. Hickmore shuffled our party of hopeful strangers into her lavish dining room. The oversized chandelier that swung gently from the high ceiling, casting flames of flickering light across the room, was the largest I'd ever seen, and the two large tables covered in blue china and polished cutlery were long enough to fill the entirety of our dining parlor at home. I stopped, stunned by the sheer number of place settings. Mrs. Hickmore had not been exaggerating the size of her routs.

"She knows how to host a party, I'll give her that," my brother Daniel muttered, stopping beside me. "I've never seen so much silver in my life."

Someone from behind jostled us and a matron passed, yanking her young daughter forward to obtain a position closer to the front. Daniel scowled at them before his

7

dark eyes focused on me. "Margaret, you cannot be serious about going through with this."

"I am." Once I was married, there would be no more rumors preventing Daniel from marrying. And I would no longer have to endure the whispers regarding the scandal of my broken engagement. Everything would finally be as it should have been two years ago.

Mrs. Hickmore clapped her hands, silencing the excited murmurs. "Now, everyone." She surveyed us with a smile so full of satisfaction it squeezed her round cheeks up, making her eyes nothing more than small slits. "To your seats. You'll find your names at your plates for tonight only. Hereafter, you may sit wherever, or should I say *with whomever,* you wish. We don't stand on ceremony here."

She spread her arms, officially welcoming us to the opening of the event. Three gentlemen strode boldly forward, nodding at her as they passed, and one of the braver women laughed and followed in their wake. Soon the group moved almost en masse toward the tables, and footmen stepped out of the shadows to assist the more timid in finding their places.

Those who hurried around us carried

anticipation in their tentative smiles and hope in their excited eyes. Yet there must be others who, like me, sought a union of convenience. Others who knew how much giving your heart to someone hurt.

A woman paused and inspected Daniel with a calculated smile. Daniel turned his back to her and clasped my arm, his voice low and insistent as he said, "Change your mind. You don't have to go through with this."

Instead of seeing this party as a means to right the wrongs that had been inflicted on our family, he viewed my coming as a rash decision made by a heartbroken sister. It *had* been devastating to discover Edward, the man I'd pledged my heart to, had entertained a string of mistresses and had only pretended to care for me because of a stipulation of his father's. He had made me look such a fool for loving him. I had been a fool. Edward's family's estate bordered our own; his sister was my best friend and the woman Daniel wished to marry. We had known each other practically our whole lives. I should have realized it wasn't real, should have seen him for what he was, should have perceived that my love meant nothing to him. That I'd meant nothing to him.

But I hadn't. He'd courted me and made me laugh and treated me with all the attentiveness I'd ever longed for. And I'd loved him.

After I discovered the truth, I of course had my father call off the engagement. Yet for a long time it was all I could do to rise from bed each morning, the darkness of Edward's deception like a lake of poison seeping through my emotions, killing my happiness and drowning my efforts to move on.

Now, though, I was no longer brokenhearted. In fact, I was no longer controlled by my heart at all. And, if everything worked as I hoped, I never would be again. I had learned my lesson well. "This is what I want," I told my brother. All would be made right once I found someone safe.

Daniel sighed. "I can see you are determined. Let's get you settled."

"Ah, Miss Brinton. Mr. Brinton." Mrs. Hickmore stepped before us, grabbing each of us by the hand. "I'm so pleased you made it."

"Thank you for extending the invitation yet again," I said.

She patted my hand. "I am delighted you finally took me up on the offer, for of all the people here, I most wish you the match you seek."

"Thank you," I replied, flattered by her concern.

"Now, Mr. Brinton," she continued, "I believe you will find your seat there." She pointed toward the head of the second table. "And Miss Brinton, if you will follow me?"

She took my arm and led me toward the first table. Leaning over conspiratorially, she said, "It would not suit our purposes to have you seated too near your brother. Relations have a way of meddling at the most unfortunate of times where young ladies are concerned. I made certain he was situated with his back to you. You will be free to converse at your leisure." She tapped her nose knowingly before coming to an abrupt halt before her husband. "Oh, Henry. Look who finally decided to join us."

Mr. Hickmore took my hand in his bulky one. "So glad you made it."

Mrs. Hickmore beamed. "Won't she just be the catch of the party?"

"She'll have her fair share of offers — I'd wager this year's harvest on it. A man would be daft not to fall for those green eyes and that mop of dark curls."

His grasp on my hand tightened. I tried to free myself while mumbling something

11

about his being too kind, but Mrs. Hickmore cut me off, her eyes wide with astonishment. "A 'mop of dark curls'? You're calling this beautiful hair a mop? And 'dark' doesn't even describe it. It's more the color of that box you bought me, the one made from that Jamaican wood. Oh, what do they call it?"

"Mahogany," Mr. Hickmore offered.

"Yes, that's it. Very rich. I dare say, Henry, I don't think describing her hair as a mop is the compliment you mean it to be." She turned back to me. "Mop, indeed. Don't pay him any heed. I never do, you know."

"No, you don't," her husband grumbled, finally releasing my hand.

Mrs. Hickmore pulled me away, directing me to an empty spot at the table. "Here you are."

The man standing to the right of my seat glanced over, his gaze sweeping over me. His dark hair was styled with disregard, as though he'd just run his hands through it. Yet his perfectly snug dinner coat, outlining his muscled shoulders and trim form, was in the latest style, and his cravat, though simply tied, was starched and pressed and without spot. He carried an air of self-assured unconcern that didn't waver as Mrs. Hickmore proceeded with the introduction.

12

"Let me present Mr. Fredrick Northam. He owns a large and well-kept estate to the south of here, as well as a house in London. He enjoys riding, hunting, and has a keen eye for business. His grandfather was aristocracy and his mother one of the kindest women I've ever met. No one can deny that he is quite the catch. However, he's been known to break a heart or two with nary a backward glance, so be on your guard."

I was always on my guard now. As for the rest, this man appeared confident and disinterested. That he possessed a country estate far enough from my own neighborhood to provide a restart in life made him nearly perfect. Perhaps he was exactly what I was hoping for.

I waited for something to draw me to him, a spark of interest warning me to look elsewhere.

No flicker of attraction came.

Smiling, I said, "I assure you, I shall keep my heart quite secured."

Mr. Northam inclined his head, his smile unchanged though he raised a brow.

"And on your other side," Mrs. Hickmore continued, "is a man with such an upstanding reputation I didn't dare leave him out." The man she indicated finished his conversation with the young woman next to him and turned to greet me. His short hair was a lighter brown than Mr. Northam's, and his eyes were blue. His clothes were not quite so fitted, though still expensively tailored. His expression was guarded, but there was an ease to his smile that made me want to smile in return.

I only just kept myself from flinching away in alarm. Whatever this man's attributes, that moment told me all I needed to know. He was not safe; he would never do for me.

"Lord Williams is, from what I understand, the very epitome of a gentleman. Well-bred, well educated, well-mannered, and a baron to boot." She leaned toward me. "He's the reason half the women agreed to come so readily. I have placed you in quite the favored position."

I smiled politely. "Thank you for such a choice seat."

Mrs. Hickmore turned to the men. "Gentlemen, Miss Brinton is the best kind of company. She is intelligent, determined, and able to hold her own. Yes, Mr. Northam, even against your wit and wiles. Though bearing no title, her family has property and means, and her mother is a true lady in action and spirit. You both must promise to be kind to her, for she is my special guest, and she has had her fill of broken hearts already."

I cringed. That last line of information would have been better left unrevealed. But being straightforward would save time, and Mrs. Hickmore was determined to see as many matches made by the end of the week as she could.

"We shall be perfect gentlemen," Mr. Northam replied.

Mrs. Hickmore raised a brow. "I'm counting on it." Then she glanced at a man approaching her. "Ah, Reverend Michaels. Let me assist you."

Mr. Northam stepped beside me as she moved away. "Please, allow me." He pulled out my chair.

This was a good start. "Thank you."

Lord Williams glanced at us. His eyes narrowed before he turned to the woman on his other side and offered her his assistance with her own chair.

After seating himself, Mr. Northam inclined his head toward me. "Mrs. Hickmore doesn't beat around the bush with introductions, does she?"

It was more of a statement than a question. "I have certainly never known her to mince words."

He tilted his head, studying me. "Is your acquaintance of long standing?"

"She is an old family friend."

"Interesting. Only I thought it rather obtuse of her to introduce you in such a way. Well, that last bit, anyway. The rest was quite flattering."

My smile relaxed into one of shared sympathy. "She did little better with you."

He grinned and settled back against his chair. "Oh, I don't mind. I think she summed me up pretty accurately."

"She practically warned me away from you."

"As she should," Lord Williams interjected, turning toward me. "Northam is a rogue."

I hadn't realized he'd been listening, and I couldn't help but resent the interruption. But Lord Williams's comment didn't seem to bother Mr. Northam in the least. He smiled. "I prefer the term *rake*. It is so much more endearing, is it not?"

A rake — that was exactly who I needed. Why hadn't I thought of it before? He couldn't deceive me, for I already knew his character. And my heart would never be in danger from anyone so profligate. I'd be safe with him.

I sat back to allow the baron admittance to the conversation, though I kept my attention directed to Mr. Northam. "You two are

16

acquainted?"

"Cousins, actually." Mr. Northam raised his glass as though in toast of Lord Williams. "Can you not see the resemblance?"

I glanced between the two. There was nothing to indicate a family likeness. "Is it in the nose, perhaps?"

Mr. Northam laughed. "And so it is. How astute of you." He leaned closer. "What on earth are you doing here? Surely someone as charming as you doesn't need to attend a gathering such as this."

Footmen came forward with soup, and I waited until they'd finished serving us before replying, "No more than a baron and his wealthy cousin." I dipped my spoon into the white liquid and took a noiseless sip. The creamy broth and crushed almonds tasted like resolve and opportunity swirled together in a perfect blend of promise.

"Touché," Mr. Northam said. "Still, I cannot say I regret your coming. This party would surely have been dull without your presence. As it is. . . ." His gaze shifted past me to Lord Williams.

I turned. Lord Williams was shaking his head but stopped abruptly. His eyes met mine before he turned away and reached for his glass. "Yes, quite dull."

Something had transpired between them,

but I ignored it for the larger question: had Lord Williams intentionally insulted me by calling me dull? "I do not believe anything dealing with Mrs. Hickmore could ever be considered dull," I countered.

"This information augurs well for the rest of the week, does it not, dear cousin?" Mr. Northam asked.

Lord Williams's frown deepened. "Perhaps for you."

I raised my brows in polite question.

"He didn't wish to come," Mr. Northam confided. "He detests social gatherings of this kind. Something to do with his title and scheming young women."

I nodded. "A bachelor with a title. I understand perfectly."

Mr. Northam shook his head as though his cousin's predicament was to be pitied. "He compounds the problem of his own volition. I have told him time and again to simply offer for a young lady and be done with it."

"My cousin is a romantic," Lord Williams said sarcastically.

"Romance is highly overrated," I replied. "You are more likely to find happiness following your cousin's advice than in the modern sentiment of following your heart."

"Was it your own broken heart Mrs.

18

Hickmore spoke of, then?" Mr. Northam asked.

"Northam," Lord Williams chastised.

Mr. Northam smiled at me. It was a magnificent smile, no doubt used upon many occasions to beg his pardon. "I do apologize, Miss Brinton. That was very ill-mannered of me."

It was ill-mannered of him, but at least he did not hide who he was. "Your question was honest and direct, two traits I admire." Two traits more people would do well to develop.

"So, you will answer the question?" Mr. Northam asked.

I smiled. "No."

"No, you will not answer, or no, you do not come to this party bearing a broken heart?"

"Really, Northam," Lord Williams broke in. "Do leave the lady alone."

Mr. Northam's attention shifted to him. "If she wanted to be left alone, she wouldn't be here."

"But I doubt she thought she'd be harassed by the likes of you all evening."

"And you think she'd rather enjoy your company than mine?" Mr. Northam met my gaze. "My cousin and I have something of a long-standing dispute, and I believe you

19

may be the perfect person to answer it for us."

"Northam." Lord Williams sounded irritated.

Mr. Northam pressed on. "He argues that women prefer a man of manners and good breeding, and that is why women flock to him. I argue that it is only because of his title that anyone shows any interest in such a tedious and tiresome person. What is your opinion on the matter?"

Lord Williams carefully set his spoon down. "You must excuse my cousin, Miss Brinton. He is worse than usual this evening, and I apologize that you are bearing the brunt of his beastliness."

Mr. Northam didn't seem disconcerted by his cousin in the least. "Attempting to contain what he terms my 'beastliness' is the only reason he's in attendance, much to the disappointment of many young women who rather hope to catch his eye — and his title."

"To be sure," Lord Williams said, the sarcasm returning to his voice.

"And will we count you among those disappointed, Miss Brinton?" Mr. Northam asked.

They both seemed to wait for an answer. I set my spoon down. It was best to be clear about my intentions from the beginning; there was no point wasting time. "I am not in attendance seeking a title, a heart, or anything similar to romance. So, no, I will not be among the throng pestering his lordship for attention. Yet to answer the other part of the question . . ." I took a breath. "I sincerely hope that I will not leave disappointed. Indeed, I am full of hope that I may be counted among Mrs. Hickmore's success stories by the end of the week."

Lord Williams studied me a moment before raising his gaze to his cousin. Again something passed between them. Whatever it was, Mr. Northam took on a determined air and leaned close enough to murmur, "You know, Miss Brinton, I believe we shall get on very well."

"I do hope so," I murmured in return.

TWO

We rose after dinner in order to, as Mrs. Hickmore called it, "enjoy a little performance or two." What she meant, of course, was to provide an opportunity for those who wished to demonstrate talent, thereby increasing the likelihood of matches being made. I turned to Mr. Northam in the hopes he would escort me into the ballroom, but Lord Williams spoke first. "Miss Brinton, would you do me the honor?"

Mr. Northam shot me a wry glance but then turned and offered his arm to a different lady. I sighed and placed my hand on Lord Williams's arm, his light cologne mixed with faint saddle oil doing nothing to recommend him.

As we moved away, Lord Williams nodded to a few people before saying, "Most women would be honored by such an offer."

I glanced behind me. A woman was speaking to Mr. Northam, but his attention

22

remained on us. "Then it is unfortunate for us both that you chose to offer your companionship to me."

"Miss Brinton." His tone turned severe, and I looked at him in surprise. "I feel it my duty to warn you against any hopes of winning my cousin's hand. He is not interested in marriage."

He had to be. Mrs. Hickmore would not have invited him if he had not expressed at least mild interest in it. "Perhaps that is only because he has not yet met the right woman."

Lord Williams looked at me with mockery in his eyes. "And you think you are that woman?"

This baron was proving less the gentleman now that we conversed alone. Still, I maintained a polite facade, for he might have some influence over his cousin. "From what I gathered at dinner, I think your cousin and I are well suited."

"How so?"

"I would change nothing in his life except his marriage status and the amount of money available to him."

Lord Williams raised his brows. "Entering into the marriage state is often considered a life-altering event, changing everything about one's life."

23

I waited until we'd maneuvered around a few stationary couples before answering. "Yes, generally. But I am seeking a marriage of convenience. Mutual respect is paramount, of course, but I wish to avoid any of the deeper connections occasionally found within the state of matrimony. If he is, as you say, a rake, I believe such a union would suit your cousin perfectly. I do come with something of a dowry; not large enough to be called a fortune, but large enough to tempt some men." Dishonorable men like Edward. And, hopefully, indifferent men like Mr. Northam.

Lord Williams drew me closer while guiding me through the crowd at the door, though he didn't seem to realize what he'd done. But I noticed.

I would not be drawn in by any man.

I put distance between us before glancing around the large ballroom. Portraits and landscapes of differing sizes lined one side of the room, their gilded frames fitted together like well-placed stones in a dry-stone wall. Windows covered with closed, heavy drapes lined the other, while rows of hard-backed chairs took up half the wood floor, set up facing a large pianoforte.

Lord Williams gestured to the middle aisle and we moved toward it. "You are certain my cousin would fill such a role after so short an acquaintance?"

I shrugged. "It is impossible for two people to grow in regard for each other without interaction, and if I have the measure of him, we would hardly ever meet, let alone spend time together. I shall pass my days in the country, he in town, or wherever he prefers. His habits all but guarantee our separation, and I will certainly make no demands that he adjust his lifestyle."

"Eventually you will grow lonely and dissatisfied. What will you do then?"

Why it concerned him I did not know. "Needlepoint."

He shook his head. "What you seek is impossible."

"And yet it is accomplished every day, especially among your peers, is it not? You cannot convince me that my plan is not a sound one."

"One cannot convince a person who refuses to see reason," he muttered.

What a pompous man. Dropping his arm, I faced him. "Do you deny that most of those who meet this week and fancy themselves in love will not discover, within a year of their being wed, that those emotions that drove them to the altar have wilted and died?"

25

"I cannot speak for others. *I* would not allow such a thing." He gestured to a chair, indicating that I should take a seat.

Only a fool would believe one could retain another's affection simply by forbidding it to waver. "You, my lord, have never been in love."

Frowning, he took my hand to assist me in sitting. "You cannot expect a person to remain so stagnant."

He was as well-bred and well-mannered as Mrs. Hickmore had claimed, but he was also rashly arrogant and overly interfering. He was exactly the sort of man who would insist on more in a union than I was willing to give, though it would always be more about gratifying his own conceit than the concerns of his companion.

I remained standing. "And you believe your cousin is inclined to such change? That eventually his disregard for someone such as me will transform into a true devotion?"

"You misunderstand me. I was speaking of you. Northam would never form a regard for you because he cares only for his own desires, and he would never desire something good. Yet were he to decide to woo you, to win your heart and make you love him, he would be successful. He takes what he wants." His gaze held mine, his expression determined.

Little did he know I was just as determined. It was time to be rid of him.

I removed my hand from his. "He may be successful with others, but he would never be successful with me. With all due respect, my lord, I thank you for your concern on my behalf. But as you can see, I am resolved, more now than ever since you yourself admit that your cousin is exactly the sort of man I require. Your attentions will undoubtedly be better served speaking with someone interested in you, your title, or your opinions. In fact, there are some women just there straining to catch your eye."

He stared at me in silence a moment before bowing. "Thank you for the honor of your time."

"I wish you all the love you seek."

He turned and walked toward the side of the room, and I finally breathed easy. Hopefully that would be the end of our interactions, excepting the wedding and perhaps holidays if things developed with Mr. Northam.

Surveying the crowd, I searched for Daniel. Guests made their way into the room, happier now that they'd been both fed and introduced to prospective companions. Many stood at the back, seemingly reluctant

27

to claim seats, either because they'd just been sitting to dine and wished to stretch their legs or because they were waiting to see where others sat so they could position themselves to advantage.

By the end of the week, the hesitation would be gone. Announcements would be made. There was no guarantee, of course. But there was hope.

I would need to branch out, make more acquaintances if this endeavor were to succeed. Placing all my expectations on the first man I met was foolish. But the others could wait for tomorrow. Tonight, I wanted to relish in the hope — something I had not felt in too long.

I located Daniel near one of the windows, conversing with a gentleman. Both wore matching scowls. They were, no doubt, discussing the ridiculousness of such a gathering and bemoaning their need to see their sisters married.

I caught Daniel's eye. He nodded his acknowledgment. The man next to him eyed me and said something to Daniel, who narrowed his eyes and said something in return. The man must have complimented me for Daniel to assume that protective older brother expression. The man wasn't bad looking. A little shorter than I would have liked, but I wasn't here to be picky.

Perhaps branching out wouldn't be so difficult after all.

There were too many people between us for me to easily reach Daniel. Besides, Mrs. Hickmore had the right of it — relations did seem to get in the way of such things, and Daniel was the rule rather than the exception. But neither could I take a seat; the room was still too empty, and it would not do to sit alone and appear undesirable. I turned and feigned interest in the portraits, resolving to study the paintings until the assembly was called to order. Then I would find a seat. Away from Lord Williams. And hopefully near Mr. Northam.

The portrait before me of a woman with a thick lace collar and dark bushy brows bore no resemblance to the man in the next portrait, sporting a tiny nose and a large clefted chin. As I scrutinized the next few paintings, I realized that none claimed a resemblance to Mrs. Hickmore's round face or Mr. Hickmore's large features. I wondered if this entire wall of paintings represented a collection of strangers, portraits brought haphazardly together, bought for a discount because those who had commissioned them disliked them or couldn't pay for them. I strolled slowly, studying the men in outdated ruffled collars and women in now-unfashionable high-necked lace, until I stumbled upon one of the smaller pictures.

Its oversized frame was easy to ignore, the filigree flaking in one corner to betray a grimy gray beneath. But the lone girl, arms spread wide, face lifted to the sky as though sunlight instead of rain spilled down from the low black clouds, held me captive. No darkness of feature hinted at secret disappointments. No downcast eye told of a past she despised. No doubt creased her brow. Instead, she radiated peace and confidence. She radiated freedom.

I had once been that free. But I could not change Edward's infidelity, nor could I go back in time and protect myself from the disappointed hopes of love. I could only promise never to repeat the situation. I would not be deceived again.

Renewed resolve rippled through me. This was why I was here. To shed my past and claim my future. One day, when my heart was safe, I would again be free.

"Miss Brinton?" A hand touched my back.

I turned, returning to an awareness of the room. Nearly everyone had been seated and the loud chattering had died to whispered murmurings.

Mr. Northam offered me a smile. "I

believe they are ready to begin. Would you care to take a seat?" He indicated a few chairs nearby.

I glanced quickly around. Lord Williams was seated toward the middle of the room. I was in no danger from him this far away.

I returned Mr. Northam's smile, his expensive cologne wafting around me like the warmth of a welcoming fire. "I would like to very much, yes." He directed me to the chairs.

"Are you prepared for the showcase?" he asked once we'd settled.

I raised my brows at his choice of words.

"Do you not agree that in every performance there is a desire to exhibit oneself to advantage?"

"I suppose." Yet there were times when a presentation of musical skill was not for display but for the pleasure of passing time amiably. Perhaps Mr. Northam did not care for such things.

His shoulder brushed mine when he leaned closer. "Have I offended you?"

"Not at all. But I confess, I am a lover of music in whatever circumstance it is presented."

"As am I. I did not mean to imply that I do not enjoy music. I enjoy music a great deal, when there is true skill. I find it more

31

difficult to appreciate mediocrity when it is forced upon me in a setting such as this."

This I could agree with. I smiled. "Yet you did not stay away."

His shoulder brushed mine again, this time with seeming intent. "No, I did not."

We lapsed into silence as a young woman arose and performed a minuet on the pianoforte. Then commenced a steady stream of singing and playing. A man performed on the violin with some talent, much to the delight of several young women. When a woman who looked barely sixteen attempted an aria that seemed particularly unpracticed, Mr. Northam's attention shifted down the row. I followed his gaze and found Lord Williams frowning at us.

Was the entire week to be overshadowed by his disapproval?

"What was my cousin so desperate to speak to you about?" Mr. Northam asked.

"He warned me against you."

Mr. Northam met my gaze with interest. "Did he?"

"Yes."

"Yet here you are."

I settled further into my chair. "Here I am."

We listened in silence a moment more before he said, "Tell me, Miss Brinton, do you play?"

"I do," I admitted, caught off guard. "But I am not much of a performer."

"Do you sing?"

"Only when alone."

He smiled at my response. It was easy to picture him breaking hearts when he smiled like that, warm and with a hint that he knew a secret he might be willing to share. "Then I will not ask you to sing. But will you do me the honor of playing something?"

I laughed quietly. "Most certainly. Perhaps tomorrow when the room isn't quite so crowded."

"There is a lull. You could play now."

I realized the young woman had finished her performance and the crowd awaited the next.

Yet had he not just exclaimed how much he disliked such a display? "You wish me to perform in front of all these people?"

"You come across as someone with great skill at the things you do. I think most of this audience would appreciate hearing from you." He stood and held out his hand.

This was too unexpected. I shook my head. "Please sit down."

"It is too late. People are beginning to stare."

I glanced around. People *were* beginning

to stare. And had I not come for this? To see if there weren't a few gentlemen in this crowd who would suit me? While it would only take one, there was that notion of eggs and baskets and all that.

"Very well." I took Mr. Northam's proffered hand and stood.

"What will you play?" he asked, guiding me to the piano.

I shrugged and looked out at the crowd, searching for Daniel. He'd moved from where he'd been before, but I located him near the back. His eyes were wide, mirroring the surprise I felt by finding myself before the crowd. My attention slipped to Lord Williams, whose expression was in its perpetual frown. He was surrounded by women touching his arm, whispering in his ear, straining to secure his notice, but the whole of his attention was directed toward me and Mr. Northam.

Though he may have found fault with my intentions, I vowed Lord Williams would find no fault in my performance. I smiled to the crowd and took my seat on the stool. Mr. Northam placed some music in front of me. "Do you know this?"

It was a song my father had purchased for me the year before. I knew it by heart. "Yes."

"Shall I turn the pages?"

"If you'd like."

He nodded and stayed standing by my side as I began to play. The crowd hushed appreciatively, and I worked to contain my smile of self-satisfaction.

A few minutes into my performance, though, murmurs rippled through the crowd. I glanced over, trusting my fingers to continue playing on their own. Lord Williams was standing, fists clenched at his side. Our gazes met and the coldness in his expression pierced my confidence.

My fingers stumbled on the keys. I stopped playing.

He stared for a moment, anger and determination in his narrowed eyes. The whole room seemed to hold its breath with anticipation of his next move.

His attention shifted to Mr. Northam and a look of disgust entered his expression. He turned and marched from the room, slamming the door behind him.

A shocked stillness filled the ballroom. The next second, the party turned as one to stare at me. Murmurs started in the back, words like "cut" and "disgraced" carrying across the crowd. Then the room erupted with conversation.

Lord Williams had walked out. On *my* performance.

This was a disaster. I could never live this down. Who would have me after a direct slight from a baron?

I searched for Daniel. We would have to leave. I couldn't stay. Even the time it took to walk from the room would be too long to spend among this company now.

Lord Williams had ruined everything.

I started to stand. Mr. Northam placed a hand on my shoulder and bent to my ear. "Keep playing."

I turned to him in astonishment. "Your cousin walked out on me, sir."

"Yes. And if you do not keep playing, it will be seen as the insult it was likely meant to be. But if you continue, if you show his leaving had no effect on you, the audience will change their opinion and instead attribute his actions to extreme rudeness. Trust me."

I located Daniel. He looked thunderous, but someone a few rows ahead of him shifted and he was lost from view.

I was on my own.

Not on my own. I had Mr. Northam. Though for how long I couldn't be certain. Surely even he wouldn't remain interested in a woman his cousin had so openly disgraced.

I picked the song up where I'd left off,

fumbling through a few measures before I again found the rhythm of the music. I struggled to pull emotion from the keys, willing everyone to forget what had happened.

It was no good, of course. The damage was done. Lord Williams had shamed me. He had ruined my chances for securing the match that was to set me free. He had stripped me of my hope. It was all I'd had left to propel me forward, and he'd stolen it on a whim.

I hated him.

"You're doing wonderfully," Mr. Northam said. "They have forgotten already."

His words made me want to laugh at their ridiculousness. Instead, my eyes stung. I fought back. I would not shed a tear over this. I had suffered shame and humiliation before. I could suffer this.

When I'd ended the song, I stood and curtsied with a plastered smile. Either Mr. Northam was correct and the people in attendance had decided Lord Williams's departure had nothing to do with me, or they were too polite to show their actual thoughts, for the applause was loud. Daniel leaned back in his chair in a relaxed fashion, though his face was still red. He nodded at me, signaling I'd done well.

Mr. Northam took my arm. "You played marvelously. Better than I had hoped. Now we will walk slowly back to our seats. If we act as though nothing happened, then in their minds, nothing will have actually happened."

"You seem to know an awful lot about managing opinions," I said.

He smiled at me. "I'm a rake, remember? Managing opinions is what I do."

THREE

Two days later, I smiled my way past a small group of guests and slipped from the parlor into the ballroom, closing the door quietly behind me. The click echoed in the empty room like the locking of a cell door. In the silence that followed, I rested my head against the cool wood of the door and allowed my false smile to finally fade.

Though my brother and I had stayed in the hopes that the week could somehow be salvaged, not even Mr. Northam had shown more than a polite interest in me since Lord Williams had walked out on my performance. Not just my performance — he'd completely left the party. More than a few women now glared whenever I passed, tittering about how handsome he'd been, how no one else compared, and how I should never have been invited. The men had been polite but distant, uninterested in a girl spurned by a baron.

The note that had arrived from our father that morning requesting our return had come as something of a relief. But it also confirmed my failure. There was nothing left but to return home and reconcile myself to the disappointment.

I pushed away from the door. Rays of midmorning sun shimmered across the empty, dark floor, inviting me to share a dance, their brightness the only illumination in the otherwise dim room. Ignoring the invitation, I hastened toward the painting of the girl, desperate to see it one last time.

She still stood alone, still stood with arms spread, still lifted her face to the sky, welcoming the rain.

I would never be her.

I closed my eyes against the truth, but it twirled through my thoughts and settled in my heart as firmly as a rock sinking to rest at the bottom of a lake.

I would never be free.

A breath grazed my neck, sending wisps of hair fluttering against my skin. Before I could turn, a trace of expensive cologne drifted in the air and a low voice whispered into my ear. "This isn't the first time I have caught you studying this painting, Miss Brinton."

Mr. Northam. Why was he here? I kept my tone disinterested and adjusted the sleeve of my coquelicot spencer. "Are you following me, sir?"

"Could you blame me if I were?"

It was easy to see through his pretend flirtations. And to come up with a few of my own. "On the contrary, it would confirm my good opinion of your taste in company."

He chuckled and stepped around me to lean against the wall. His tall figure, dark green coat, and black hair proved an alluring contrast to the portrait of the yellow-coated elderly gentleman hanging above him. "When do you leave?" he asked.

"Within the hour, I expect."

"You do not appear disappointed to be departing early. Are you not concerned I shall be miserable without you?"

"Miserable? A lady can always hope." We would have been so perfect together, our meaningless banter filling whatever time we were made to spend in each other's company. And yet, what was the purpose of such banter now? "In all honesty, I am glad to be leaving."

His eyes darkened. "Williams is a black-guard."

The disdain in his voice was gratifying, and yet it was time to move past the morti-

41

fication of it all. Lord Williams would most likely live his life never knowing how he'd ruined mine. And I already knew how futile it was to harbor grievances against such people. "It's of little import. I shall never see him again."

"Dance with me?" Mr. Northam asked suddenly.

I glanced around the empty room. He'd closed the door behind himself so that we truly were alone. "One couple is not enough for a dance," I said.

His lips curved suggestively. "It is for a waltz."

The dance had been introduced in London a few months ago, and though the papers termed the dance scandalous, there'd been whispers that Mrs. Hickmore was not opposed to its being danced this week. However, being alone with Mr. Northam was enough to shred my already tarnished societal status. Dancing the waltz with him was certain to ruin my reputation permanently, and I still had my honor; Lord Williams had not robbed me of that.

I shook my head. "You will have to content yourself with a bit of conversation. Considering we are without a chaperone, it should satisfy your craving for scandal until I am gone."

Mr. Northam's voice dropped to a whisper. "I could *convince* you to dance with me." His eyes gleamed with the promise that I would not regret accepting his invitation.

For all his attempts at persuasion, I remained unmoved. I had Edward to thank for that. "If you merely wish to dance, I am afraid your efforts would be futile."

Mr. Northam shoved off the wall, removing the distance between us with a step. His eyes bored into mine; the laughter left his smile. "And if I wish for more?"

I hesitated, quelling the flush of anticipation as quickly as it had arrived. I had already resigned myself to leaving without a proposal. Unwilling to allow myself hope, I shrugged. "Our time together has run out."

"There is still time to make it a success."

He no doubt measured success very differently than most. "By Mrs. Hickmore's standards or by your own?"

"Both."

My breath caught. Whatever else he meant, he meant to propose. It was the only event Mrs. Hickmore would ever consider a success. Had my imminent departure made him realize how perfect we would be together? Had he finally understood what a quick and easy match we could make?

43

He tucked two fingers beneath my chin and tilted my face toward his. "A kiss to seal the deal?" His gaze shifted to my lips.

I placed a hand on his arm, forestalling his kiss, needing to hear the words that would bind us together. "What exactly are you proposing?"

"You have an apt way of choosing words." He leaned closer.

Boots clicked on the floor behind me.

We'd been caught. Alone. In a somewhat compromising position. Only a frank proposal could save me now.

Mr. Northam's attention shifted above my head and his smile disappeared. He dropped his hand but didn't step away.

"Margaret, there you are." The edge in Daniel's voice was unmistakable. Even so, relief filled me that it was only my brother who had discovered us instead of someone else in the party. He clamped a hand on my shoulder, its pressure sending me stumbling back a step. "The carriage is waiting. Excuse us, Mr. Northam."

I couldn't leave. Not yet. I looked at my brother, hoping to catch his eye. If he knew how close I was to a proposal, he might delay our departure. But his anger was focused on Mr. Northam, whose smile had become hard and mocking.

44

"Of course, Mr. Brinton. I was merely bidding your sister farewell."

Wasn't he going to tell Daniel? Wasn't Mr. Northam going to say the words?

Daniel's fingers dug into my shoulders. I attempted to shrug them off, but his grip tightened. "Come, Margaret. We are finished here."

I didn't yield to his pressure. I would not give up hope just yet.

Mr. Northam's amused gaze lowered, meeting mine. His expression grew unexpectedly intimate. This was the moment.

"I am sorry we were interrupted. I look forward to continuing our conversation soon." He captured my gloved hand and slowly lifted it to his lips.

He hadn't asked.

But he wanted to continue the conversation. He still wanted to propose.

"I would like that very much, Mr. Northam," I replied, praying my smile was encouraging instead of disappointed. I had waited this long. I could wait a bit longer.

Daniel ripped my hand away and slipped it around his arm but refrained from speaking. He would air all his censures once we were alone in the carriage.

I didn't care. As we turned to leave, I shifted my parting grin from Mr. Northam to the painting of the girl welcoming the rain.

"What were you thinking?" Daniel demanded, not caring that I was struggling to secure my bonnet as he pulled me down the front steps to the tree-lined gravel drive and our waiting host and hostess.

I ignored his question, smiling and dropping a curtsy at the Hickmores, grateful they provided a temporary distraction from Daniel's reprimands. "Mr. Hickmore, Mrs. Hickmore."

"Ah, you found her," Mrs. Hickmore exclaimed, her round face lighting up. "No doubt in the middle of a large group of very downhearted young gentlemen."

"I wish I had," Daniel muttered, shaking Mr. Hickmore's bulky hand.

Mrs. Hickmore glanced inquiringly at me. "Thank you again for inviting us," I said quickly to avoid questions.

Mrs. Hickmore's lips pressed into a small frown. "I am sorry it started off poorly. I shall never invite that Lord Williams again. Behaving so rudely toward you. His actions are not to be excused. I do regret that things did not turn out as you had hoped." She leaned in until I could see each pore on her nose. "Perhaps we shall have another gathering and invite only the one young man who proved most promising." She gave me a knowing smile and winked, then straightened, her head bobbing in agreement to her own comment.

Daniel tensed at the reference to Mr. Northam. After clearing his throat, he said, "We should be on our way."

Mrs. Hickmore frowned. "I wish you an uneventful ride home, Mr. Brinton."

"Thank you, Mrs. Hickmore. I assure you we shall be quite safe." He placed a firm hand on my back.

"Give my regards to your father," Mr. Hickmore said.

"And mine to your mother," Mrs. Hickmore added.

I curtsied once more before allowing Daniel to direct me to the waiting carriage. He assisted me in, climbed up behind me, and shut the door. I settled onto the cushioned rear-facing bench while he sat opposite and rapped on the ceiling. The carriage jerked and slowly drew down the drive.

Hours of traveling stretched before us. Earlier, the thought hadn't disturbed me. Though my younger sister Alice was sure to be disappointed not to have a new brother-in-law in the making, I missed my morning walks around the lake on our estate and the quiet evenings being in the company of only my family. But now the hours of sitting would be fraught with images of what might have been had Daniel not intervened.

Struggling to resign myself to the journey, I turned my attention to the window and the Hickmores' diminishing house. A figure stood on the stairs. It took only a second to realize Mr. Northam had followed us outside, his unmistakable silhouette unmoving against the pillared white building. I gasped with delight.

Daniel glared out the window, then huffed as he sat back. "Have you gone mad?"

The carriage turned and Mr. Northam disappeared behind the trees. I closed my eyes so Daniel's sour expression wouldn't tarnish that final image of Mr. Northam on the step watching me drive away. It was all I had to feed my hope.

"Margaret!"

I peeked at Daniel through half-shut lids. "Shh. I'm dreaming."

"Dreaming? Of Northam? Or of how it felt to be kissed again?"

I shot up in my seat. "Excuse me?"

"You're lucky I was the one who discovered you instead of one of the guests or even Mrs. Hickmore. What would you have done then?"

He thought we'd kissed? My face burned. I had not realized Daniel would assume I was so lacking in morals. "He didn't kiss me."

"But it was your intention to allow him to, was it not?" His tone turned derisive. "You needn't have made a fool of yourself. Northam is a rake. If you had asked, he would have given you a good kissing the first night."

My insides roiled at the suggestion. "I would never permit a man such liberties without being engaged to him."

"Are you saying you were not about to let him kiss you?" Daniel leaned toward me, emphasizing his point.

I drew back and crossed my arms. "I do not believe it is any of your business what I was or was not going to allow."

"On this trip you have been my sole matter of business," he responded through clenched teeth.

I rolled my eyes, but since he had come only because I had wished it, I yielded. "Fine. Yes, I would have allowed Mr. Northam to kiss me, if you hadn't stridden into the room, in all your holy glory. But only after he'd proposed."

Daniel's brows shot up before knitting together with concern. "Northam is not the marrying type. Whatever he said, it wouldn't have been followed by a proposal. But even if he did propose, I would never permit you to marry him."

I scoffed, irritated by his assertion. "Fortunately, I am not in need of your permission. Father won't refuse, not when Mr. Northam is a gentleman."

"He will once I inform him of Northam's reputation."

The restraint on my frustration gave way. "If I do not care about the rumors, I see no reason why they should matter to you! You cannot want me dependent upon you, Daniel. Do you realize how humiliating that would be? And what will become of Alice? My remaining unwed may all but ruin her chances for a good match."

"Anyone other than Northam, Margaret."

"At least with Mr. Northam I'll know what I'm getting. Say what you will, but it would be a fine match for both of us. Mr. Northam is not so wealthy that my dowry would go unappreciated, yet his estate is reputed to be quite breathtaking. He would obtain a wife who would not pester him with romantic sentiments, and I would finally obtain the status of married woman."

Daniel opened his mouth, closed it, settled back against the seat, and crossed his arms.

"He would never love you. You will never be happy without love." His voice was quiet but certain.

I shifted and stared out the window at the passing meadows of sheep. It was true that marriage to Mr. Northam was the opposite of what I had desired two years earlier, when I had giddily agreed to Edward's proposal and my family's expectations of our union. But it was exactly what I wished for now.

FOUR

The carriage became stuffy and cramped as the hours passed and the sun remained high in the sky. The scene outside stayed nearly unchanged, flashing between sheep, fields nearly ready for harvest, and occasional villages. And still Mr. Northam's image did not leave my mind.

Suddenly, the carriage jerked and tilted sharply to the side. My hands shot out for balance as our coachman John cried a warning. Daniel's head slid forward, the pillow he'd propped under his head sliding with him until it slipped and his head whacked against the wall. He bolted upright, only to be thrown back by the carriage's sudden stop.

"What is going on?" he demanded.

I shook my head in ignorance, straining to keep from sliding out of my seat.

Daniel shuffled along the bench toward the door, but it swung open before he reached the handle. John's weathered face peeked inside.

"Apologies, master, miss, but the carriage lost a wheel."

"A wheel? Our carriage has lost a wheel?" Daniel grabbed at the door frame and heaved himself out.

"Yes, sir," John replied, his voice moving around the back of the carriage. "Not sure how it happened."

"Hmff."

"Someone will have to be fetched to fix it," John continued.

I sighed. If only the wheel had fallen off while we were still at the Hickmores'. I could even now be walking the gardens, my hand on Mr. Northam's arm, the kiss of his proposal warm on my lips.

"How long will we be delayed?" Daniel asked.

"Hard to say, sir, but I'd expect most of the day."

Daniel's face reappeared in the doorway, consternation etched in the lines around his mouth. "We're going to be here a while. You might as well get out."

"I would like nothing more." I clasped his waiting hand and he assisted me down the abnormally large drop to the ground. Placing my hands on my hips, I glanced around.

The road was worn but not large. Trees lined one side of the lane, and a wide, open field stretched along the other. It was peaceful.

I frowned. For once, I would exchange a peaceful road for a heavily traveled one if it meant receiving aid and arriving home sooner. "Where are we, John?"

"About three miles east of Welborough, miss."

Welborough. But that meant —

I grabbed Daniel's arm. "Daniel, did you hear? We must be very near Rosden!"

"Yes, miss," John said. "Not but two miles at most."

"Oh, Daniel, let's go. I would love to look at the lace. The shops near home never bring in anything near as lovely."

Daniel's expression soured. "I have no interest in lace, Margaret."

"But we have nothing for Alice, and I promised I'd bring her a present. I had planned to find something when Mrs. Hickmore took me to town, but then we left today. I cannot return home without a gift."

"You and your promises." But his sternness faltered, undoubtedly from picturing the disappointment on our ten-year-old sister's face when she realized it was his

54

fault we hadn't brought her a present.

I narrowed my eyes and waggled my eyebrows. "And I am certain Louisa would adore a lace handkerchief." Though no announcement had yet been made, Daniel and my best friend were in love, and a general expectation of their union had existed for some time.

His frown deepened. "Fine."

"You will have to fetch my reticule." Daniel reached around inside the carriage. "No, Daniel. Right back — no — down there. Yes. Thank you."

He shoved my reticule into my arms with a grunt. "John, we'll hire a carriage in Rosden to take us home."

"Are you sure you'd prefer to walk, miss?" John asked. "You could wait till someone passed by."

"I'm afraid we would be waiting all day," I said, retying my bonnet. "I don't mind the exercise. The road is lined with trees, and we shall walk in the shade." I slid my hands farther into my kidskin gloves, waved goodbye, and followed Daniel as he trudged down the road. He set so brisk a pace I had to pull on his arm to slow him to a comfortable stroll.

Before we had walked far, the sight of horses approaching from the direction of

Rosden drove us to the side of the road. A carriage much finer than our own, with a coachman and two footmen in livery, slowed to a stop next to us.

I scarcely had time to note that its coat of arms indicated the carriage belonged to one of the aristocracy before a footman with a rather long nose stepped down. "Pardon me, miss, sir. His lordship means to inquire if you are in need of assistance."

Daniel moved forward, but I placed my hand on his arm to stop him. Peers of the realm did not stop to offer assistance to strangers. While Daniel might not have much to fear from the encounter, the idea of being in an unfamiliar carriage with an unknown aristocrat was not a comfortable thought for me.

Daniel glanced at me. "Please thank his lordship for the inquiry, but we are enjoying a stroll to Rosden."

"His lordship would ask you to allow him to convey you to your destination."

My grip tightened on Daniel's arm. Why was this man being so persistent?

Daniel shook his head. "Again, we thank his lordship, but my sister is quite intent on walking."

"You do not wish to be conveyed in his lordship's carriage?" The footman lifted his chin and peered down his nose at us. It was impossible that he could still see us when he assumed that stance. His nose had to get in the way of his vision.

The handle to the carriage door turned and the footman scrambled to grasp it. I stifled a gasp as Lord Williams stepped out.

With such a condescending footman, I should have known.

Daniel bowed, jostling me, and I bobbed a stiff curtsy before meeting Lord Williams's icy blue glare with one of my own.

"It would be my honor to assist you," Lord Williams said with a slight bow. His words were clipped, his tone formal. I could only imagine how annoying it must be for him to lower himself by offering us assistance.

"No, thank you." The sharpness in Daniel's response was gratifying. "We would not wish to inconvenience you."

"I assure you it would be no inconvenience at all." Even as he spoke the words, the baron rolled his shoulders back as though steeling himself against the probability of having commoners in his carriage.

Arrogant man. All three of us would have been much better off if he had refrained from stopping.

The sound of wheels approaching from

the other direction turned my attention. An empty hay wagon had maneuvered around our broken carriage and rumbled toward us.

"Daniel, this man appears to be traveling toward Rosden. Perhaps he will be so good as to provide us with transport so that we need not impose upon his lordship."

The driver pulled to a stop. "Is one of you needin' a lift? The coachman down the way indicated you might."

Daniel stepped forward. "My sister and I need to catch a stage in Rosden. Would you mind greatly?"

The driver glanced at me. "My wagon ain't fittin' for a lady."

"Oh, I am not afraid of a bit of straw," I replied.

Lord Williams stepped forward. "You should not ride in a dirty hay cart when there is a carriage at your disposal."

Given his rudeness at the Hickmores', I should not have been surprised that he was so impertinent as to tell me what I should and should not do. His eyes narrowed at the driver and his lips pulled into a frown, as though his disapproval alone could send the driver on his way.

Struggling to hide my indignation, I said, "There is no place to turn your carriage, my lord, and that dirty hay cart is headed in the direction we need to go. If, however, you are intent on rendering your services, perhaps you would be so kind as to provide our coachman with conveyance to Welborough. We would certainly be in your debt."

Without waiting for a response, I walked to the back of the wagon. "Daniel?"

Daniel frowned and glanced between me, the baron, and the driver. I tapped my toe to urge him to hurry, but suddenly the baron was beside me. "At least allow me to assist you into the cart."

I jerked away from him. "No! I mean, no, thank you. I am able to manage for myself."

His lips thinned and he stepped back. I turned my attention to the wagon. Its bed was as high as my thighs and there was no step attached, eliminating any means of easy access. I cursed Daniel's slowness, knowing I would look foolish insisting on his help after the baron had offered.

I searched for anything upon which I could step to hoist myself up, but nothing availed itself for my use. My only option appeared to be shuffling in by sitting on the edge of the wagon and swinging my legs up in a most unladylike manner. The floor of the wagon was littered with straw; I would be filthy before I was even able to stand.

There was no way to enter without help.

"May I?" The baron hadn't moved, but his lips were curved into an amused smile.

I would rather walk for miles than accept his assistance. "On second thought, this wagon is much dirtier than I anticipated, and I find I am rather looking forward to the walk." I turned my back on the men.

"Margaret, here." Daniel appeared next to me and hefted me into the wagon so unceremoniously I fell to my knees.

The driver quickly extended a hand and helped me to my feet. "Might be best if you remain standin'."

I tried to smile, but it felt more like a grimace.

The wagon rocked as Daniel climbed in. I peeked at the baron through my lashes and found him frowning at me, disapproval expressed in every feature of his plain face. It rankled that he should have so unjustly ruined my future. But as a person of title, he probably never thought about those of us below him in status. I, at least, had shown how little regard I held for him.

A blossom of smugness replaced my humiliation and I smiled brightly. "Good day, my lord."

He met my gaze with the same icy stare as before, which only made my grin bigger.

Perhaps one day he would learn to take more care with those around him.

The footman positioned himself behind the baron, and even though my head was now quite above his, he still managed to look down his nose at me. I had never met such a pair of supercilious people.

The wagon's sudden movement forward threw me off balance. I grasped the railing.

"You made quite an impression," Daniel said, stepping next to me and grinning.

"If I did, I owe it all to you," I muttered.

"Do you think he'll offer his aid to John?"

I shook my head. "He won't stop for a servant."

"Let's wager on it."

"A wager?" I searched my mind for something worth the wager.

"Yes," Daniel said. "I'll wager for one lace handkerchief."

A lace handkerchief wasn't enough. "No. You must take Louisa out on the lake. Just the two of you."

Daniel scoffed. "She'll never agree."

"Then you have nothing to lose."

"Fine. And you'll have to go with Mr. Lundall."

"Daniel!"

"Those are the terms."

Was it worth the risk of losing and having

to take a boat ride with a man who refused to accept our incompatibility? I glanced back down the road. The baron's carriage wasn't slowing. It was worth it if it got Louisa and Daniel alone together; maybe he'd finally propose. "Agreed."

The baron's carriage passed our own broken carriage. Smirking, I elbowed Daniel. "You lost."

"No, look." The carriage had stopped. The long-nosed footman got down and spoke to John, then moved to the side of the road. John walked to the carriage and took the footman's place.

The baron had offered a ride to John after all. It made no sense.

"Enjoy your solitary time with Mr. Lundall," Daniel said.

FIVE

The next morning I wound my way across the lawn and down the steps leading to the garden and, a little farther, the path to the lake. We'd arrived home too late for much more than goodnights. I hadn't even been able to give Alice her present on account of her having already gone to bed with a cold.

A breeze blew through the trees. Birds called and insects buzzed among the reeds. The calm water, lapping at the shore as though offering a caress, reflected white billowing clouds. A few rocks jettied into the lake, tempting me with the promise that by walking on them I could walk away from all the trouble men like Edward and Lord Williams created. Unwilling to resist their beckoning, I stepped along the dead-end path until water threatened to wet my boots. The air tasted wet and clean. This is exactly what I had missed by being away. This is exactly what I needed today.

"Margaret!"

Startled, I flung my arms out to keep from falling into the water and turned to see a chagrined Louisa, her hand covering her mouth. "I'm so sorry," she exclaimed, her quiet voice barely audible. "I didn't mean to surprise you."

"Louisa. Just the person I hoped to meet." I made my way back to shore.

"But what are you doing here? You should be gone at least another few days. Unless —" She gasped with delight. "You are engaged?"

I shook my head. "I never got the chance." We walked the path along the shore and I tore a leaf off a tree as I relayed everything that had occurred. "I was so close. Mr. Northam is truly the most perfect man I have ever met."

"Is he indeed?" Louisa bent and broke off a flower, adding it to her bouquet. "Have you told your family of him? That much perfection would make me uncomfortable."

"You understand I mean perfect for me. I hardly think most would even consider him a good match. And, no, I haven't told my family. I want it to be official before I give them hope." I studied her. "You don't think Daniel is perfect?"

"No." Her light skin pinked at her cheeks.

"Everyone has faults."

"Daniel's is to make people miserable."

"You shouldn't say such things."

"Why not? It is the truth. He made me miserable with his actions, striding in just as I was about to finally rediscover happiness. And he makes you miserable every day by refusing to formally ask for your hand." If only Daniel wouldn't allow Edward's actions to affect his own, he and Louisa would be happily settled and I wouldn't feel guilty for my role in it, unintended though it was.

"Please." She touched my arm. "Let's not speak of it."

I shrugged. "Well, you may not wish to speak ill of him. And I own that he's a good enough person when he wants to be. But I consider him very high-handed. He even went so far as to tell me that even if Mr. Northam proposed, he wouldn't let me marry him."

"But he has no say in the matter."

"Yes, and I reminded him of it, too. I believe he thinks I am getting desperate. He doesn't understand."

"Your brother is protective because he cares for you. He wants what is best for you." She stopped to add another flower to her bouquet.

It didn't matter the reasons behind Daniel's actions. "Making someone live the way you think they should is not caring. He should encourage me —"

"Margaret! Over here!" Daniel waved from the top of a large boulder that lay half buried in the water. He was barely visible through the trees. His arm froze when Louisa stepped next to me. He jerked his hand down, stepped back, stumbled off the rock, and disappeared into the water.

"Oh, dear!" Louisa exclaimed.

Daniel reemerged, gasping, clearly uninjured though his hair was plastered to his face and his clothes clung to him.

"I think I should go," Louisa whispered. But she didn't move, her attention fixed on Daniel. It must have been a riveting sight for the man she loved to be standing so ridiculously wet before her. A titter escaped me.

Louisa turned bright pink. "I — oh." She thrust the flowers into my hand, turned, and fled back down the path.

I would definitely tell this story at their wedding dinner.

As I walked to the boulder, Daniel slogged to the shore, looking more ridiculous than I had ever seen him. Served him right.

I tried to hold in my amusement, but a snort sounded at the back of my throat. I

66

threw my hand over my mouth as laughter erupted from me. Daniel had embarrassed himself more effectively than any scheme I could have ever executed. If I had been at all adept at painting, I would have immortalized Daniel exactly as he appeared then, cravat hanging limp, coat and vest clinging to him. Then I would have hung the portrait in our entry.

No. I would have given it to Louisa for a wedding present so she could hang it in her entry.

"Margaret, this is not funny!" Daniel strode out of the water, his boots squishing with each step.

The sound made me laugh harder. "Yes, it is." I leaned on the boulder, no longer trying to restrain the laughs.

Water suddenly ran down my hair into my face. I gasped and straightened. "Daniel!"

He smirked, shaking out the coat he had twisted above me. He draped it over his arm and propped an elbow on the stone. "Refreshing, isn't it?"

A swampy smell now clung to me as water trickled down my back. Anger and laughter battled within. "No! It's revolting and wet and — and —" The image of Daniel stepping off the rock flashed and I gave up on anger. "And highly amusing."

Daniel scowled and struggled out of his waistcoat as though it were a competitor in a wrestling match. "I assume Louisa ran off *after* my . . . accident."

"Admit it," I said, setting the bouquet next to me. "The whole situation is laughable."

His lips twitched. "You're absolutely correct." He lunged and wrapped his arms around me in a tight hug. I shrieked at the sudden damp.

"Just wanted to assure you I harbor no ill feelings." His own chuckling rang through the air.

I shoved against him, breaking free of his grip. "Ill feelings for what?"

"For surprising me with Louisa's presence. Now help me off with my boots."

"It was not my fault you were perched on that boulder," I objected.

He lifted a leg and held it out to me. His boots were covered in gooey mud.

"Daniel, they're filthy. I'll ruin my dress."

"You're wet, so you already have to change. Come on."

"My being wet is completely your fault, as is the condition of your boots. Don't blame your clumsiness on me." But he was in obvious discomfort, so I stepped forward to help.

Once the boots were off, he dumped the water out of them and looked at me. "You look like you've been rolling in the mud."

My dress was covered in green and brown slime. I threw my hands in the air in exasperation.

His smile turned more genuine. "Thank you for your help."

I held out my now mud-splattered dress to assess the damage. "At least this wasn't one of my favorites."

He stripped off his dripping shirt and threw it on top of his vest, coat, and necktie. "That's better."

He was now bare from the waist up. "Daniel, what if someone sees you? You should at least retain your shirt."

"Who's going to see me?"

"Louisa?"

He shook his head. "I'll be lucky if she ever returns." He wrestled his feet back into his boots. "We need to hurry if we're going to change before breakfast."

Piling his clothes in one arm, he threw his other arm over my shoulder and we headed up the path, sniggering at the squish of his boots.

By the time the roof and upper floor of our pink-stone country house rose into view, Daniel's hair had frizzed from drying in the sun. A smile of contentment covered his face. It was as good a time as any. "Why don't you formally ask for Louisa's hand?"

His smile faltered. His arm slipped from my shoulder and dropped to his side.

"Make it official," I pressed.

The smile disappeared. "Not yet."

"You don't want her suffering through another season, do you? What if her parents determine she's waited long enough and begin to doubt your intentions?"

He shook his head. "They'd never doubt my intentions."

How he could believe that, considering the actions of their own son, was beyond me. "Daniel, they would be foolish not to after what Edward did."

"I am not him," Daniel said firmly. "I will ask her once I have a solid income. You know that."

"You are set to inherit this." I swept my hand through the air to indicate the house and all the land surrounding us. "Surely Father will help you. And with Louisa's dowry —"

"I would not touch her dowry for anything. It will go directly to jointure and portions. No one will accuse me of marrying her for money."

This was why he wouldn't ask. Because Edward had pretended to love me to obtain my dowry and access to his father's funds.

"No one will even think such a thing. Unless you have a mistress hidden somewhere, biding her time until —"

"Miss Brinton? Miss Brinton!" A man's voice called from up the path, interrupting me. A horribly wheezy, horribly familiar voice.

I froze, my only movement an automatic intake of air.

"Miss Brinton?" the man called again.

I grabbed Daniel's arm and pulled him backward.

Daniel's brows rose, but when the man's perfectly combed blond hair peeked over a bush, Daniel actually had the nerve to smile. The styled hair jarred me into a realization of my predicament. I was a mess, and I was about to be confronted by one of the dandiest men of my acquaintance. I clutched Daniel's arm tighter. "I cannot be seen," I hissed.

Daniel glanced at me but ignored my comment. Instead, he scrunched his nose. Then he sniffed theatrically. Twice.

"Daniel," I chided.

Mr. Lundall appeared on the path before us and halted. There was no escape now, but that didn't stop me from stepping behind Daniel. If he was a good brother, he would devise a means for allowing me to return to the house unhindered, perhaps by creating some excuse so I could slip away.

"I had best greet him, don't you think?" The twitch in Daniel's lips belied the civil tone in his question. He was going to abandon me.

"Daniel, you wouldn't dare. Please." I glanced around, but the only way to the house was now blocked. Without Daniel, I had no means for escape.

Daniel shook off my grip and moved forward, his arm outstretched in greeting. "Mr. Lundall, what a pleasure it is to sme— see you again. I had not thought we would be meeting you again so soon." *Sniff.*

"Egad! What happened?" Mr. Lundall stepped back, ignoring Daniel's proffered hand. He lifted his quizzing glass and surveyed Daniel with widened eyes.

Daniel lowered his hand and glanced at me with a smirk. "Will you excuse me, Mr. Lundall? As you can see, I have suffered a slight mishap and wish to change before breakfast."

I made to grasp Daniel's arm, but as if reading my thoughts, he took another step away from me.

Mr. Lundall glanced at me. "You don't seem to be the only one." He returned to his inspection of Daniel. "Though, really, your lack of clothes — it will be more like dressing than changing . . . but by all means. . . ." Mr. Lundall offered Daniel a dismissive bow.

Daniel paused under the arbor at the base of the stairs, produced his wet handkerchief from the pocket of his coat, and held it out to me. I didn't move. He shrugged and, putting it over his own nose, turned and walked up the stairs leading to the lawns surrounding the house.

"My dear Miss Brinton."

My gaze flew back to Mr. Lundall. His cravat was outrageously ruffled and the points of his collar almost poked him in the chin with their stiffness. His gloves were perfectly white, his shoes spotless and shiny. I straightened, every speck of dirt on my dress burning into my flesh.

He stepped toward me, and the acridness of too much cologne barely masking body odor nearly gagged me. I raised Louisa's bouquet to my nose and inhaled deeply. "Mr. Lundall." I curtsied.

"You look radiant this morning, even with. . . ." He waved his hand, indicating the whole of me. His nose wrinkled. "What happened?"

I feigned a small cough to bring my hand to my mouth, discreetly plugging my nose and inhaling another giant breath. After filling my lungs, I ignored his question and said, "Please tell me, Mr. Lundall, how it is I find you wandering my estate this morning."

His smile grew. "I thought it the best place to find a flower such as you, and I have been so desperate to speak with you." Grasping my hand in his, he hastened it to his lips.

I ripped my hand out of his and stumbled back, away from his nearness and his overpowering stench. The smell was definitely worse than last time. "How intuitive of you."

"Yes, it was. I knew you would be in this little wildernessy section this morning as I knew we belonged together that day I saw you wandering through the park. Do you remember?" His exaggerated sigh made my stomach churn. He could not be doing this again. I had been absolutely clear the last time.

This had to end. His affection was wasted on me. "Mr. Lundall —"

"Wait!" he interrupted, placing a finger on my lips to quiet me. I froze at the rashness of his touch. "Please. Before you say anything." He tapped my lips to accentuate each word he spoke. "I wish to apologize for our last meeting. I believe it was a bit much. I did not mean to be so . . . ."

I pushed his hand away. "Tiresome?"

His eyes widened, then his gaze fell. "Yes. Precisely. You can see I have come today bearing no gifts whatsoever. And we are in a private area where no one can observe us."

"Yes, it is much better than having a donkey laden with packages delivered to me in a public park while the whole town is strolling about."

"I wanted the world to know how I feel. My heart beats only for you. There is no sun in my day without you near. I have been struck —"

"Please, sir."

"What I came to say is —" He grasped both my hands. "Miss Brinton, please do me the honor of marrying me."

I shook my head and tried to wriggle my hands from his grip without dropping my flowers. "Mr. Lundall, you don't know what you're saying. Release me." He dropped my hands but did not back away. His eyes pleaded for the answer I could not give. "Mr. Lundall, as I have said before, I cannot marry you and I never will."

"But the violence of my affections demands it!"

"I have no such feelings toward you."

"My passions are great enough for the both of us."

"Mr. Lundall, you fail to understand. I am sorry, but I refuse to marry someone whose sentiments are so different from my own." I would never bind someone to a loveless marriage the way Edward had tried to bind me.

He looked away from me and sighed. Then he straightened. "I will wait."

Did this man never quit? "Have you not been listening? My answer is no. Please do me the honor of believing me when I say I shall never marry you."

"Margaret," my father called from the top of the stairs. "It is time for breakfast."

I sighed with relief. "I must ask you to excuse me, Mr. Lundall. As you can see, I am in no condition to receive guests, and considering our conversation, I dare say you would rather be on your way."

"Yes, I suppose that would be best."

"I can show our guest to his horse, Margaret," my father said. Bless him and his impeccable ability to come to my rescue.

"It's a chaise, actually," Mr. Lundall said. "I never ride horses. Abominably dirty animals."

I curtsied. "Perhaps we shall meet again, Mr. Lundall."

I made to step around him, but he grabbed my hand and quickly kissed it. "I will not give up, Miss Brinton." He turned and bounded up the stairs.

My father rocked back on his feet as Mr. Lundall passed, then shot me an astonished glance. I shrugged and lifted the bouquet back to my nose. His lips twitched and he turned, following Mr. Lundall around to the front of the house.

Six

Alice met me at the back door, her nose red and her face a little pale though her blonde hair was done up in ringlets; she must have gotten over her cold. Her expression was serious but her eyes held excitement. "Did you see Mr. Lund— you look worse than Daniel! Did you fall into the lake as well? Daniel said it was your fault. What did you do?"

"It was not my fault." I sat on the bench and began unlacing my shoe. "I wasn't even near him. But this," I indicated my dress, "is completely his doing. How are you feeling?"

"Better. It was only a little cold. You'll have to hurry if you're going to change. Cook is already having the food brought in."

I slipped my feet out of my boots and made for the stairs.

"Did you see Mr. Lundall?" she asked

again, following me. "Mama told him it was too early to call, but I saw him slip around the side a minute later."

"Yes. I rather wish he'd listened to Mother."

"Did he propose again?" She giggled.

I stopped and faced her. "He did. But I do not think it something to laugh over. I would not wish a refusal on anyone."

Alice instantly sobered. "He should stop asking."

"He should." Why he didn't I couldn't understand. "I brought you a gift. Give me a moment to change."

"Is it another book? I read some while you were gone. I hope you don't mind. You left at such an interesting part. You should have come in last night, after you got home."

"I did. You were asleep. But I'll read to you tonight."

Alice nodded and headed down the hall.

I stepped into the breakfast room just as everyone was sitting down, a different dress, old but clean, concealing most of the morning's events. As I slid into my seat across from Daniel, I glared. "You left me."

He took a sip from his glass, hiding his mouth. It did nothing to hide the laughter in his eyes.

"I'll exact revenge," I promised.

"Unnecessary, seeing as you already have — preemptively, so to speak."

"Louisa's witnessing your debacle was not my fault."

"As Mr. Lundall's appearance was not mine."

I reached for a piece of toast. "The two are not the same, Daniel."

"Did you bring my gift?" Alice asked from across the table.

"Of course." I handed her the small, wrapped package.

"May I, Mother?"

Our mother nodded, and Alice began to meticulously untie the string. When the wrapping fell away, she gasped and reverently fingered the pattern on the lace handkerchief. "It is so lovely. Where did you get it?"

"Rosden. And, look." I held up my matching handkerchief. "I purchased one exactly like it for myself."

"You were in Rosden? Why did you not return with Father? He was home just after noon."

I glanced at Father. "You were in Rosden?" He'd mentioned nothing about it last night. Ever since the pneumonia he'd contracted the previous winter, my father's health had never regained its robustness, and he rarely left the village on account of it. A trip to Rosden was the type of excursion he would have brought up, especially after Daniel and I had recounted our adventures of the day. We might even have laughed at our missing each other.

Father remained fixed on his paper. "Yes. Your mother and I would like a word with you after breakfast."

With me? Alone? This did not bode well.

I glanced at my mother. Her brown hair was pulled into an immaculate bun, her posture was impeccable, and her gown, a vibrant green morning dress, matched her eyes.

Everything about her was a contrast to how I appeared. I straightened my own back and shoulders, but there was nothing I could do at present about my hair or the old dress I had flung on.

Perhaps they were upset about this morning. Or, worse, my failure at the Hickmores'.

"Yes, sir."

Eventually, Daniel escorted Alice out of the room with talk of a game outside. My toast and marmalade lay on my plate, my tea untouched. My father lingered over the paper and my mother sat over her plate as full of uneaten food as my own.

This did not bode well at all.

After a moment, my mother looked up. "Colin," she said with a sigh.

My father turned to the last page before setting his paper down. With a frown tugging at his mouth and without looking my way, he rose and walked to the window, his back to me, staring out with his hands clasped stiffly behind him.

I shifted in my seat. "Father, I know I promised you that attending the Hickmores' party would end in a proposal, but I can assure you the lack of one is not my fault. I was close, and I did try —"

"Margaret, I am not concerned with what occurred at the party. Indeed, I am content circumstances turned out as they have."

"Yes, dear," my mother said. "We have happy news." She smiled, but it didn't reach her eyes.

"Oh?" I asked tentatively. Neither of them seemed particularly overjoyed.

My mother glanced at my father. "Your father has found you a husband."

I furrowed my brows. "I beg your pardon?"

"A very good match, too," she continued. "He comes from an old, well-respected family. The estate is supposedly quite stunning."

I shook my head. "Mother, you cannot be serious."

Her lips thinned with dismay. She was very serious.

It was as though *I* had fallen into the lake, only it was winter and the water ice cold. This wasn't the way things were supposed to happen. I was supposed to make my own match, carefully selecting the man to ensure the future I needed. "There must be some mistake."

"Your father has arranged a marriage for you, Margaret. There has been no mistake."

The dishes scattered across the table painted a picture of comfort and happiness that mocked me. I focused on my father. "To whom? Why have you done this?"

He faced me, his expression set. "You are desperate to marry, are you not?"

I shook my head. "*Desperate* isn't quite how I'd put it. Determined, perhaps, but —"

My father cut in. "The nuances don't matter. It is a good match. And we will finally be settled with this whole business."

The air in the room vanished. My father blamed me. Not for Edward, of course, but for the rumors that kept Daniel from proposing. And for the time since the engagement, for not securing a husband on my own. But it had taken time to recover, time for me to understand what I needed.

83

"Father, I'm sorry for the way things have turned out. But surely we haven't arrived at this point."

Yet my father's expression and my mother's clasped hands testified that we had, indeed, arrived at this point.

I clamped down on my rising fear, desperate to push past it and this situation. Perhaps I could still work something out.

A movement outside the window demanded my attention. Daniel's face appeared, out of view of my mother's sharp eye but clearly visible to me, his nose pressed against the pane as he surveyed the room. His eyes met mine and I suddenly thought of Mr. Northam. He was the key to my release.

I refocused on my father. "Go back to this man. Inform him I am no longer available. I didn't tell you last night — it was so late. But I found someone while at the Hickmores', a Mr. Fredrick Northam. He is perfect. You'll think so, too, I promise. He is coming here to ask your permission. He will most likely visit this week — maybe even today. I am certain it will be soon. He is quite the gentleman, with a large estate. So you see? This match is unnecessary. I shall be married before year's end."

"What?" My mother started forward in

her chair, then muttered, "Oh, my." She leaned back and closed her eyes. "Colin —"

"No, Eloise," my father interrupted. "I am sorry, Margaret. But it is already done."

I flinched back in my seat. "The settlement has been arranged? The contract is drawn up?"

"The circumstances are very much in our favor. I believe you will be happy." He said the last part quietly, as though it were more of a hope than an expectation.

I could never be happy if I wasn't safe. How was I to ensure I would be safe?

"Margaret, don't look at me like that. It's a good match." My father stepped toward me as though to comfort me.

I scrambled out of my chair, sending it wobbling. Grabbing the chair to steady it, I slid behind it and dug my nails into the floral relief etched along its rim. "Please, do not do this. Not while there's still a chance to make things right."

My mother sighed and stood. "I wish we had known —" She glanced at my father and stopped. Taking a breath, she continued, "I am so very sorry. But it really is too late. He arrives tomorrow."

"Tomorrow?" They hadn't even given me time to get used to the idea, to make a plan.

My mother nodded. As I looked from her

to my father, they suddenly appeared unfamiliar, as people I should have known but didn't.

The room grew smaller, the walls inching toward me, compressing the air so tightly I thought I would drown. Too many things could go wrong; there were too many unknowns in marrying like this. I couldn't go through what I'd gone through with Edward again. But what could I do? "I understand," I whispered, and I rushed from the room.

Seven

I stopped at the back lawn and stared at the sky, trying to ignore how my heart thumped in my head. I needed to escape, to go someplace that would expunge all I had just heard. I longed for the solitude of the lake, just visible through the trees, certain its verdant surroundings would feel more familiar at the moment than my own home. But even it could not undo my parents' actions.

I turned my back on its sparkling surface and strode the path skirting the yard, tracing the edge of the woods.

From out of nowhere, Daniel stepped before me and grasped my arms. "Margaret, what is it? What happened?"

I struggled against his hold. "Let me go. Please."

"I saw you from the window. You were white. You still are. And your eyes — are you going to cry? You never cry. What —"

I wrenched myself from his grasp and turned away. "Leave me alone."

He put a hand on my arm, stopping me. "Margaret, tell me what is going on."

"Where's Alice?"

"I sent her down the path to that old fort we put together. Do you remember it?"

"The one with the tree swing John hung for us?"

Daniel nodded.

"She shouldn't be alone, Daniel."

"I'm joining her. Just as soon as you tell me what is going on."

I forced a smile. "You've gotten your wish. Any man but Mr. Northam. Isn't that what you said?"

Daniel's eyes widened. "What?"

"Father has found me a husband. He arrives tomorrow."

"He found you a husband? Who is it?"

"Does it matter?"

The pity in his look made me grit my teeth. I turned away, continuing down the path. Daniel was soon by my side.

"I cannot believe they would do this," he said.

I thought hearing disbelief in his voice would make me feel better, his incredulity a validation for my dismay, but it didn't. It only made the void within me grow.

"After all my efforts to reestablish myself, to make people forget. . . . Everyone will say they aren't surprised this is the only way I could get a husband."

"Well, you haven't married. So, in a way they would be correct."

"Daniel!"

"Sorry, I shouldn't have said that."

He was callous at the worst moments. I kicked at a pebble. "I was so close. A few more days and I —" I clamped my lips together. It would do no good to let Daniel know how I'd hoped for Mr. Northam's appearance.

Daniel raised an eyebrow. "Is that how long Mr. Lundall gave you this time? Do you really intend to marry him?"

"Mr. Lundall didn't say when he'd return. But even if I wished to, I am no longer at liberty to accept him." And yet this other man was sure to be worse than Mr. Lundall in every way, except possibly smell.

"What do you know of this man?"

"Nothing." A featureless face rose before me and I shivered. What was wrong with this man that he had to turn to me to find a match? "Do you think father knows him well?" The words came out strangled.

Daniel stopped and gripped my arms, turning me to face him. "Margaret, our father would never allow you to marry someone he didn't esteem as the best of men."

"This wouldn't be the first time Father has been mistaken."

Daniel frowned and stepped back. "I believe we all learned our lesson, especially Father."

"But this man is obviously only after my dowry. What else could it be? So it is the same. Only worse. I've never even met this man!"

"And how is going along with Father's plan any different from your marrying Northam?"

"It's completely different. Mr. Northam would be my choice, and I'd know exactly what I was getting. My marrying Mr. Northam would be mutually beneficial. I get nothing from marrying this stranger." I knew how to protect myself with Mr. Northam, while with someone else there was no guarantee.

"You don't know that." Daniel's eyes narrowed. "What is it you're so afraid of?"

I turned away.

"Margaret," Daniel said gently. After a pause, he spoke. "Perhaps it isn't about the money at all. Perhaps he has a limp and is bent with deformity."

Horrific images of mangled men raced through my mind before Daniel's teasing chuckle made me fix him with my meanest glare. Couldn't he ever be serious?

Instead of cowing, he continued, "How about an accent of some sort? Ooh, a Frenchman. No, wait. A Russian! They are so popular these days. He could have an accent. 'Margaret, my dear, vould you like to go out tonight? To ze opera, perhaps?'"

Daniel grasped my hand. I strained against his grip, but his fingers tightened. He slouched down until his face was level with mine and stared at me with an expression of mock sincerity.

I narrowed my eyes and pulled again on my hand, but he didn't release me. He waggled his brows, then winked. Years of habitual reaction worked against me. My lips twitched until the corners of my mouth lifted into a small grin.

"I take dat as a yez."

It was despicable, the way he could get me to smile. This was not a circumstance to laugh at. I gritted my teeth. "Daniel, you don't sound very Russian."

He ignored me and placed my hand on his arm. He didn't stand up, though. Instead, he remained low and hunched over. As we moved forward he dragged one foot behind him. The scrape of his foot along the path sent chills through me even as I swallowed a laugh.

Of a sudden, he lurched forward to grab a large stick, jostling me off balance. He placed the stick upright like a cane.

"Daniel, stop," I begged. I didn't know if I wanted to laugh or cry. I wanted both.

"How am I to vin your love if I stop? No. I must continue. Forever."

Forever. I would be married to this man until death did us part.

I might never be free again.

EIGHT

The next day, Parson Andrews droned on about repentance and change, but I hardly heard a word, dividing my time between staring at Louisa's back, willing her to feel my impatience to speak with her, and the slow movement of the colors splayed across the altar from the stained-glass window above. Sometime during the night I'd realized what I had to do — I had to find a way out of this engagement before anyone learned of it. Then everything could return to the way it had been before, and Mr. Northam and I could marry as we wished.

But I had no idea how to get a man so desperate as to seek out a wife sight unseen to turn around and call it off.

When the stained glass reflection finally hit the floor, the sermon ended and Parson Andrews shuffled down the aisle to take his customary place at the door, enabling him to bid farewell to his parishioners. Louisa and her family slipped into the aisle before I could catch her attention, and of course Daniel, who sat on the end of our pew, waited for them to pass before moving into the aisle himself.

I tried to shove past him, but he intentionally blocked my way.

"Anxious to leave this morning, are we? Cannot wait to discover who is waiting for you at home?"

I smiled sweetly. "Certainly. Anything is better than sitting next to your stink all morning."

Skepticism flashed through his eyes, but he discreetly tilted his head to smell his armpit. His distraction provided me just enough space to squeeze by him, and I blew him a kiss as I passed.

The Rosthorns were already making their way to their carriage. I ran up to Louisa. "I need to speak with you," I whispered, feigning a smile at the Johnsons, who were gathered around waiting for their mother to finish speaking with Louisa's. "Behind the bushes," I added. The old holly, situated conveniently out of earshot of casual eavesdroppers, was a place we met whenever there was something we needed to discuss while our parents socialized after services.

Louisa's brows rose and she gave a slight

nod, but as we took a step back, Mrs. Johnson's second daughter, Catherine, intercepted us. "Miss Rosthorn, how lovely you look this morning." Her shrewd gaze swept over my hair and dress. "And Miss Brinton."

"Miss Johnson, such a pleasure," I replied, forcing my tone to be polite. Though she was a year older than us, we had all been childhood friends until we had come out into society. Catherine had then become the epitome of ill-will, acting as though each man in the village — and each new one who appeared — was somehow her personal property and Louisa and I the thieves. She'd even had intentions for Daniel at one point.

"Did I overhear your brother mention that you are expecting a guest?"

Curse Daniel for telling people. "We are."

Her lips dipped into a frown. "How refreshing. Family, I assume? Is your guest staying long?"

Catherine knew perfectly well we had no family who would visit. My mother's only sister had passed a few years before without marrying, and my father was an only child. None of their parents were living. Catherine was just being nosy, and my patience was running thin. I needed to speak with Louisa.

"Not family. Someone my father knows. I am certain the man will be a dead bore. But if you would like to see him for yourself and try your hand at winning his affection, you are more than welcome to visit."

"Thank you, but we have plans." She looked at Louisa. "Good day, Miss Rosthorn." She turned her back to us and rejoined her family.

"Margaret, that was rude," Louisa said.

"It was," I acknowledged. "And of course I am sorry. But I do not wish to discuss Catherine. I have something more pressing to speak to you about." I led the way to the bushes.

"What is it?"

My parents were conversing with some neighbors, their smiles a further betrayal to me. They should at least appear morose about confining their daughter to such a predicament. "The man, the guest who's coming — Louisa, my father intends for me to marry him."

"What? Is it Mr. Northam?"

"No, it is someone I have never met."

Louisa paled. "Oh, no."

"You have to help me. I must find some way out of this. I cannot hide his arrival from the town, but if I can find some way out of the arrangement tonight, it might be possible to keep gossip at a minimum."

She nodded with understanding. "What will you do?"

"I have no plan as of yet. I am too anxious to think clearly. I was hoping you would suggest something."

She shook her head sadly. "I wouldn't know what to do. You cannot very well go against your parents' wishes without tainting your reputation. Perhaps you could tell him, in confidence, that your heart is already engaged elsewhere?" At my skeptical look, she amended, "Well, not your heart, but your interest?"

"The type of man to enter into an agreement of marriage without even first seeing his bride will not care two whits about her wishes or interests."

"You will think of something. I know you will." Louisa glanced back at the crowd. "I have to go. Mother is searching for me."

Her mother was indeed searching the faces around her for her daughter, while her father's expression no longer held the smile it had sported while speaking with the Johnsons. Glancing across the crowd, I saw why. My father inclined his head to Sir Edward, but then turned his back. Though they had never been friends, our fathers had at least conversed. Any semblance of civility had evaporated with the failed engagement.

Louisa placed a hand on my arm. "I will come tomorrow, if I can."

I nodded. She squeezed my arm comfortingly before walking back into the crowd, leaving me alone to wrestle between my heated defiance at accepting this engagement and the despair of its inevitability.

NINE

Upon returning home, I retreated to the drawing room and closed the door. Once seated at the piano, I ran my fingers up and down the keys, the scales I had detested practicing as a child now calming the disquiet within me. I tried not to think about the man I would shortly meet, but each chiming of the clock testified my time was dwindling. When the room began to feel like a coffin, I left to seek consolation outside.

My mother stopped me in the hall. "Our guest will arrive in half an hour."

I started. "I thought he was coming late, for dinner."

"Please see to your appearance. Your hair has come loose."

My hand automatically went to my hair. I nodded and scurried up the stairs to my room, fixed the lock that was loose, then slipped back down. Mother's and Alice's voices from the parlor sent me out the back door. I hurried across the lawn and down the stairs, slowing to run my fingers along the wooden arbor at the base of the stairs, marking the entrance to the garden. There wasn't enough time to go to the lake. But I hoped to find a bit of solace here, away from the house.

A bench positioned across the garden near the path was just the thing. I sat and tilted my head to rest against the back of the bench.

The long flowing clouds lacing the sky looked like hovering claws ready to swoop down and snatch up whatever offended them. I shivered at a breeze playing at my skin. Bringing my feet up onto the bench, I wrapped my arms around my legs for warmth and laid my cheek on my knees, staring at nothing.

I couldn't believe this was happening. Within moments I would meet the man my parents expected me to marry. And I would have to do it unless I found a way out.

One thing was certain: I would never like this man. If he developed a tendre for me, he'd have to deal with it himself. I'd made myself a promise, and no random middle-aged hunchbacked Russian was going to convince me to break it.

A familiar noise made its way through my numb mind, though it took me a moment to recognize the sound of a carriage.

Dropping my feet to the ground, I twisted down low on the bench and held my breath. The bench, though not directly next to the road, could still be seen from the front of the house. I remained huddled until the sound of the wheels stopped and the welcoming voices of my parents had gone silent.

Only a few minutes would pass before my mother discovered my absence and sent someone to call for me. If I hurried, I could glimpse the man through the window in the parlor. Then I could be prepared. I would have the upper hand when we were introduced.

I scrambled off the bench and raced up the stairs. Bending low to avoid being seen, I raced across the lawn and climbed onto the low wall surrounding the house. With my arms outstretched for balance, I shimmied toward the parlor windows, trying to avoid falling forward into the prickly bushes growing between the wall and the house. When I found a good spot, I adjusted my feet, inhaled deeply, and peered inside.

My mother stood nearest, though she was angled away from the window as though watching the door for my arrival. My father stood a few steps from her, facing the other side of the room. They both looked uncomfortable, my mother furtively glancing to the door, my father unmoving with a small frown on his face. I leaned closer to the window, trying to see who else was in the room, but I couldn't maneuver past the unruly yew bush growing next to the house and over the wall.

The only other person visible was Daniel, standing by himself in the middle of the room. I waved my hand to catch his attention. When he noticed me, he frowned and shook his head. Why was he so serious? It wasn't his future that was being destroyed. I made a face. He didn't respond, though I imagined I heard him clear his throat to stifle a laugh. I gestured to the side of the room, wanting to know what the man was like. Daniel didn't move. Undeterred, I hunched over, pressing one hand to the small of my back while holding a pretend cane in the other. I took a step along the wall and shook my pretend cane at him in imitation of his Russian from the day before.

Suddenly a man appeared between us and looked directly at me. The intensity of his blue eyes threw me off balance. My arms flung out, flailing for anything to stop my fall, but there was nothing to grasp. My feet slipped and I fell backward onto the lawn. After struggling to regain my breath, I looked at the house. I had fallen too close to the wall to see the window, which meant no one could see me. I was safe.

Except, I was not safe. I knew those icy blue eyes. They were Lord Williams's eyes.

It couldn't be.

I lifted myself onto my elbows and peeked over the wall.

It was.

Lord Williams was in my home, standing in my window, though he'd turned and now his back was to me. Even the way he carried himself, formal yet relaxed, testified to his belief that all should bow before him.

Surely this couldn't be the man my parents had spoken of. He must be here for some other reason. To disabuse me to my parents? To warn them of his cousin since I'd refused to pay heed to him before?

If it was the latter, the joke was on him. My marriage plans had already taken a tumultuous detour.

I would not stand for any more meddling from him, whatever his purpose. Especially not when I was already consumed with deciding how to eradicate a soon-to-be-arriving fiancé. Ladylike or not, I would confront him and let him know exactly what

I thought of him. And then I would throw him out.

I stood and, without looking again at the window, walked calmly to the front door, straightening my skirt. Taking a deep breath, I pushed the door open and almost collided with Alice.

"I was just coming to get you," she said excitedly, her eyes sparkling. "The baron has arrived, Margaret. Isn't it thrilling?"

The baron? She said it as though he were the only baron in all of England. I bit back a remark and shook my head, instead grasping Alice's hand and forcing myself toward the parlor. Just before I reached the open door I paused.

"Do I look presentable?" I asked.

"Yes, you look very pretty. Are you nervous?"

"To face Lord Williams? I should think not." I rolled my shoulders back, lifted my chin, and strode into the room.

All eyes fixed on me as I entered. Keeping my head up, I quickly surveyed the small party. No one had moved from their positions of a moment before. The only difference was that there were now red splotches on Daniel's cheeks as he struggled for composure, no doubt the effect of witnessing my fall.

My mother bustled up to me wearing a mask of pleasantness, but her eyes were tight at the sides. I felt the smallest hint of sympathy for her. Lord Williams's presence in our house, or anywhere in the county, for that matter, was enough to make anyone unhappy.

"Margaret, let me introduce Lord Williams." She placed a firm hand on my arm and directed me to the middle of the room.

Lord Williams moved in front of me and bowed. It would have been a very gracious bow, except his eyes never left mine.

He must have been watching for my reaction. I wouldn't give him the satisfaction of seeing anything but displeasure. I dropped a shallow curtsy. "Lord Williams and I are already acquainted. Or, rather, we have already had the opportunity to become acquainted."

"You have? I mean, you are?" my mother stammered in surprise, glancing toward my father.

I relished this opportunity to discredit the baron. Smiling sweetly, I said, "Yes. We were both at the Hickmores'."

The baron nodded and smiled at my mother. "Unfortunately, I had to leave quite suddenly, before we had the opportunity for much conversation."

He made it sound as though we had merely exchanged names before he ran away, instead of bestowing me with his austere and high-handed advice before humiliating me. I was not going to allow him to get away with his deception. "And here I thought the conversation we shared had been most stimulating. Or, at least, instructive to us both. And then there was all of dinner as well." I shrugged. "No doubt my sentiments are faulty, a result of my refusal to see reason."

He met my gaze. "No doubt."

He dared insult me in my own home?

My mother glanced from me to Lord Williams and back as though trying to puzzle something out, then placed a placid smile on her face. "It is fortuitous you have already met." She glanced at my father with a small narrowing of her eyes.

Daniel cleared his throat. "Perhaps you should serve the tea, Margaret." He indicated the service set upon a side table.

"It was fortuitous," I said, ignoring Daniel, "as I was able to discover some of Lord Williams's finer attributes. I was especially impressed by his respectful manner in offering advice and his articulated taste in music." I smiled, but unless he was a complete dolt my words would hit their mark.

"To what do we owe the honor of this visit?"

Lord Williams looked to my father with some surprise before returning his gaze to me, his expression containing a hint of uncertainty. "I have come to better acquaint myself with your family."

To acquaint himself with my family? Whatever for?

"Well, here we are." I made no attempt to hide the disdain from my voice. "I am confident we are all very pleased by your arrival. However, we are expecting another visitor and I must ensure everything is properly prepared. Please excuse me."

I curtsied, but before I could turn Daniel grasped my arm so I couldn't move. When I glanced at him in surprise, he gave a small shake of his head.

"Margaret," my father said, "Lord Williams *is* our expected visitor."

I frowned and looked at my father over my shoulder. "But what about —" Daniel pinched me.

"Daniel, why'd you —" My gaze shot back to Lord Williams with understanding. *He* was the man? Lord Williams and I were — engaged?

With dread pooling in my chest, I surveyed the baron's expensively-tailored clothes and icy blue eyes. My first misgivings had been correct.

But no. We couldn't be together. It was impossible. He despised me and I hated him.

Surely this was taking his warning too far. Did he expect to ensure I would never marry his cousin by marrying me himself?

That was ridiculous. No man would throw his life away in such a stupid manner. Yes, it would be convenient. But we would certainly never respect each other. Even mutual toleration was out of the question. My life would be unbearable.

I could not marry this man.

My mother stepped forward. "Allow me to introduce our other daughter. Alice, dear," my mother said, "this is Lord Williams."

"How do you do?" Alice responded behind me.

"It is a pleasure to meet you, Miss Alice," Lord Williams replied with a deep bow and a smile.

I frowned. Maybe I was wrong altogether. Maybe he wasn't here for any reason other than to prove a point, to show that his title commanded all to bow to him and be subservient to his wishes. In which case there was no reason to fear. Because I would never bow. Neither would I allow him to hurt my family.

I stepped next to Alice and placed an arm around her shoulders.

My mother motioned toward the door. "You must be weary after your travel, my lord. Please allow me to show you to your room."

"Thank you." Lord Williams nodded to Daniel and bowed to me. I turned away.

The moment he was out of the room I spun to my father. "How did this happen?"

Daniel stepped next to me. "Margaret, perhaps —"

"Daniel, you know he is here only to flaunt his power over us."

"You think he wants to marry you solely because we didn't accept the ride he offered?" Daniel asked. "That's ridiculous."

"No, because I wouldn't give heed to his words at the Hickmores'." I turned back to my father, not quite keeping the desperation from my voice. "Father, he is condescending and a liar. He humiliated me at the Hickmores'. He's the reason we —"

"Margaret," my father broke in. "You will not speak ill of a guest in this house."

His decisive tone should have stopped me, but he needed to be made aware of the true nature of the man he had allowed into his home, of the ruin he was capable of. "But —"

"I am ashamed at the lack of character you displayed. It will not happen again. You will show our guest every courtesy while he is here." His eyes bored into me, demanding a response.

There was nothing else to be done. "Yes, sir."

TEN

Daniel put an arm around my shoulders. "Why don't we go outside? Lord Williams is sure to be occupied in his room for the rest of the day. You won't have to worry about meeting him again until dinner. Alice, come with us. How about a game of bowls?"

Alice smiled. "Oh, yes. I would love that."

I remained silent until we stepped onto the lawn. "This is unbelievable," I finally said, wrapping my arms around myself.

Daniel nodded. "I had not thought to ever see him again."

"It makes no sense. Why would Lord Williams do this?"

"Perhaps he is as determined to live a life of misery as you are," Daniel said.

I ignored the comment. The situation had all the appearance of a cruel joke. I could hardly stand to be in the same room with this man. How was I to endure his visit — or worse, marriage? I would never be able to do it. "What am I going to do?"

"Well, to begin with, you're going to ignore me for a moment." Daniel stretched his hand forward and tugged at the side of my hair.

I wrenched away from him. "What are you doing?"

"Retrieving this." He held up a blade of grass.

My hand flew to my head. "That was in my hair?"

He nodded.

I glanced up at the window to the baron's room in mortification. The curtains were drawn, but I could easily imagine him in his room laughing at me. "What a perfect day." It certainly could not get worse.

"A little competition will ease your anxiety," Daniel said.

I trudged after him to our playing spot across the lawn. "Margaret," Alice said tentatively, "would you like to deliver the jack?"

I looked at her in surprise. She always tossed the little white ball that then became the target of the larger ones. Lawn bowls was her favorite game.

My surprise turned to chagrin. I shouldn't have allowed my feelings of the moment to overrun my sense of decorum. My father had been correct. I had shown a want of character and, worse, I had done so in front of Alice. No matter how abhorrent the circumstance, my reaction was inexcusable. "No. You do it. I assume Daniel and I are on a team?"

She nodded, then bent in concentration and tossed the jack. It landed a bit closer than usual, but she stood with a smile.

"Alice, would you like your turn first or last?" Daniel asked.

She picked up one of her balls. "First."

"I cannot imagine a worse situation." I spoke quietly enough that Alice wouldn't overhear.

"Oh, come, Margaret. The situation isn't that bad."

"How is it not?"

"The baron's not an unpleasant-looking fellow, is he? He isn't old. And he doesn't smell."

"I could more easily wear a clothespin on my nose than abide Lord Williams's presence for days on end."

Alice's ball landed some distance from the jack. "Bad luck, Alice," Daniel said loudly. He picked up one of our balls. "You don't mean that. And, though you don't agree, he is a better choice than Mr. Northam."

"The two are not even comparable."

Daniel tossed the ball. He hit Alice's, knocking it farther from the jack. "Looks like your luck is taking a turn for the worse, Alice." He turned to me. "Sorry, you'll have to fix that." He gestured toward Alice's ball. "But you are correct, they are not comparable. No matter how he acts toward you, Lord Williams is a far better match for you."

"How is an arrogant, unintelligent, rash baron a good match for anyone?" Alice picked up her next ball, and I decided to watch, for if her toss landed poorly, I would need to fix that as well.

Daniel glanced at me and straightened. "Margaret —"

"No, Daniel. I'm serious. I can't imagine Mr. Northam ever walking out on a lady's performance."

If only Mr. Northam had proposed at the Hickmores'.

"Margaret!" Daniel hissed.

"Fine. Don't relent. But I'm not giving up on him. Mr. Northam is perfect. Everything I want. He is handsome, engaging, and much too intelligent to ever —"

"My lord, would you care to join us?" Daniel cut in.

I rolled my eyes. There was no way I was falling for that jest. "Really, Daniel. Can you think of nothing better than that?"

"I wouldn't care to intrude on a private game." The deep voice came from directly behind me, and a faint scent of mild cologne and saddle oil wafted in the air.

My face flamed with embarrassment. I hadn't been speaking loudly, but it was very probable the baron had overheard my speech.

"Your company would be welcomed," Daniel replied.

I had to make some effort. I had promised my father. Without turning, I said, "Yes, please join us."

Daniel smirked at my efforts at civility. "As you can see, my lord, our teams are unequal. Alice, would you mind Lord Williams joining your team?"

"Oh." Alice's face reddened and she looked down at the ground. "I would be delighted."

I shot Daniel a glare for placing our sister in such an awkward position, one she couldn't refuse without being rude. "Alice, if you would feel more comfortable with Daniel or —"

"No," she said quickly, looking up at me. "It's all right."

It shouldn't be all right. She should not have been paired with a stranger, especially not with the baron. But if I said anything

115

more I would appear ill-mannered, and Lord Williams had already claimed that description for himself.

"It is our turn now, my lord," Alice said, "but since you've just arrived, you can take your turn after Margaret to gauge her skill. It may give you some advantage."

"A very good idea," Lord Williams agreed.

I moved to the starting point. Daniel and I would have to clean up the baron's mistakes as well as Alice's misshots. I was not going to allow his presence to keep Alice from winning. I angled the ball and tossed. It raced wide, then curved and knocked both the jack and Daniel's ball. Though Daniel's was now farther away, Alice and I were tied.

"An unfortunate delivery," the baron said, stepping next to me with a ball in his hands.

He was referring to the game, of course, but I couldn't help thinking that his appearance was, indeed, unfortunate. "Quite." While pretending to assess the play, I quietly continued, "Do not distress yourself on your game, my lord. Just try your best. Daniel and I will fix any poor shots to ensure Alice wins — and now, by default, you as well." I turned and took up my position beside Daniel.

"That was a poor shot, Margaret," Alice

said. "You knocked Daniel's ball away. I'm sure you would have won if you hadn't done that."

I nodded my head. "Fate certainly seems to be stacked against me today."

The baron's tossed ball settled between mine and the jack. It was a good shot. A very good shot. And a difficult one. An amazing stroke of good luck.

Daniel didn't share my belief about it being luck. "Well done, my lord. It appears, Margaret, that you may actually have a bit of real competition."

"Are you very accomplished at bowls, then, Miss Brinton?" Lord Williams stepped back to join our little group.

His question was surely meant to mock, since no woman of culture would claim a sport among her refined talents, even if she was skilled at it. Besides, I couldn't be honest with Alice listening. "I do not believe bowls would be listed among my accomplishments."

Alice shook her head in agreement. "She isn't very good, but it's more that she's unlucky. The only time she wins is when she plays against Daniel." Alice looked suddenly concerned. "Margaret, am I bad luck for you?"

"Of course not. You are a good luck

charm, which is probably why his lordship's ball placed so perfectly. And I only win against Daniel because he lacks focus. Any small comment ruins his game. Silence, too, because then his mind wanders."

Alice nodded solemnly. "He isn't very good, is he?"

Daniel's gaze shifted heavenward in an act of long-suffering.

Lord Williams smiled. "It sounds as though you are the champion bowler in the family, Miss Alice."

She smiled. "I do enjoy it."

I rolled my eyes. Flattery would get the man nowhere.

Daniel leaned close to me and taunted, "You won't get out of this one." Then he addressed Lord Williams. "Margaret is excellent at bowls. She surpassed me years ago. I would very much like to see the two of you matched."

Never had I believed Daniel would turn on me so easily, openly placing me in such an awkward position.

Alice threw her ball wide.

"Daniel, it is your turn," I squeaked, trying to redirect the attention away from Daniel's suggestion.

His jaw set in concentration as he took his stance, ball in hand. But when he released, he flinched, and the ball went wide. I groaned but refrained from saying anything that might provoke him into insisting on the proposed match between me and the baron.

Lord Williams had more luck, tapping the jack so his two balls and one of Alice's remained closest, securing them three points if I shot badly. I hesitated. It was obvious the baron played with more than luck. That last shot was much more difficult than his first, and he had accomplished both with ease. I wanted Alice to win, but the baron's skill rankled. I couldn't allow him to believe he was better than I was because I purposefully lost. It would be best to knock the jack away from the baron's shots and closer to Alice's. Then none of his shots would count, but Alice would still win.

I shifted my stance slightly and tossed. The ball went straight, knocking the baron's out of the way. However, it also knocked the jack farther from Alice's ball. Mine was closest — which meant Daniel and I won.

"A winning shot," Lord Williams said, his tone laced with irony.

I turned in horror to Daniel, then focused on Alice. "Oh, Alice." I couldn't think of anything to say.

To my surprise, she smiled. "Perhaps this is a lucky day for you, Margaret."

I glanced away. There was nothing at all lucky about this day.

"Shall we play again, Miss Brinton?" Lord Williams asked.

"Thank you, but no."

"Of course you should," Daniel said. "Deliver the jack, Margaret. And then, since yours was the winning shot, the first toss falls to you."

I glanced from Daniel to Lord Williams, who indicated the starting spot with a sweep of his hand.

"Oh, yes, do play," Alice said.

"Alice." Daniel put his arm around her shoulders and turned her toward the house. "Why don't we watch from the seats on the portico?" He motioned toward the bench and chairs situated next to the house.

In desperation, I turned back to the baron. "I'm certain playing lawn bowls is not how you would like to spend your afternoon. You probably long for some exercise after your travels. Perhaps you wish to see the estate?"

"That would be agreeable, if you wish."

He had obviously misunderstood. "I wouldn't be going."

"Oh?"

"Daniel would be the best escort for such an excursion. I am sure I would only slow you down."

"Tomorrow will work for seeing the estate. Let us begin our game."

He was either so conceited he couldn't imagine my not wanting to be around him, or he was dense. He was very likely both. "My lord, I am certain my mother would be appalled if you spent your afternoon playing a lawn game."

"Are you afraid to lose, Miss Brinton?"

The directness of his challenge made any further attempt at escape impossible. I lifted my chin. "Of course not."

"Then, please." He again gestured toward the starting point.

Gritting my teeth, I strode to where the balls sat on the ground, picked up the jack, and tossed it. I would play one game, but that was all. And I would not speak to him.

My first toss was a good shot, but Lord Williams's toss was equally good. I knocked his ball away with my second, but he moved the jack on his second, regaining the lead. I threw my third ball a little gentler and it stopped just in front of the jack, blocking any thought he might have had of moving the jack again. To my surprise, his next toss knocked mine to the side of the jack while his rolled into its place. Allowing myself a quick glance at him, I found him wearing a very self-satisfied grin.

No gentleman should ever look that way when playing against a lady.

There was only one thing to do. I aimed for his third ball, intent on knocking it away. Instead, mine rolled wide and short. I had lost.

Lord Williams picked up his ball and, with his toss, knocked his ball away from the jack. I had won after all.

I scowled. "My lord, please do not mistake me for one of those women who require a man to lose. That last shot was intentionally not in your favor."

"You think I deliberately lost? Perhaps we need a rematch."

I stepped back. I wouldn't play another game. Why was he even here? "There has obviously been some mistake. Certainly you never meant for this to happen."

"We'll consider that game a practice. Now that we have taken the measure of each other's skill, let us see who truly is the better player."

He was being purposefully obtuse. "My lord, I am not speaking of the game."

His cold stare met mine. "Our being together is no mistake."

"Why are you doing this?"

"I have my reasons."

Ire flared within me. "And I am not to be

privy to those reasons? I gather I am supposed to be honored by your offer because most women would be and not question your actions?"

"We've already established your lack of sense when it comes to behaving as other women, as well as how little regard you have for my opinions. So you will forgive me for not confessing my reasons. It is your turn."

My hands clenched into fists. "Excuse me, but —"

My father walked around the corner of the house, as though to remind me of his words. I cleared my throat. "Perhaps you would like to go first this time?" I shot the baron a smile, then turned to watch my father disappear into the stables.

"Your father is gone," Lord Williams said quietly, so close that his chest almost touched my shoulder. I looked at him in surprise and stumbled a step away. "There is no longer a need to appear civil." Amusement filled his eyes.

My body warmed from embarrassment and anger. He was laughing at me, finding humor in my discomfort as though everything that had happened today had been orchestrated to entertain him.

"Thank you for your permission, my lord.

Please excuse me." I spun and strode to the house.

124

Eleven

I paced my bedroom, bemoaning my fate and cursing my ill luck, stopping just short of wishing I had never gone to the Hickmores'. I wasn't fool enough to wish that undone, for if I hadn't gone, I would never have met Mr. Northam. And I would never regret meeting Mr. Northam.

If only he'd proposed. Or come yesterday. Or this morning. Any of those options would have sufficed.

But would it have done any good? My father had already made the arrangement by then.

A sudden thought stopped my feet. What if he came now? What would I do? Surely Mr. Northam would honor his cousin's engagement.

Yet he'd called Lord Williams a blackguard, which implied his disapproval of him. If Mr. Northam did, in fact, hate his cousin as I did, as I hoped he did, then I could

125

count on him to help rescue me. But if they were friends as well as cousins —

If they were friends, Mr. Northam would certainly relinquish any claim he felt he had.

It was best not to gamble with the chance of Mr. Northam's arriving until I found a way out of this engagement. I had to get word to him somehow, urging him not to come. But such a note could never come from me — not unless it was contained inside another letter written by a man. My thoughts automatically flew to my father, but he would never write such a note under the present circumstances. Which left only Daniel. Who would also never help.

I began to pace again, then stopped. If I told Daniel to inform Mr. Northam that he should stay away because there was no point in his coming anymore, surely he would do that. It would be playing to Daniel's desires. This could all work out wonderfully. I would speak to him about it tonight.

For dinner I wore my plainest yellow evening dress adorned with no more than a simple gold necklace and my hair in a bun, all in the hope to drive home the message of my lack of interest in impressing the baron. Ignoring my mother's look of disapproval at my attire, I silently followed my family into the dining room.

"Lord Williams," my father said, indicating a place at the table. Next to mine.

I halted mid-step.

Lord Williams nodded and moved to his seat, resting his hands on the back of his chair while waiting for everyone to take their places. I couldn't move. I would have to sit next to him. And not just for tonight. I would have to sit next to him for every meal throughout his stay.

"Margaret." My mother's voice jarred me to the recognition that everyone was looking at me. I shuffled to my chair.

The table was beautifully laid, the servants having worked all day to make this dinner perfect, and I made a mental note to compliment them later, though I wished there were at least one small, repulsive something on the table that would make the baron uncomfortable. I wondered how difficult it would be to discover a dish he found particularly abhorrent and ensure it was served as a main course while he visited.

As the meal began, Alice's observations about the day were interspersed with Daniel's bark of laughter, my mother's comments, and even Lord Williams's occasional remark. I took no part in the conversation. To do so, to pretend that everything was normal when that man was sitting next to me, smiling and conversing with my family as easily as though he were a part of it already, seemed a falsehood too deep to attempt.

I picked at my food, spreading the fish around on the plate.

Then I stopped. Why should I allow the baron's presence to alter my habits? Doing so surely granted him some power over me. I shoved my queasiness aside and gingerly placed a bite on my tongue. It melted and my stomach relaxed. I smiled at my immunity to the baron and took another bite.

"Lord Williams, do you by any chance speak Russian?" Daniel asked.

I nearly spit my food out on my plate. As it was, I coughed into my napkin and quickly took a drink.

"I'm afraid I don't," the baron responded, eyeing me as though with a desire to scoot his chair farther away.

"A pity," Daniel said. "Margaret has a great love for the language. I do hope you enjoy the opera, though."

"I do. Miss Brinton, you enjoy the opera?"

"I have never been," I replied, glaring at Daniel from under my lashes.

Daniel shook his head sadly. "No, she hasn't. But she is determined to like it nevertheless."

If the opportunity ever presented itself, I wouldn't hesitate to shove Daniel in the lake. And I would make certain he knew it was on purpose.

"I would suggest going later in the season if you particularly wish to enjoy the occasion," Lord Williams offered. "Never on opening night, as the theater is thronged with gossips who have no intention of viewing the performance."

Only an idiot wouldn't know that about opening night at the London opera. No doubt the baron thought us nothing more than country bumpkins. I set my fork down.

"Very good to know. Thank you," Daniel responded, catching my eye roll.

After a moment, Lord Williams leaned toward me. "You do not enjoy fish?"

His quiet question caught me off guard. "Yes. I do." I readjusted the napkin in my lap.

"Hm. I'd hate to see how you treated food you didn't like."

"It isn't the food I find disagreeable." I clamped my mouth shut. I was allowing myself to be as rude to him as he had been to me and, though he may not object to his character, I vehemently opposed it. I needed to hold my tongue and be polite, like Louisa could.

I reclaimed my fork. If my mouth was full, I wouldn't have to speak.

"You seem to find many things disagreeable, Miss Brinton. Perhaps not all of them are deserving of your criticism."

"I do not find many things disagreeable. But when I do, it is usually because the thing has provided me with no other option."

I speared a piece of fish with my fork.

Before I could take a bite, however, Lord Williams leaned toward me. "Or perhaps it is simply because you yourself are disagreeable."

I gaped at him. He smiled and shifted away to converse with my mother.

Horrid man. Is this really what he wanted for a marriage? He was a baron; any number of women would have been ecstatic for such an offer. Why had he chosen to ruin my life in particular?

The dinner dishes were cleared away and a dark dessert topped with cream was placed on the table. I hoped it was laced with just enough poison to make the baron ill.

"Margaret, you will play for us tonight," my father said.

I glanced up from the table. I couldn't play in front of the baron again, not after the debacle of last time. "Father, Lord Williams had the opportunity to hear me play at the Hickmores'. I'm afraid he found it rather lacking and not in the least enjoyable."

My father raised his brows.

"Besides," I continued quickly, "Alice was looking forward to Daniel reading to us."

"Oh, yes, Papa," Alice exclaimed. "Please."

My father nodded his assent and I sighed with relief at avoiding another catastrophe.

The men lingered remarkably long after dinner. I tried to sew, but between wondering what the men were discussing and my anxiety to speak to Daniel regarding Mr. Northam, my stitches were wide and misshapen. I began to unstitch everything and start over.

The moment the men joined us, I sidled up next to Daniel. "I need to speak with you."

He gave me a questioning look.

"I need you to send a message to Mr. Northam."

Daniel scoffed and turned to Alice. "Have you chosen something for me to read?"

"Please, Daniel," I whispered. "Just tell him not to come."

He looked back at me. "You don't want him to come?"

I shook my head.

"Why not?"

I couldn't have him guess the real reason. "There's no point. And it would just cause awkwardness."

Daniel nodded. "I'll see what I can do."

I smiled my thanks. My attention slid to Lord Williams. He was watching me with his horrid blue eyes.

I straightened, retrieved my sewing, and didn't look up again the rest of the evening.

TWELVE

The next morning, I opened my door and peeked out. The hall was dark, the house silent except for the occasional sigh that country houses make. Grabbing my half-boots off the floor, I slipped out of my room and crept down the hall, my hand skimming the wall for balance, my other hand pressing the boots against the skirt of my walking dress to keep it from swishing. When the floor squeaked under my step, I yanked up my foot, tense, waiting. Nothing stirred. I slowly let out my breath and inched more carefully toward the stairs.

Five stairs down, I stopped, my hand clasped on the railing. I had forgotten to close my bedroom door.

Only my fear of waking someone kept the groan from escaping my lips. For one fleeting moment, I entertained the idea of going on anyway. But if that odious baron decided to take a self-guided tour of the house, I did not want him seeing into my bedchamber. Clenching my jaw, I slipped back up the stairs to my room.

When I had finally made it to the bottom of the staircase, I sat and laced up my boots. The brightening light crept though the windows, hurrying me. I wanted to catch the morning rays as they began their daily dance on the lake. I ached for a few moments alone, to escape into the silence of nature, into the solitude of non-human things.

A door clicked shut above me and I froze, but only silence echoed in my ears. Then I heard footsteps.

I fumbled through my last knot and raced out the door. As I stepped around the side of the house, light hit my face, stopping me. I breathed in the morning sun, willing it to diminish the shadows of yesterday's misfortune. The crisp morning air, the sun warming my skin, and the ruckus of birdsong all filled me with resolution. Today I would find a way to be rid of the baron. I would start right after my walk.

I danced down the steps and ran my hand along the fencing when I passed under the arbor. As a girl, I had fantasized that the arbor led to a world of make-believe and magic and, once I was a little older, love. I used to spin through the paths and imagine a rainbow of fairies wreaking havoc in the shrubbery. Then I'd sit on the bench, tilt my head back, and watch the clouds drift away. It had been so easy to believe that anything was possible.

This morning the air recovered a bit of that magic, and I smiled. Tilting my head back, I closed my eyes and inhaled, the smell of childhood contained in the scents of the flowers and bushes around me. The lake would be beautiful this morning. I would have to hurry if I was —

"Excuse me, Miss Brinton. May I join you?"

The magic vanished. My eyes flew open and my breath whooshed out of me. I turned slowly, willing him to disappear before I saw him, praying he wasn't really there.

But he was. The baron's face was freshly shaved, his hair neatly combed. His clothes were immaculate but simple, after the same fashion as the day before with a dark green coat, lighter green vest, and tall black boots. He must have been up earlier than I, since I had merely dressed and wound my hair in a bun.

He could at least have had the decency to sleep in. "Do you always rise early after a long journey?"

"Generally. I find I accomplish more if I do."

What did he hope to accomplish this morning?

"May I join you?" he asked again.

He couldn't possibly join me. I was on my way to the lake, to regain a portion of the magic he'd destroyed. "I prefer to walk alone in the mornings."

He nodded. "Company is another thing you find disagreeable?"

He would not win this battle. "Not at all, my lord. The company of friends is always agreeable, no matter the hour."

He stepped next to me. "Will you not put aside your quarrel with me for a moment? While witty banter and veiled insults have their proper place, and you excel quite handsomely at both, I find myself without the ability to keep pace so early in the morning."

Only he could offer an insult as a compliment in such a way that to refuse would appear ill-mannered. Fine. I would agree. It only meant that the opportunity to begin persuading him to leave had arrived early. However, there was no way I was going to walk all the way around the lake with him. A stroll around the garden would have to do. "If you wish." I turned and moved onto one of the garden paths. He stepped beside me and adjusted his pace to mine.

After walking a bit in silence, he said, "This is a nice walk."

Nice was not a word one should apply to nature. Exquisite, yes. Peaceful, definitely. A sanctuary from problems, a provider of hope — these were the things a person felt while walking outside. *Nice* was quite near to calling it ugly.

I turned onto a different path.

He didn't miss a step. In fact, he kept so close his hand brushed mine. I clasped my hands behind me to avoid any more accidental brushing.

"It is on the small side," he continued, "and quite formal for my taste, but it fits the house and property."

I stopped. "I am sorry you find the small size of our house and estate straining. No doubt you are being deprived of many luxuries to which you are accustomed. My family is certain to understand if you wish to make an early departure. And as for this," I continued, sweeping my hand in a wide arc to indicate the beauty around us, "it is perfect just the way it is, whatever your tastes may be." I moved on, hoping rather than believing he wouldn't follow.

He followed, resuming his place next to me. "I believe my tastes are considered refined."

Was there no end to his arrogance? "No doubt a conclusion to which you alone so impartially arrived."

"On the contrary, it is what I have been told."

"By whom?"

"Single ladies seeking my attention. And their mothers."

I stopped again, this time my mouth falling open in disbelief at his temerity. "It is a wonder you did not choose to ruin one of their lives instead of mine. It seems it would have suited everyone much more agreeably."

"Not everyone." His lips twitched and his eyes took on a teasing glint.

My own eyes narrowed. "Lord Williams, if it is your intent to mock me and insult my home, I would prefer to be left alone."

He quirked an eyebrow and his lips relaxed into an easy grin. "You already mentioned you'd rather be alone. I suspect you feel that way whether I comment on your home or not. But I was not insulting it; on the contrary, I was complimenting it."

"You have a very strange manner for complimenting." He didn't address my accusation about his mocking me, though, and

I again felt as though I was no more to him than an entertaining way to pass time. I would not be his plaything. I would not bear his company a moment longer. Solitude inside was preferable to his company outside, no matter how stifling the house could be. I spun and headed in the other direction.

"We were walking this way," he called out.

"I am returning to the house."

He trailed me. "Do you eat so early?"

"No. I am going to . . . sew."

He was beside me a moment later. He would probably follow me even if I broke into a run. I kept my gait steady, resisting the urge to test my theory. The stairs were just down the path.

He wasn't in the least troubled by the quick pace. "You find sewing an invigorating pastime, I must assume, since you are so eager to give up this fine morning and sew before breakfast. However, if this is your normal routine, I would advise you to allow for a little more exercise in your day."

I stopped, my hands clenching into fists. "My lord, if you must know, I detest sewing. But I'm finding this walk too taxing for me this morning."

"You are ill?" To my astonishment, he clasped my elbow with one hand, my hand with his other, and propelled me backward onto the bench. I fell with a plop. "Can I get you anything? Would you like me to fetch you a glass of water?" He retained my hand and crouched before me, meeting my gaze with his own steady one.

What had just happened? Was this another way for him to ridicule me? Yet he seemed sincere. "No. You misunderstand. I am not unwell." I slipped my hand from his grasp. "My lord —"

"Gregory."

"I beg your pardon?"

"My name is Gregory. I'd prefer for you to call me Gregory."

"I am not going to address you by your Christian name."

"Why not?"

He had to be jesting. This was all just part of his game to make me look ridiculous. "I do not know what you are about, but I believe this carries it too far."

He tilted his head. "It is, perhaps, uncommon. But given our circumstances, it is not carrying things too far."

"I do not believe it will ever be appropriate to address each other by our first names."

"Seeing that we are engaged —"

I jumped up. "We should not be engaged,

and you know it."

"Margaret?"

I looked with dread to discover a very astonished Louisa standing in the path a little way from us.

"Louisa!" I had to wait for Lord Williams to stand so I could maneuver around him. The slowness with which he did so prolonged the awkward situation Louisa had stumbled upon, causing my face to heat. When he'd finally stood, I scrambled around him and strode to my friend. "How are you? Have you come to join us for breakfast? My family will be delighted."

Louisa glanced at me meaningfully, then looked steadily at Lord Williams. I sighed.

"Louisa, allow me to introduce Lord Williams." Louisa's brows shot up, but I continued, "Miss Rosthorn is a particular friend of the family, my lord. Her family's estate borders our own."

"Miss Rosthorn, it is a pleasure to meet you."

Louisa curtsied with an elegance of which I had always been jealous. "I did not mean to intrude. Margaret's morning walks around the lake are as routine as the rising sun, and her absence this morning left me worried. However," she continued, her gaze flicking to me, "now that I see you are in perfect health, I shall return home."

"Oh, please stay for breakfast." My voice was calm and natural, but I tugged at her arm.

"Will it not be too great an inconvenience?"

"You know it would be no inconvenience whatsoever."

"What would be an inconvenience?" Daniel's voice made all three of us look to where he'd just appeared around a bend.

"I am trying to persuade Louisa to join us for breakfast," I replied.

Daniel's eyes widened and his shoulders straightened as though he'd just noticed her. "Good morning, Miss Rosthorn." His tone was unusually formal.

"Mr. Brinton," Louisa answered quietly.

Daniel cleared his throat. "Margaret, if she does not wish to stay, don't pester her. Miss Rosthorn, please give our regards to your parents."

"Of course." Louisa said, pulling her arm out of my hand.

"But —"

"I will visit you later," she interrupted. "I had best return. My parents will wonder. . . ." She fled down the path back toward the lake and her own home.

I spun around. "Daniel, what is the matter with you? Why did you not convince her to stay?"

"She is a grown woman who can make her own decisions. You should not work so hard to get others to bend to your will." He turned and strode up the stairs.

Daniel's insulting correction of my behavior left me stunned.

"Shall we return?" Lord Williams asked, offering me his arm.

Daniel's harshness no doubt had something to do with the baron's presence, and it was with him that the blame should lie. "Yes." Ignoring his arm, I strode ahead of him into the house.

THIRTEEN

The first thing I noticed when we entered the breakfast parlor was that my chair was much closer to Lord Williams's chair than it had been at dinner. Daniel's smirk left little doubt as to who had moved it. Unable to think of any immediate action I could take to exact revenge on Daniel without embarrassing myself as well, I vowed to find some horrible way to repay him. Quickening my pace, I determined to slide my chair away without anyone noticing, but Lord Williams reached it at the same time I did and pulled it out for me. I had no choice but to sit.

We were uncomfortably close. I tucked my elbows into my sides as much as I could while eating, but still my arm occasionally brushed his coat. I blew out some air in frustration, causing my mother to glance at me. I sent her an "I didn't do this" look and her stern expression settled on Daniel, but it was wasted since he was too engrossed in eating to notice. I wouldn't have minded a public set-down for him; he certainly deserved it. But my mother would never vocalize her disapproval considering the present company.

Immediately after breakfast, Daniel and Lord Williams went out to tour the estate. I paced the morning room in my spencer, bonnet, and gloves, anxious to get out and finally have my walk around the lake. But I couldn't do so until I was certain there was no chance of meeting the gentlemen outside. When I deemed enough time had passed, I slipped from the room.

The sound of a carriage arriving greeted me when I opened the front door. Panic shot through me.

Mr. Northam was already here.

I slipped back inside and slammed the door, cringing as the sound echoed in the hall. Then I raced to the window and drew back the curtain. But instead of the expected coach or chaise, a tilbury driven by two women pulled to a stop in front of the house. Peering closer, I groaned and dropped the curtain back into place.

Catherine and her mother had arrived, no doubt in an attempt to poach Lord Williams. If only they'd come a few minutes earlier, I would have thrown the door open myself and left them to it. But without the object of their visit being present, the Johnsons were sure to be sour company.

I turned on my heel, intent on sneaking out through the back.

The bell rang just as I passed the morning parlor. Inside the room, my mother glanced up from where she was giving Alice her morning lessons. "Margaret, who is at the door?"

Cursing my luck, I turned. "I believe it to be Mrs. Johnson and her daughter Catherine."

My father stood from the breakfast table, folding the paper he had only picked up once the baron and Daniel had left. "Excuse me." He strode past me toward the study.

My mother rose from her chair. "I was expecting this. Margaret, ring for tea. Alice, please continue this lesson in your room. I want to see that you have mastered it by the time our guests leave."

I pulled on the cord to alert the servants as Alice gathered up her things.

My mother glanced at me. "Margaret, you are still wearing your bonnet."

"I was going out."

"The arrival of guests changes that, does it not?"

I waited until Alice had slipped by me

before saying, "Mother, please don't make me stay. I have yet to take my morning walk."

She shook her head. "You spend too much time out of doors as it is. And I have never understood what occurred between you and Catherine. Surely you do not think so ill of her as to refuse her when she calls."

My shoulders fell. "No, of course not." I slid off my gloves and bonnet and was just removing my spencer when the Johnsons were shown into the room.

Mrs. Johnson glanced at me sharply. "I hope we are not intruding."

I curtsied, shadowing my mother's movements. "Not at all," my mother replied. "It is always a delight to have company." She indicated a few chairs.

I sat in the chair I always occupied when company called. It was situated so as to allow me to look out the window behind the guests without divulging where my attention truly lay. I couldn't see the lake from so low an angle, but I could see the top of the beech trees surrounding it. I tried to determine if they were swaying or not. No breeze had cooled the air that morning, but perhaps one had picked up, in which case I might need a different jacket.

When the usual fifteen-minute time allotment for a call passed, I shifted my attention back to the conversation. Mrs. Johnson was relaying some anecdote regarding one of her sons, who had recently moved to Bath with his wife. I focused back out the window. The trees definitely seemed to be moving. But perhaps it was a warm wind.

"Your daughter seems anxious for a certain someone's return," Mrs. Johnson said, jolting my attention back to her. A knowing smile covered her face. "Can this have anything to do with your mysterious aristocratic visitor?"

They had heard of the engagement?

No. There would have been no point in their visit if they knew we were engaged. I could still make this work. "Not at all, I assure you. I was merely lamenting the passing of such a perfect day. I do not think we shall see many more of them this year."

"Ah, yes," Catherine broke in, a small sneer curling her lip. "Ever the avid admirer of nature. Much more at home outside than with friends, even."

Catherine could not possibly still consider us friends, could she? We were barely more than acquaintances these days. "I do take pleasure in my daily exercise," I said, refraining from adding that the sooner she and her mother left, the sooner I could enjoy it. I had a sudden thought of a way in which I could both repay Daniel for this morning's chair incident and ensure that if the Johnsons heard the rumor of the engagement they wouldn't believe it, all while sneaking in an attempt to pawn the baron off on someone else. "I believe our guest feels the same way, as he walked this morning in the gardens and is now riding about the estate with my brother. It is regretful that you have missed him. Perhaps you will return in a day or two and join us for dinner."

Catherine frowned, her transparent expression relaying her distrust in my invitation. But Mrs. Johnson seized the opportunity. "How very thoughtful of you, Margaret. I don't believe we have any engagements for tomorrow night."

I smiled. "Wonderful." Catherine could spend the night flirting with the baron, and, with any luck, drive him clean away. And Daniel would detest having her in the house. Her previous attempts at winning his affection had resulted in his despising the sound of her voice. Perhaps I could even convince her to sing.

My mother rose and I rose with her. "Well, we shall plan for tomorrow, then."

They said their goodbyes and I even went

so far as to see them out the door, waving as they drove off.

"Margaret," my mother said as soon as the door closed, her tone demanding to know why I had extended the invitation.

I shrugged. "You are always telling me to be friendlier with Catherine. I thought this as good an opportunity as any."

My mother's eyes narrowed, but she said no more on the subject. I retrieved my bonnet and gloves and left.

FOURTEEN

That evening, I took a book down from the shelf behind the door in my father's study and turned it over in my hands. It wasn't that I wanted to read. But it was nice to find a quiet corner where I was certain not to be disturbed by the baron. Situated where I was, even if he looked in this room, he wouldn't see me. It was the perfect place.

I set the book back. It wasn't the one I wanted. My favorite book of poetry was missing.

The door opened and Daniel walked in. "He has some excellent ideas regarding the estate," he was saying to someone. "We rode over the entire property today."

My father and Lord Williams entered behind him. Even here was not safe, it seemed.

"I would like to hear them," my father said.

I rolled my eyes. Daniel and my father

were fawning over Lord Williams simply because of his title. It was absurd. If any other man had offered suggestions, no one would have paid half as much attention.

The men took seats around the desk. Though Daniel was still in his riding clothes, the baron was dressed for dinner in a conservative blue jacket. I glanced down at my blue gown and frowned.

"He has this idea regarding the crops. Well, why don't you tell him yourself, my lord?"

"The first thing to do would be to drain the lake and use the water that feeds into it —"

"What?" I stepped forward. "You cannot get rid of the lake."

The men all turned and Lord Williams quickly rose.

"Ah, Margaret," Daniel said. "Will you excuse us? We have some estate business to discuss, not a matter for women." Not waiting for a reply, he turned back around in his chair.

"There is no reason to drain the lake," I reiterated, nodding that Lord Williams should sit back down. He did so with a small frown.

"Of course there is. It's little more than a dead pond as is," Daniel replied. My father didn't look convinced, though he returned his attention to Daniel. Lord Williams's attention, though, lingered on me, a thought-filled expression on his face.

I ignored him. My father allowed Daniel to take on occasional projects he deemed necessary to allow Daniel the experience for when he had the management of the estate. I had to find a way to ensure that draining the lake was not one of those projects. "No. This is absurd. You've had some interesting ideas in the past, Daniel, but this wins the prize as the worst."

Daniel kept his attention on our father. "It's not useful. It's nowhere near any of the crops or livestock. It isn't even stocked with fish."

"It most certainly *is* useful," I replied, striding forward. He *would* listen to me. This was one matter in which I would not back down. "And, as I am sure Lord Williams will inform you, what with his tastes being so very refined, the lake is the only tolerable aspect of our estate, according to modern standards."

Lord Williams cleared his throat.

"Margaret, shouldn't you be getting ready for dinner?" Daniel asked.

"I am ready. Father, you can't possibly contemplate such an action. That lake has stood as a landmark on our estate for generations."

My father sat back in his chair. "I would like to hear what Lord Williams has to say on the matter."

I moved around the desk, my back to Daniel and Lord Williams. "Why?" I asked quietly. "Riding over the estate doesn't provide a person with a knowledge of the day-to-day workings of the land. He can't know what he's saying."

"Perhaps," Daniel said loudly, "it would be best to discuss this after dinner." Which meant he wished to continue the discussion when I was not present to voice objections to whatever scheme he and Lord Williams had concocted.

Mother entered. "Colin, Daniel. Dinner is in half an hour."

"That is my cue to dress. Thank you, Eloise." My father stood.

Behind me, Daniel and Lord Williams stood as well.

"Please, father," I said quietly. "Please don't do this."

"Margaret, I know how important the lake is to you. Nothing will be decided tonight, but I would like to at least hear Lord Williams's ideas."

"Did you know, Margaret," Daniel interrupted, "that Lord Williams is quite fond of music and has studied a bit himself? Perhaps you will entertain us all with a song later."

I turned to him in shock. I rarely sang for anyone outside of the family. I could not endure the thought of the baron's reaction to my singing when he had found my playing so atrocious. "I am certain that if Lord Williams is so very fond of music he will find no pleasure in listening to me."

"Quite the contrary, Miss Brinton," Lord Williams said.

"You are too kind, my lord. But you will have to excuse me."

He bowed his head in consent and followed my father and brother out of the room.

My mother stayed at the door. "You should at least play for him."

"You would understand why I cannot if I were to tell you of his behavior at the Hickmores'."

"I am listening."

Surprised but grateful for my mother's willingness to hear my story, I relayed everything that had occurred.

When I'd finished, she said, "This engagement has never sat well with me. I will endeavor to learn more about our guest."

Relief washed over me. My mother was

on my side. She was going to help me escape. "Thank you."

A half hour later, we assembled in the parlor. Now was the perfect opportunity to get Daniel away from Lord Williams and ask him for an update on his letter to Mr. Northam. I walked over to a pile of books on a table and rifled through them. Under the pretense of indecision, I said, "Daniel, I believe you have read most of these. Will you assist me?"

"Actually," he said, "that is a stack Lord Williams has recommended for me. You will have to ask his opinion on which one you should read, though I doubt you will find any of them very interesting."

I stepped back as Lord Williams rose from his chair. Why was every attempt to distance myself from him backfiring?

"There are no novels here," he said apologetically, coming to stand near me.

"I read more than just novels," I retorted.

"I am glad to hear it."

It was lamentable that anything I did made him glad. "You disapprove of novels?"

"Not at all, though I believe some novels are of more merit than others."

"No doubt you are one of those who rank sermons on conduct much more highly than novels."

"No." Lord Williams selected a book and turned it over in his hands. "There are far too many women who know the arts of conduct." He handed the book to me.

I glanced at the spine. It was my favorite book of poetry. I would have blamed the incident on Daniel, but I doubted Daniel even knew I treasured this collection. "What is this?"

"A collection of poems I admire."

I frowned. "I am surprised you find pleasure in poetry."

"You may be surprised by a great many things about me, Miss Brinton." He turned and resumed his position next to Daniel.

FIFTEEN

I sat on the bench out front after breakfast the next morning, pretending to read a sermon on conduct. The talk of the morning had again focused on changes that should be made to the estate, and my residual agitation made it almost impossible to sit still, let alone focus on the words of the book. But I didn't give up my pretense for fear that the baron would catch me without an occupation and request my company.

A small noise on the gravel drew my attention and I glanced up, careful to make it appear I was still reading in case the noise arose from Lord Williams. Louisa's figure rounded the bend, and I tossed the book aside and ran to her. "Oh, Louisa! You came!"

"Of course. Tell me everything."

"Come sit with me."

To my surprise, she pulled away. "Perhaps

we could walk?"

"Why?"

"I think it better if I do not meet with your brother."

"What has happened?"

Louisa studied her gloved hands. "The last time we met he seemed ill-pleased to see me. If . . . something has changed . . . regarding his intentions —"

I suddenly understood. Daniel's reaction at the stairs had caused her to believe his affection had transferred to someone he'd met at the Hickmores'. "He loves you, Louisa, and no one else."

She wouldn't meet my eyes, so I continued, "He has been acting peculiar ever since Lord Williams appeared. But yesterday morning he was upset with me because he thought I was pressuring you into staying. He did not wish for you to stay if you had no desire to."

"I understand." She smiled, but doubt still shone in her eyes. Then her smile turned to a frown. "Tell me — your guest, Lord Williams — he is the same man you told me about?"

I nodded.

"What is he doing here?"

I surveyed our surroundings. No one appeared to be outside, but still I dragged her across the lawn to a bench on the path near the woods, relaying how the baron was the man my father had arranged for me to marry and everything that had occurred since.

"Oh, Margaret." She clasped my hands. "What are you going to do? What does your brother think?"

"Daniel is practically in love with the baron himself. My whole family is enchanted by him."

Louisa frowned, a line of thought creasing her brows as she murmured, "He did appear quite attentive yesterday when I chanced upon you."

I rolled my eyes. "When you discovered us, I had been trying to make my escape. The baron mistook my desire to return to the house as a bout of illness and forced me onto the bench to rest." I hesitated, debating whether I should tell her how he asked me to call him by his first name. I decided against it, fearing that if I told her, his lack of insistence on formality would appeal to her. With my family so against me, I needed her support.

"Margaret, what I fail to understand is why Lord Williams is even here."

"I told you —"

"No, I mean, why does he wish to marry

you?" At my expression, she rushed to add, "You know I didn't mean it that way."

I laughed. "Of course not, but. . . ." I shrugged. "I have no idea. It makes no sense. I even asked him, but he's disinclined to tell me. I can only think that he either means to keep me from his cousin or he means to teach me some lesson."

"Neither of which warrant an engagement." Louisa stopped and stared over my shoulder. I followed her gaze to find Daniel and Lord Williams strolling toward us across the lawn.

I stood. "Let's walk."

She hesitated.

"Hurry," I urged.

We moved along the path skirting the yard, heading toward the lake and away from the men.

"What have you heard of Mr. Northam?" she asked.

"Nothing." I sighed. "My hope is that Daniel has written to him and asked him not to come. It wouldn't do to have him appear while Lord Williams is here. It might ruin my chances with him."

"Do you have a plan?"

I shook my head. "I've tried everything short of being malicious myself — and perhaps even a little of that. You would have

161

abhorred the way I've acted."

Daniel reached my side. "Abhorrence at the way you act is nothing new." He smiled at Louisa. "May we join you?"

I stopped walking and glared at Daniel. "No," I replied at the same time that Louisa quietly responded, "Of course."

I sighed. "For Louisa's sake," I amended.

"It is a pleasure to see you again, Miss Rosthorn," Lord Williams said.

Daniel crossed his arms and glanced from the baron to Louisa with a frown.

He was jealous. It would do him some good to feel jealous. If I could get Lord Williams and Louisa to walk alone together, perhaps that would spur Daniel to action. The lake seemed the best route; Lord Williams would never consider draining the lake once he had experienced its beauty up close.

"We are walking to the lake." I linked my arm through Daniel's. His frown deepened, but I ignored it and tugged on his arm.

"What are you up to?" he asked when we reached the bottom of the stairs.

"Up to? I'm saving your relationship with the only woman who'll have you." I glanced over my shoulder, pleased that Lord Williams and Louisa were conversing.

Daniel huffed.

"You do not believe me? Would you believe we were hurrying through the yard because she was afraid to encounter you?"

"Of course not."

"Well, you should. Your behavior toward her since our return has been less than encouraging."

Daniel tensed. "Margaret, the last time we met I fell into the lake."

I took in his slightly reddened cheeks and couldn't help but laugh.

He scowled. I put a hand on his arm to placate him. "Daniel, if embarrassment is the reason for your cold greeting yesterday, speak with her. She thinks it is something serious."

"Having her witness such a misfortune is serious."

I shook my head. "Your injured pride is not serious. Her thinking you met someone at the Hickmores' is."

Daniel stopped walking. "But — that — she thinks that? Did she say as much to you?" He glanced behind us to where Louisa smiled at something Lord Williams said.

"You need to speak with her," I urged.

He kicked a rock on the path and sent it racing into the grass, then set his shoulders with resolve. But I had not discussed with him the other thing weighing on my mind, so I tugged on his arm to continue our walk. "I need to speak to you of something else."

"What?" he asked, glancing over his shoulder again but walking with me.

"Did you write to Mr. Northam for me?" Daniel yanked his arm away from me. "Why does it matter?"

"Daniel, please. I cannot have him coming here while Lord Williams is present."

He sneered. "What makes you think he'll come at all?"

"What if he did? Whatever you think, he was about to propose. What if he comes and demands he had the prior claim?"

"You've decided Lord Williams is the better choice?" Daniel asked in disbelief.

I shook my head. "Never."

"Then you are an even greater fool than I thought. I should tell Lord Williams of your stupidity while he still has time to back out."

We came to a stop again and I stared at Daniel, hurt by the betrayal of his allegiance, but not denying the opportunity it provided. "He already knows and has wasted no time in telling me as much himself. However, I wish you would reiterate it. Please, see that he is gone within the hour."

"You do not know what you are asking."

"Yes, I do."

Daniel glanced back at the approaching couple. "He is the best thing that has ever happened to you. If you would only open your eyes you would see it, too."

At that moment Louisa laughed quietly at something Lord Williams said. He was winning her over as well. That wasn't supposed to happen. "Why can no one see that he is all pretense?" I asked in frustration.

Daniel shook his head and turned away, studying the lake as Louisa and the baron caught up with us.

Well, whether Daniel aided me or not, I would still help him. Flashing my brightest smile, I said, "Lord Williams, perhaps you would enjoy a bouquet of flowers from the garden in your room. I have been remiss in my duty, as it is a habit of mine to ensure each of our guests is greeted with an arrangement." I stepped between him and Louisa, forcing Louisa up the path next to Daniel. "Upon reconsideration, it is rather fortuitous that I waited, is it not? Else you would have found yourself waking each morning to a disagreeably formal selection of blooms, and now I will be sure to obtain some wildflowers instead."

"Indeed. I do not know how to thank you for your neglect," Lord Williams replied in his characteristic ironic tone.

I shot him a glare. He raised a brow in return.

"Miss Rosthorn?" Daniel held an arm out to Louisa and she hesitantly took it. Lord Williams made to follow them but I placed a hand on his arm, stopping him until they were several feet in front of us. When Louisa finally turned her face to Daniel and spoke, I clasped my hands behind me in satisfaction.

"Well done," Lord Williams commented.

He couldn't have known what had transpired. "Excuse me?"

He indicated Daniel and Louisa.

Perhaps he understood more than I gave him credit for. I shrugged and followed after them. "There was a simple misunderstanding."

He kept pace with me. "I would that all misunderstandings were so easily rectified."

"Yes, indeed," I muttered. Though his presence didn't quite qualify as a misunderstanding.

"Miss Rosthorn appears to be a very amiable friend."

"She is the best sort of friend."

"Does she have siblings?"

His question made me stumble, but I quickly recovered my footing. "Yes. An older brother."

Lord Williams nodded as though I had confirmed something.

"Are you acquainted with her brother?"

"No, we have never met."

That was a relief.

His question gave me pause, though. If Lord Williams had siblings, people who depended on him, I could use them as another reason against his marrying me. Certainly our union would be frowned upon by any relatives.

"Do you have siblings, my lord?"

"I have asked that you call me Gregory."

"And I refuse."

He sighed. "No, I do not have siblings."

"Cousins aside from Mr. Northam, then?"

"None." He glanced at me.

It was as though his life had been orchestrated to be as unhelpful as possible. "Does Mr. Northam know of your being here?"

His brow furrowed. "I should hope not."

Now we were getting somewhere. "Then you are not so very close?"

"I do not have the rapport with him that you appear to have with your siblings and friends. Though we do converse on many matters, there are some confidences that are best left unshared."

Had he really not shared the engagement with his own family? What possible motivation could he have for omitting such information? "You are rather like siblings, then, as there are many things I would not share with either Daniel or Alice. Do you support each other in your decisions, as siblings should?"

He tilted his head. "What are you driving at?"

"Oh, nothing." I smiled. "Only, I do hope Mr. Northam is like a sibling to you. I could not imagine life without the little contests and irritants that siblings provide."

He looked at me sharply. "What contests?"

I frowned at his reaction. Daniel and I had numerous ongoing competitions, little games started as children that we had never seen fit to outgrow. The best games were played in public, awarding extra points when we pinned the other to some promise or errand by making the request in the company of others where a refusal was impossible. Such as Daniel forcing me to speak with Mr. Lundall alone or his ensnaring me into the game of lawn bowls with Lord Williams. "Everything. Anything. A game of chess, a wager on who could throw a rock farther, whether you would stop and help our coachman. . . ."

His expression eased, but a brow rose. "You wagered on whether or not I would help?"

"Of course."

"Did you win or lose?"

"I lost."

"I am sorry to have cost you a win."

I shrugged. "It was no great loss."

After a brief pause, Lord Williams said, "My cousin has always been a great admirer of competition. Sometimes he is a little too enthusiastic."

"Cuts of cloth," I muttered.

"I beg your pardon?"

"It seems you two were cut from the same cloth. I would say you are a little too enthusiastic about some things."

"Such as?"

"Well, you were rather insistent regarding a game of bowls together."

"Yes, and I believe I was labeled a cheater because of that game."

I shrugged and grabbed a leaf off a tree. "You should not worry yourself about it. You have obviously endeared yourself to my family."

"But not to you."

I laughed. "Surely you do not care what I think of you."

"I believe it is customary to care what one's intended thinks of one."

I shrugged. "I don't care what you think

of me."

"Yes. I know."

I turned and studied him. Was he mocking me again? He didn't seem to be in earnest, yet the taunting smile was absent from his expression. "You cannot object, nor be surprised. Our circumstances are not customary in the least."

"As you remind me at every opportunity."

I refocused on my leaf. "There is a solution, of course."

"Flowers, gifts, kisses. That sort of thing?"

I stopped, aghast that he'd suggest anything as intimate as kissing. "No. Of course not."

"No?" The smile was back.

I narrowed my eyes. "I want nothing of the sort from you."

"Then what do you want?"

Now was my chance. I took a deep breath. "Retract the agreement that exists between us. You cannot want this marriage any more than I. I have no knowledge of the circumstances that drove you into it, but whatever they are, I can promise you that they will not make you as miserable as marriage to me will."

Lord Williams fell silent. I forced myself to look at the lake so as not to pressure a response from him. I needed him to deliberate on the truthfulness of my words, for surely he must see that our very characters were at odds with each other.

He finally said, "If I were to do this, I would find myself absolved of whatever has led you to create such an unfavorable opinion of me?"

I turned. He couldn't possibly be ignorant of his ill manners. But perhaps he was so accustomed to untitled people holding him in awe that no one had displayed their dislike for him before. No doubt they were all better accomplished at schooling their features and hiding their emotions than I.

However, all that was beside the point. "Yes, of course." The excitement of a possible victory — of regaining my freedom — made me optimistic. "Oh, and you must convince my father to keep the lake."

He studied me. "You would have me do this even if draining the lake is in the best interest of the estate?"

The leaf crumbled in my fist. "It is not in the best interest of the estate's occupants."

He shrugged dismissively. "That is something your father will have to decide."

I would not be dismissed. "The idea would never have occurred to him if you had not taken it upon yourself to suggest it."

He started walking again. This time I kept pace with him.

"What is it about this lake that is so vital to your happiness?"

I gestured to the water in frustration. "It is not just my happiness. Our entire family derives enjoyment from it, as do many of our neighbors. We have grown up playing in the water, picnicking along this shore. We used to swim here as children."

"You wish to retain it for nostalgic purposes?"

How was I to make him understand? Not only understand. I had to convince him that it was important enough for him to argue my point against Daniel while still retaining his compliance in ending our engagement. But it would mean exposing my feelings, and I had no reason to believe he would not mock me for them.

Yet, what did I care if he mocked me? Hadn't he been doing just that from the time he'd arrived at my home, and even before? Still, my voice was quiet when I explained, "This lake is more than just a body of water or even a place of entertainment. I have found peace here when I could find it no other place. There is a tranquility one derives from the sound of lapping water, the rustling of a breeze through the trees, which is soothing and reassuring in moments of distress. A lake — our lake — has, at times, provided more comfort than a friend's company or a parent's embrace."

"I venture to believe you are the only one in your family who feels this way."

"No. Daniel might not wish to admit it and Alice is probably not aware of it, but the lake is a part of them. My father, as well. Up until a little while ago, he and I walked here together every morning, a tradition we started while I was a child."

"How long has it been since he joined you?"

I was about to excuse my father's absence on account of his illness but paused when I realized our walks had stopped before the illness, when I had, for a time, slipped out of the house early so that I might walk alone. They had stopped because of Edward's betrayal. I could not think of an instance since when I had seen him walk down here. "Longer than I'd realized."

"If they discuss the topic again in my presence, I will remind your father and brother of your feelings. However, though understandable, the sentiments you have expressed do not change my opinion."

This man was unendurable. "This whole landscape would suffer because of your opinion. Does your arrogance know no bounds? You speak and act with complete disregard to those around you, as though we are nothing more than plants in your yard to be moved or destroyed according to your whim. Yet each person you trample has a life full of hopes and regrets that you will never understand. It is the same with what surrounds us. Can you even appreciate anything beyond how it serves you?"

He frowned as though in disapproval of my thoughts. I'd had enough of his disapproval. "I am a fool. I hoped too much in expecting you, a man with title and money and haughty opinions, to understand. A man who is willing to marry a woman against her will cannot possibly be expected to comprehend such things."

His eyes flashed and he was suddenly directly in front of me. "I will ignore your slight against my sensibilities, Miss Brinton, since you seem determined to think ill of me. But, whether or not you believe I comprehend such things, I will not mislead your family with unsound advice."

"Who are you to give us advice? You think because you are titled we should bow before you and be grateful for whatever notice you bestow upon us? Keep your advice. And your offers and insults. They are not wanted here." I glared at him, our faces inches from each other, the air between us charged as though the space separating us held its breath. His blue eyes burned with cold disdain while my own body felt afire with anger. He had given me a perfect understanding of my position with him. He would never adjust his opinions to accommodate my desires. If we were to marry, I would have to bend my will to his.

I would never do that.

"Margaret!"

Startled, I turned toward Daniel's voice. The space between Lord Williams and me exhaled, returning to nothing more than dirt and air and light. My brother and Louisa stood near the shore a short distance away.

"I'm calling in what you owe. Take Lord Williams out in the boat so he can see the lake better."

I scowled. "That was not the agreement."

"Would you really rather it be Lundall?"

Being alone with Lord Williams with no possibility of escape was the last thing I wanted. "His lordship does not wish to ride out on the lake."

"You know nothing of my wishes," Lord Williams said quietly. "Please do not speak for me." He moved off to help Daniel turn the boat over.

I walked to Louisa. "I can't do this."

She touched my arm sympathetically. "Lord Williams appears to be quite the gentleman. Your brother thinks very highly of him."

"Daniel has known him for less than a week, Louisa. Our family has already proved to be quite gullible when it comes to suitors for me."

Louisa dropped her hand and I registered what I'd said. I turned in horror to my friend. "Oh, I'm so sorry. I didn't mean — what I meant was —"

"It's all right, Margaret. I know how strongly you are repulsed by this. But perhaps you should give him a chance. From what Daniel has told me, he seems to have nothing to gain by this association."

I bit my lip. Her brother had also seemed to have nothing to gain by the association. The baron wasn't here without a reason. I just didn't know how to discover what that reason was.

SIXTEEN

"The boat is ready. Margaret?" Daniel held his hand out to assist me. I shot Louisa a pained look and walked to the boat.

"This fulfills the bargain?" I asked.

Daniel nodded.

I stepped into the boat. Once I was settled, Lord Williams and Daniel pushed the boat into the water. Lord Williams hopped in at the last minute and settled on the seat opposite me.

"Whatever you do, my lord, do not let her row," Daniel called as Lord Williams drew us away. "You will end up soaked!"

I turned and looked out over the water.

We rowed in silence. Tilting my head back, I closed my eyes, determined to ignore the baron. The rustling of the trees, though fainter in the middle of the lake, never truly faded. The sun's comforting touch lightened my spirits. I let out a slow breath. "Say what you will, but there is a peace to be found here that is unique and cannot be found elsewhere."

When Lord Williams didn't respond, I opened my eyes. He was watching me with an expression of confusion and something else I couldn't place. I grew uncomfortable under his scrutiny and turned away to dangle my fingers in the water. The ripples trailed in a line behind us.

The silence grew unbearable and guilt began to eat at me. No matter what his words and actions, I should not have reacted with so much feeling.

"I apologize, my lord," I said after a few moments. "I am not normally this argumentative."

"I am certain this must be very difficult for you."

Whether he referenced our supposed union, his continual presence, or the potential draining of the lake, I did not know. I glanced at him, but his expression revealed nothing. I decided it didn't matter. "Yes. And I am afraid I have not proved equal to the task." I looked back at the water and rested my head on one arm, plunging my other hand into the lake.

"Miss Brinton, I cannot release you from the agreement. I am sorry."

I sat up in horror. The sun glittered

blindingly off the water and I had to raise my hand to block the glare. "What do you mean? Of course you can. When we return to the house, tell my parents you have changed your mind. I give you leave to lay full blame upon me. Tell them — tell them you cannot tolerate me. They will believe you."

"I cannot do that."

"Why not?"

"Because it is not the truth."

"It isn't?"

He slowly shook his head.

Oh. "Well, it should be. We despise each other."

"It doesn't have to be this way."

Yes, it did have to be this way. I'd made a promise to myself, and I wasn't about to let Lord Williams destroy me more than he already had. "It will never be anything else."

The boat had turned so I faced the sandy stretch of shore from which we had launched. Daniel and Louisa were no longer there. I quickly glanced around and spotted them walking away down the path. I motioned toward them with my hand. "Lord Williams, get them to stop. They cannot leave us here alone."

Lord Williams looked in the direction I pointed. "What would you have me do?"

179

"Call to them! They must be stopped."

Lord Williams turned in the boat and stood up. "Brinton," he called, but not loudly. Daniel and Louisa did not even look in our direction.

"Oh, for goodness' sake." I stood and climbed over the bench.

"Miss Brinton, please sit down."

"Someone has got to get their attention and —"

"Miss Brinton, sit down!"

I lost my footing and fell onto the ridge of the boat, my arm plunging into the water with a loud splash. Yanking it out, I scooted quickly to the other side. The boat rocked with my movement. I grasped the edge before noticing the empty seat; Lord Williams had disappeared. I crept toward where he had been sitting.

A hand sprang out of the water and clasped the side of the boat.

"Oh, my!" I scrambled to the side of the boat and looked over the edge into the wet face of Lord Williams. "I am so sorry, my lord." Grabbing his hand, I tried to pull him into the boat.

"Miss Brinton, please let go of me."

"But —" The sternness of his expression cut off my words. I released him and sat back.

"If you would be so kind as to assist me out of my coat, I believe I can manage the rest."

The rest of what? Was he going to undress in the water? "My lord, surely you do not mean to stay in the water. Let me help you back into the boat."

"My coat, Miss Brinton." He held out his arm to me. I hesitated, then grasped the cuff of his coat so he could slip his arm out. "Thank you," he said.

I took that as my cue to release the garment. Lord Williams shifted in the water for a moment before flinging the coat into the boat, splashing water on me as he did. I flinched away from the sudden moisture.

"I beg your pardon," he said. Then he pushed off the boat, heading toward the shore.

"Wait, why are you swimming?"

He didn't respond.

I grasped the oars and headed after him. When I reached the shore he was already walking out of the water. Grabbing his coat, I stood and walked carefully to the front of the boat, as near to the dry sand as possible. I would have to get my boots wet no matter what, but I had to at least try to spare my dress.

He glanced at me as he bent a leg and

grabbed his shin. "If you would wait a moment, I will assist you." He leaned forward and water poured out of his boot.

I stopped. Lord Williams had just offered me assistance in a rather calm tone while soaking wet as a result of my actions. It was not at all how I'd expected him to react. He had every reason to be upset. Furious, even. His boots were likely ruined, his clothes, especially his silk waistcoat, destroyed, and he smelled like lake water — though he may not have realized that last bit yet.

I certainly wouldn't wait for his assistance; he was quite likely intending to pick me up and toss me into the water as repayment. I sat on the rim of the boat and threw my legs over the side so they dangled above the water.

Just as I was about to jump down, he placed a hand on my shoulder. "Miss Brinton, are you always this impatient?" His tone sounded mildly annoyed. I glanced up, ready with a quip, but water dripped from his hair, running down his face to the edge of his chin, and his white sleeves, so wet they clung to him, poured a steady trickle of drops into the shallow water below.

My remark drained away. "Yes," I mumbled.

Lord Williams tugged the boat until it was

safely on the shore, then offered me his hand. I took it and his fingers closed around mine, confident but gentle. As he assisted me off, I had the unmistakable feeling that the baron's grip personified the man himself.

Seventeen

The moment my boots were out of danger, Lord Williams dropped my hand to tug the boat higher onto the shore.

"Thank you." I wiped my hand in the folds of my dress, hoping to somehow rub out the eerie feeling of safety that lingered with the memory of his touch.

He left the boat and strode to a nearby fallen tree, untied his cravat, and slung it over the log. The slope of his shoulders drew my attention to the way his shirt clung to his muscular arms as he bent each leg behind him again, spilling more water from his boots onto the ground. He ran his fingers through his hair, making his shirt cling to his arms even more. He was much more muscular than his clothes, when dry, revealed. His hand dropped, displaying his clenched jaw. The muscle popped, accenting the angle of his chin, then disappeared.

A bird's call brought me to my senses. I

was staring. I dropped my gaze from his face only to discover that he had unbuttoned his waistcoat and was untying the collar of his shirt.

"What are you doing?" I flung his coat at the boat and rushed up to him, putting my hands on his chest in an attempt to keep his vest closed.

He glanced at me. "I am removing my clothes."

"You cannot do that!"

"Miss Brinton, I will not remain in these wet things."

I filled with apprehension. "You cannot mean to remove *all* your wet things." I glanced over him quickly. Everything was soaked. Even my hands, pressing against his waistcoat, had droplets of water running down them.

Lord Williams lifted an eyebrow and a small smile curved his lips. "Oh?"

I stepped back in alarm.

He chuckled. "No, Miss Brinton. I plan only to remove those items that are unnecessary."

My cheeks grew hot. Lord Williams would soon be standing in only his breeches. What was I supposed to do then? I had never been in a more embarrassing situation. "I assume you would like assistance in removing your boots." I glanced down at the mud-streaked shoes and sighed. It wouldn't matter that I had kept dry before. I was about to ruin yet another dress, only this time it was a dress I actually liked.

"Miss Brinton." Lord Williams's words rang with rebuke. My gaze flew to his in surprise. "My boots are filthy. I would never ask you to do such a thing."

I stared at him. He would rather be uncomfortable than have me sully my dress? Why? This didn't fit the man who'd told me what to do, ruined my chances of marriage, and then ensured the end of my plans through forcing my hand.

Was this a new twist in his plan?

Or . . . I frowned. Was it possible I had been mistaken?

No, nothing about what had happened could be misinterpreted. But why had he done it all? And why was he here now, acting the gentleman, when we both knew this wasn't who he was?

A smile lifted a corner of his mouth. "If I'd known all it would take to catch your attention was a swim, I'd have insisted on a boat ride the first day."

He was flirting with me.

My cheeks flamed. "You haven't caught my attention." I picked up his coat from where it had landed, half in the mud. "Your coat. It's a bit dirty."

His gaze held mine as he took the coat. "Thank you." His voice was soft and coaxing.

I stepped away. "I am sure you'd like to get on with your —" I gestured to his clothes. I would not watch him disrobe. A nearby tree provided a perfect support, and I leaned my forehead against it and closed my eyes.

"I am sorry this makes you uncomfortable."

Not only was my face on fire, but my neck also, burning as I struggled to push images of the state of his attire, or lack thereof, from my mind. "It is no more than I deserve, I am sure."

At least we were alone, and no one else was near to witness this spectacle. My mother, surely, would have fainted from shock. The situation may have proved embarrassing enough for even my father to feel lightheaded with shame.

"I am ready."

I pushed off the tree and forced myself to look at him, prepared for a wholly improper scene. Instead, surprise and gratitude left me speechless. He had retained his shirt, though he'd rolled his sleeves up to his elbows, as well as his waistcoat, which, though unbuttoned, must still have been quite uncomfortable. His coat and cravat were slung across an arm. His hair, no longer dripping so profusely, had actually curled a bit.

In that moment I understood why the ladies at the Hickmores' party had been disappointed by his early departure. His lack of formal attire made him appear relaxed and approachable and quite worth sparing more than one passing glance on.

A slow smile spread across his face. His eyes, more welcoming than I had ever seen them, began to sparkle as though with barely contained amusement.

Fear flitted through me. I was allowing him to draw me in. How was it possible that someone who behaved so abominably could at the same time be so charming?

I spun toward the path. "I am ready as well." I didn't wait, knowing he'd catch up. And I needed a moment to myself, however brief, because whatever had just passed between us made me feel off balance, as though I was still standing in the boat, only a storm was rising on the lake and the boat was quickly becoming unsteady.

As we neared the garden, Lord Williams said, "I am afraid I failed to find much peace at your lake. While a swim could be termed refreshing, there was nothing tranquil or soothing about this afternoon."

I looked up. His face was completely serious, but a twinkle in his eyes betrayed him. He was jesting.

I wasn't quite sure how to reply. "Being refreshed is something."

"Yes, it is." He smiled, his first genuine smile.

That smile was worse than our arguments. At least in a disagreement the battle lines were clearly drawn. But the way he grinned, warm and welcoming, did something inside that made me want to answer with a grin of my own.

I was becoming as ridiculous as my family. I would not allow him power over me.

I yanked my attention back to the path. We climbed the stairs from the garden to the lawn and I stopped. It would do no good to be caught with him half dressed. If Daniel and Louisa saw us, there would be no end to the teasing. If my parents were to discover us, I was in for more than a mere lecture. "I need to see where everyone is."

He lifted a brow but uttered no disagreement.

I made him wait by the large yew bush while I stood on the wall. Louisa and Daniel sat with my mother and sister. My father wasn't visible in any of the windows.

I sighed. "We will have to risk it. However, it would be best if we entered the house separately."

"Why is that?"

"You want us to be discovered with you looking like . . . with you half-dressed looking like. . . ."

"Looking like I fell into the lake?" He shrugged. "You cannot tell me it has not happened before."

"Not to a guest. And certainly not to a baron. You go in by the front door. I'll walk around to the back." I held out my hand, waiting for him to assist me down.

"Anyone who sees either of us will guess what happened." To my surprise, he grabbed me by my waist and lifted me off the wall. Clutching his arms to keep my balance, I swallowed a shriek that would certainly have brought my mother and sister rushing to the window. In a harsh whisper, I demanded, "What are you doing?"

He set me down. "The last time you climbed that wall, you fell off, and I have a suspicion it was partly my fault. I could not allow that to happen again."

His tone might make one believe that having a man lift a woman from a wall was the most natural thing in the world. But there was nothing natural about the way his hands burned imprints into my sides that I was certain would never go away.

I stepped out of his grasp. "Next time, the assistance of *one* of your hands will be enough."

He nodded and started walking away.

"Where are you going?"

He paused. "To change. As much as I enjoy spending time with you, I think it best if I return to a more proper state of attire." He disappeared around the side of the house.

He enjoyed spending time with me. Was he serious? Did it matter? Confusion wore at my resolve. The man from the Hickmores' would never have handled me so gently. He would never have been kind after being knocked into a lake. And his touch would never have left me feeling warm and unsettled.

This side of Lord Williams was definitely more dangerous than the man from the Hickmores'.

EIGHTEEN

The ringing bell signaled the Johnsons' arrival five minutes earlier than expected. Those were five minutes I had planned to spend in my room to await the last possible moment to descend in an effort to keep my interactions with Lord Williams to a minimum. No good would come from being around him more than absolutely necessary.

This afternoon had only reiterated how important the selection of my future spouse was; there could be no yielding on this.

I glanced in the mirror and arranged the chain of my necklace before leaving to greet our guests.

Daniel stood at the top of the stairs, blocking my way, staring down to the entry below, his hands grasping the railings.

"Daniel, shall we descend? I believe our guests are here."

Catherine's laugh echoed up to us. He whipped around to face me. "Did you invite them?"

I shrugged and pretended to study my glove. "It was either them or Mr. Lundall, and considering I have already had my fair share of time alone with the latter, I thought it only fair to provide you the same opportunity with the former."

"You invited them to get back at me for leaving you with Mr. Lundall? Dragging things out a little far, aren't we?"

I narrowed my eyes, all sense of good humor evaporating. "Not just for that. This is for the game of bowls you made me play with Lord Williams. And for scooting my chair next to his. It is for the song you tried to corner me into singing and for leaving us in the middle of the lake in a boat. It is for every awkward, backstabbing move you have made since Lord Williams arrived. I thought I could rely on you — my own brother — but now I know that at the first possibility for amusement you will throw me to the wolves."

"There are no wolves in England, Margaret."

I don't know why his response surprised me, but the annoyance in his voice inflamed me to anger. I shoved past him. I had no need of his help. I would do this on my own.

Pasting on a wide smile, I strode into the

parlor. To my surprise, Catherine's father, who was the town doctor, and her elder brother James had also come.

Catherine had already attached herself to Lord Williams's side. James came forward to greet me.

"Miss Brinton, how good to see you again."

There was a falseness in his too-cheery voice. I realized at once why he had been included. The Johnsons had had the same idea of attaching Catherine to Lord Williams as I'd had, and James was there as my distraction. I could have laughed.

"Mr. Johnson."

Daniel entered and dinner was announced. James offered me his arm. Though Lord Williams glanced at us and my mother frowned, I accepted his offer and whispered, "I believe you and I are fighting on the same side, sir."

"Are we indeed?"

I waited to see whether Catherine would catch Lord Williams as her escort or be left with Daniel. Either would have satisfied me. What I did not expect was Lord Williams to willingly extend his arm to her. I was further surprised when he requested Catherine sit next to him. I sat in my regular seat next to my father, James between me and his sister.

Across from me, Mrs. Johnson beamed at her daughter.

After dinner was served, James leaned close. "You were saying, Miss Brinton?"

I peeked around him. Catherine was completely engrossed in a conversation with Lord Williams, her plate forgotten. Lord Williams appeared to be just as engrossed in the conversation. What could they possibly be talking about? Catherine couldn't have many interests in common with Lord Williams, since her only interest was finding a man to marry. Though, come to think of it, he seemed to have marriage as his primary interest as well.

I straightened. Why was I the only one he insisted on being disagreeable to? "I was saying there is no need to pretend an interest in me. I know what you are about, and I will not interfere."

"You think my interest is feigned?"

I rolled my eyes. "Mr. Johnson, we have known each other too long to play games."

He smiled. "Exactly."

"I do not take your meaning."

"My meaning is that people change. Feelings change. Why does it seem so impossible that my intentions toward you may not have changed?"

I stabbed a potato with my fork. "Are you

saying that you have developed a tendre for me, Mr. Johnson?"

"I'm only saying that it isn't impossible." He lifted his napkin, pretending to wipe his mouth.

He was unsuccessful in masking his grin. "You forget that I have a brother," I said. "You may tease me as much as you wish, but I will not be fooled by your antics."

Mr. Johnson replaced his napkin, fully revealing his smile. "Your brother is extremely blessed to have a sister such as yourself."

"Perhaps you should remind him of his good fortune."

Daniel grimaced at something Catherine had said and commenced picking at his food. He should not display his irritation so openly. Although, had not I done the same the night Lord Williams had arrived?

"Mr. Brinton, your guest certainly appears to be a charming young man," Mrs. Johnson said. "It was very kind of your daughter to extend an invitation to dine while he is here."

"Yes," my father replied. To his credit, he gave no indication of the annoyance he must have felt at the situation.

"And he is here merely visiting as . . . ?"

"He has come to consult on improvements to our estate."

I raised my brows. My father had not mentioned the engagement. Why not announce it? Surely he meant for the banns to be read this coming Sunday.

Mrs. Johnson glanced at me. "I see. Miss Brinton, what do you think of your guest?"

Would she not even attempt to disguise her intent? "I think him an honorable acquaintance."

She examined me a second too long before she looked back down the table. "He seems quite amiable. His estate is to the north, I believe?"

She no doubt knew more about Lord Williams than I did. Being isolated from the town these past few days, I had not had the advantage of village gossip to inform me of all the facts and rumors regarding Lord Williams. But when Mrs. Johnson refrained from making any more inquiries, I began to doubt that word of the engagement had gotten out.

In the sudden hush at our end of the table, I heard Lord Williams say, "I very much enjoyed the company of Miss Rosthorn today. Is she in any way related to Mr. Edward Rosthorn?"

The room stilled, Dr. and Mrs. Johnson both glancing at me while James set down the bite of food that had been halfway to his mouth. My father cleared his throat. "Uh, yes. Edward is Miss Rosthorn's elder brother."

Lord Williams nodded. "I thought there might be some connection. The family should be very proud. Though I have never met the couple, I hear he and the former Lady Swenson are very happy."

"No doubt her large fortune aided in their felicitous union," I muttered.

Next to me, James chuckled. My comment must have been louder than I expected, because Lord Williams said, "I understood that, though her family was against the union, the couple could not be separated, that theirs was a love match. Miss Brinton, you believe it to be otherwise?"

It did not matter what I believed. Nor did the shadow of the old ache in my chest matter. Nothing about Edward, his mistresses, or his hasty marriage to the former Lady Swenson mattered. "No. You must be correct." And for the former Lady Swenson's sake, I hoped he was.

My mother said something then, to which Dr. Johnson responded. I forced myself to eat, though the whole table was now doing its best to pretend I didn't exist.

Mrs. Johnson endeavored to restart conversation, and my father and James rallied to the task. Even so, I heard Daniel ask, "How was the boat ride, my lord? I hope you heeded my warning and did not allow Margaret to row. I would hate for you to have suffered a drenching."

Did Daniel know? Even if he didn't, there was no reason for Lord Williams not to confess what had happened. This had to be one of the most humiliating dinners I had suffered through.

"No, your sister did not touch the oars while I was in the boat," Lord Williams replied. I waited, but he failed to elaborate. The conversation turned to the remarkable weather we'd been enjoying.

Lord Williams hadn't outed me. He'd respected my wishes that the incident remain undiscovered. And he had kept the secret without lying.

Why?

Alice was waiting for us when we retired to the drawing room. Catherine greeted her briefly before making her way to the piano. Mrs. Johnson ignored Alice completely and imprisoned my mother in conversation.

I sat next to Alice and answered her questions regarding the dinner with more excitement than I felt.

When the gentlemen entered, Catherine

stood from the piano to greet them. I knew what she was about. By her position, she associated herself with music, yet in refraining from playing when the men entered she gave the pretense of modesty. She was practically begging someone to ask her to display her musical talents.

She wasn't disappointed. James and Daniel made their way to me, but Lord Williams hesitated only a second before striding to Catherine.

"Do you play, Miss Johnson?"

"A little."

"Perhaps you would do us the honor."

She would. Catherine would never pass up an opportunity for display.

She lowered her gaze to the floor. To a man her maneuver might seem bashful, but I had studied the same arts she had and knew she was merely pretending. "I would not wish to displace Miss Brinton."

I nearly snorted. She'd derive great pleasure in doing just that.

I waited to be addressed so that I might assure them of my disinterest in performing. But Lord Williams didn't consult me. He didn't even look my way. "I think you will find Miss Brinton is rather averse to the idea of playing before the present audience."

"Really?" Catherine studied me as though

trying to discern my true motives for passing on such an opportunity. "In that case, I would be happy to sing."

Daniel let out a low snort of impatience. Before he could say something rude, I said, "Miss Johnson, we would be delighted if you would honor us with a song." Better her than me.

Her eyes narrowed as though she thought I planned to undermine her. I responded with a genuine smile. Still looking distrustful, she sat at the piano.

She had improved since I had last heard her. Her fingers stumbled over a few notes, but she hid her mistakes well by singing over them. It was a decent performance, one that demanded praise.

Lord Williams stood next to her the entire time, his attention never wavering.

He was wearing the blue coat he had worn the previous evening; it accented his eyes wonderfully. Catherine's gaze lingered when she looked up at him, and I wondered if she could fathom the strong shoulders and arms his coat concealed or if she would appreciate his even temper and thoughtfulness if she knew of them.

Of course she would. Any woman would. And given that he had not displayed the least inclination to bolt while she sang or even frowned in her direction, she might not understand the humiliation he was capable of inflicting.

"You seem somewhat excited, Miss Brinton," James said, interrupting my musings. "Is everything all right?"

I glanced at him, startled. "You are mistaken. I am perfectly at ease."

James tilted his head to the side. "Hm. Either you have acquired a rather nervous habit of twisting your hands since we were last together or your fingers are very anxious for their chance at the piano."

Lord Williams glanced over at us. I stilled my hands. "Neither, I think."

"Do you really intend not to perform at your own gathering?" James asked.

Daniel leaned in front of me. "You'll have to excuse her, James. She had a rather traumatic experience last week and is too timid to play before the present company."

"I am not timid," I said.

"Of course not." Daniel straightened with a smirk.

"I'm not," I repeated.

Lord Williams and Catherine moved to the book of music and began discussing various pieces. Frustration welled within me. Though I had invited Catherine as a diversion for Lord Williams, I had not expected him to take to her quite so quickly. Or so completely.

Alice walked up and stood next to me. "Aren't you going to play something?"

I glanced to where my mother and father and Dr. and Mrs. Johnson sat comfortably on the settees, Mrs. Johnson beaming at Catherine, Dr. Johnson in low conversation with my father.

My mother nodded at me, urging me to perform. Perhaps she had sent Alice over.

"Are you going to play or not?" Daniel asked. "If you aren't, perhaps we should bring out the cards."

"If you would sing, I would consider it a privilege to accompany you," James offered.

I shook my head. "Thank you, but no."

"Well, you have to do something," Daniel said. "You arranged for this party, after all." He cleared his throat. "My dear sister Margaret has decided to honor us with her playing."

James flashed me a sympathetic look.

Perhaps it was best to get it over with. If I played, Daniel's game of constantly volunteering me to perform would end.

Catherine moved to her brother's side and whispered in his ear while I shuffled across the room. To both my annoyance and satisfaction, Lord Williams remained near the piano.

"What will you play?" he asked.

His question brought me up short. I didn't know what to play. "Perhaps you should suggest something so I can avoid the re-action I received the last time I attempted to entertain you with music."

"We both know it was not me you were attempting to entertain. But I promise to remain in this spot throughout the duration of your performance."

"How kind of you." I couldn't determine if I found his nearness vexing or calming.

This was all Daniel's fault. And then I smiled. I knew exactly what to play.

I played Daniel's least favorite song, a plaintive air that he'd insisted I'd played too much after Edward. Daniel's groan of objection was satisfying, but I hadn't counted on the music dredging up the old pain, the memory of how at one time I had been blissfully in love.

Would I never be free of the dishonesty?

Lord Williams was true to his word. He didn't move throughout the song. When I finished, I was embarrassed to find him watching me closely. I stood, hoping he hadn't seen what I'd felt.

"Ugh, Margaret," Daniel said. "If I'd known you were going to play that I would have insisted on cards. Play something else. Something less doom and gloom."

"Will you play something else?" Lord Williams asked more quietly.

I shook my head. "I believe hearing me play once is more than enough entertainment."

"Not for me."

I couldn't tell from his expression if he'd truly appreciated my playing or if he was merely trying to make up for the rudeness of last time. I hoped it was the first.

No. That wasn't right.

"Margaret," Daniel said, "if you're unwilling, perhaps Miss Johnson will delight us with another."

Catherine's gaze settled on Lord Williams and something in my chest tightened. I needed to be alone a moment to smother my emotions and gather my wits.

I retreated to the stack of music.

Lord Williams joined me. "Do you have a song in mind?"

Why had he followed me? "No." I flicked through the pages, barely glancing at the songs. I should just let Catherine play. That's what she was here for.

Lord Williams's hand suddenly settled on mine. Startled, I looked up, but he was focused on the paper before us.

"Would you play this?"

It was the song from the Hickmores', the sonata he had walked out on. I slid my hand, which had been growing pleasantly warm under his touch, from under his and hid it in my skirt. "You've already heard it."

"I'd like to hear it again. All of it."

"I don't think —"

"Please."

His tone, so earnest, stopped my immediate refusal.

"Excuse me, my lord," one of the servants interrupted. "This just arrived." He held out a letter.

Lord Williams took it. "Thank you." He read the inscription. "Pardon me, Miss Brinton, but —

"Not at all. Do not delay reading your letter on my account."

"Thank you." He moved a step away and broke the seal. A smaller folded paper slipped from the letter. Lord Williams caught it and frowned as he read whatever was scribbled on its front before turning his attention to the main letter's content.

I glanced around the room. Daniel and James chuckled at something while Catherine stood mutely next to them, her focus set on Lord Williams, no doubt as curious about the contents of the letter as I was. Or perhaps she was curious about the man as well. Alice had returned to her seat near our mother, who narrowed her eyes at me and nodded at the music. Pretending not to notice how she wished me to play another song, I turned back to the music and feigned interest in it.

Lord Williams balled the letter in his hand, his jaw muscle popping.

It was such an astonishing display of discomposure I stepped toward him. "I hope you have not received something up-setting."

"It is from my cousin."

"Mr. Northam?"

Lord Williams's eyes narrowed and I realized I'd allowed too much interest to show in my voice. "I thought he didn't know you were here."

"I didn't know he knew. Someone must have told him." He eyed me as though I was that person.

I looked to Daniel. Had he actually come through for me?

"There is a note here for you, as well."

Mr. Northam had written to me?

Lord Williams handed me the folded paper with my name scrawled across its front. I unfolded it, turning slightly to block the writing from his view.

My dear, I curse my folly that I did not secure you when I had the opportunity. Only tell me that I am still wanted and I am yours. ~F. Northam.

I stared at the words. He regretted his silence. He was still mine.

I could still succeed.

Lord Williams stepped closer and lowered his voice. "What does it say?"

I quickly folded the paper and looked up, trying to pretend the note hadn't meant anything. "It is a trifle, that is all."

"My cousin never trifles in matters of import," Lord Williams said.

Was he saying I was a matter of import?

He stood so close it was difficult to think. "You still wish to marry him instead of me?"

I shook my head. Then I nodded. Then frowned. "It's why you are here, is it not? To make a union between me and your cousin impossible?"

"That is not the only reason," he said.

"Well, whatever the other reason, I'm certain it has nothing to do with me. You've proved you don't care about my wishes at all." Except that wasn't true. He hadn't told the others about the lake.

So he did care?

I searched his face, trying to discern what

208

I saw in his steady gaze before I remembered — it didn't matter if he cared. It was worse if he cared. Because I could never care.

"Margaret," Daniel called. "If you're not going to play anymore, let's set up the cards."

Lord Williams didn't move. "My cousin is not to be trusted."

I tilted my head. "And you are?" There was too much vulnerability in my voice for it to be the quip I'd meant it to be.

His brow furrowed, but he hesitated a moment too long.

"I believe Daniel is anxious for your company." I turned and pretended interest in the music.

His hand touched my back as he leaned near my ear. "Your performance at the Hickmores' was flawless." Then the warmth of his breath and the gentleness of his touch were gone.

NINETEEN

Lord Williams was absent when I joined my family in the parlor the next morning. The clock testified he still had a few minutes before breakfast. I glanced at the door.

"Missing your love already?" Daniel smirked.

I forced my features into a calm, untroubled appearance. "Not at all, I assure you."

"Well, you needn't worry. He was out early and will be delayed only a few minutes."

I rolled my eyes. "I cannot tell you how comforting that is."

"Do you really not like the baron, Margaret?" Alice asked.

After yesterday, I no longer knew how to answer that question. "Can we please speak of something else?" I glanced at my mother for help, but she was engrossed in a letter. On pink paper. There was only one person who ever wrote us on pink paper. "How is

Mrs. Hickmore, Mother?"

She waved a hand, instructing me to be quiet, and turned the page over to continue reading. I hadn't realized my mother found Mrs. Hickmore's letters so interesting. I directed my gaze outside. The trees sat still and the sky was bright and clear except for a few clouds in the distance.

"Margaret, what is the meaning of this?" my mother demanded a second later.

I frowned in confusion. "Of what?"

She read from the page. *"I have every reason to expect a union between your daughter and the man in question; only time will tell if it is to be a happy one. Perhaps, in Margaret's case, it will be, for though I would normally advise any mother to keep her daughter far away from Mr. Northam, I think this union is exactly what she is looking for. For my part, I wish it weren't."*

I stared at her. "You wrote Mrs. Hickmore about Mr. Northam?"

My father lowered his paper. "Eloise, I specifically forbade you from —"

"Did you really expect me not to, Colin? Our daughter deserves to be happy. Or am I the only one who feels that way?" She returned her attention to me. "Mr. Northam does not appear to be the kind of man who would bring about such happiness, though, does he?"

"He isn't," Daniel interrupted. "Mr. Northam is a rake of the worst kind."

"And what do you know of it, Daniel?" I asked dismissively, trying to ignore the pool of foreboding forming in my stomach.

His eyes narrowed. "I know enough. I caught him, Margaret, the first night we were there, creeping out of the house with a girl too young to know better."

My face heated, but I shrugged. "Every woman at that party knew better. Besides, what do I care what he does when he isn't with me?"

My mother gasped. "Margaret, you cannot be serious."

"Why not? All it means is that he is like every other man of our acquaintance. Unlike Edward, though, Mr. Northam doesn't pretend to be someone else. So at least with him I know what I am getting."

"Margaret," my father chastised.

I glanced at him. "Should I not say such things, even though they are true?" I turned to my mother. "It doesn't matter anyway, since it makes no difference how I feel. Everything has already been ruined."

"Unless you content yourself with Lord Williams," Daniel said. "He is obviously determined to have you. And he is nothing like Edward."

"He is exactly like Edward — pleasing and gentlemanly when he wants to be, yet ruining people's lives without a second thought when he deems it fitting." My voice was louder than I'd meant and I took a deep breath to calm down.

Daniel rolled his eyes. "Oh, come, Margaret. If you had met Lord Williams before the misunderstanding with Edward, you would be madly in love by now."

"That's enough, both of you," my father interrupted. "This is not a conversation to have in the parlor." He glanced at Alice, who was standing behind my mother, her eyes wide.

My chest heaved with the injustice of my situation. But I shouldn't have spoken so in front of Alice. "I apologize," I said to her.

My father nodded. "I think we have waited long enough for our guest. Margaret?" He gestured toward the breakfast table.

I shook my head. "No, thank you. I find I've lost my appetite." I strode out of the breakfast room and out of the house.

A trail of decimated leaves followed me around the lake. When I reached the boulder that Daniel had fallen off the morning after returning from the Hickmores', I climbed onto it. The clouds in the distant sky had gathered, promising an impending storm, but for now only a slight breeze blew, pulling strands of my hair loose while its caress played along my skin. I scooted to the edge of the rock and leaned over.

The lake's surface rippled and waved, but I searched it anyway. Faint traces of myself — a flash of skin, a hint of an eye, the trail of a curl — flickered into view. But mostly only the blues and greens of the ruffled water reflected back. I stretched down and dipped my finger into the lake, stirring it to produce my own wake, but my ripples were almost instantly consumed by the ones generated by the wind.

Daniel's words ran through my mind even as I struggled to force them out. I couldn't deny that Lord Williams, as he acted here, amongst my family, was someone to be admired. Mostly. He was still arrogant and unyielding. But he was also gentle and attentive. Under duress, his behavior betrayed a kind and patient man. He even displayed moments of humor and wit, and his unyielding manner meant he didn't back down from an argument.

He'd insisted I call him by his first name. That wasn't something the man from the Hickmores' would have done.

The truth was, if we had met before Edward, I quite possibly might have been in love.

In love with *Gregory.*

How easy it was to think of him by that name.

I yanked my hand out of the water. It did not matter how Gregory or Lord Williams or that man made my pool of buried dreams spill across the dam I had erected to keep them contained. I was not going to be deceived again. Mr. Northam was the man for me.

"See, my lord? I told you we would find her here."

I spun around. Lord Williams and Alice walked toward me, Alice with a grin of triumph on her face, Lord Williams with a frown set with determination.

"I knew you'd be here, Margaret," Alice repeated.

I glanced down to make sure my dress covered my ankles before sliding off the stone, trying to appear relaxed and unaffected by their sudden appearance. "Yes, I came out to . . . I needed a walk."

"It's going to storm," Lord Williams said, indicating the clouds still some distance away.

I shrugged. "The rain will do us all a bit

of good."

"We should not be caught outside in it."

I didn't blame him for not wanting to ruin any more clothes. "It is still a ways off. But if you are worried, you needn't remain."

"Perhaps it will only be a light rain and we can play in it," Alice chimed in.

"Yes, perhaps," I replied. "Though from the looks of it, we should plan for something heavier."

Lord Williams nodded in agreement.

"Alice, shouldn't you be at your studies?" The hours after breakfast were usually devoted to her education.

She smiled shyly. "I came to show Lord Williams where you were. Mama said it was all right."

"I wager she made you promise to return right away, though, didn't she?"

Alice frowned. "Yes, she did. But we were only studying history, and I know it all so well already. I would much rather be out here with you."

Lord Williams smiled. "Ah, you already know the whole of history? You must be quite brilliant."

"Well, I don't know *all* of it," Alice admitted.

"Why don't we return together?" I pushed off the rock and stepped toward Alice.

"Actually, Miss Brinton, I would like a word with you. In private," Lord Williams said.

Did this have to do with the letter? "Alice, tell Mother we will be along directly."

Alice glanced between us, something akin to eagerness lighting her eyes, and nodded. "All right."

As she retreated up the path, I frowned. She had never been so easily persuaded to return to her studies, especially history. What was she about?

"Miss Brinton."

I turned my attention to Lord Williams.

"Last night, when I mentioned Edward Rosthorn, I had not realized his connection to you and your family. I assumed you were acquainted, given your close friendship with Miss Rosthorn, but I was not aware that you and he had formed an attachment. I must apologize."

My eyes widened in surprise. "My lord —"

His sigh interrupted me. "Please call me Gregory."

Gregory. I shook my head in refusal. "Mr. Rosthorn and I were raised practically as brother and sister. You have nothing to apologize for."

He stepped closer. "There is no need for

pretense. I know of your former engagement to him."

Suddenly light-headed, I leaned against the boulder for balance. Why was he bringing this up now? "I'm sorry, my lord, but I assure you —"

"Your sister told me everything," he insisted, his voice cutting through mine.

I frowned. "I do not know what Alice told you, but you should not give credit to all her words. She was a child — only eight years of age at the time. Events are sure to have been distorted through misunderstanding."

"Are you telling me that you were not engaged to Mr. Rosthorn?"

There was no way around such a direct question. "No. It is true. I was engaged to him."

"And he broke it off?"

"No. I did."

"Why?" He was determined to know. It showed in his eyes, in the firm set of his jaw.

I realized that the truth I was about to share was probably the surest way of guaranteeing Lord Williams's retreat. I should have told him everything that first day.

He would judge me. People always did.

I squared my shoulders. Let him judge

me. "He had a mistress — or perhaps a stream of them. His father wouldn't allow him access to the estate funds until he'd married and settled down. As I told you that first night, I have something of a dowry attached to me. Marriage to me was an easy way for him to gain access both to his father's funds and to a little extra on the side — my dowry is enough that it would have allowed him to keep his mistress, or mistresses, without much difficulty."

"Then how is it he came to marry Lady Swenson?"

I shrugged. "No doubt he tricked her into falling in love with him." The same as he had me.

The lake reflected the darkening clouds, the water almost as black as my days had been after Edward.

"Did you love him?" The anger in Lord Williams's voice confused me, forcing me to return my gaze to him. His brows were creased with deep lines, matching the frown of his mouth.

It was an intimate question, one he had no right asking. "This is not a conversation to be having given the brevity with which —"

"No need. I understand. You loved him. He broke your heart. You thought to protect yourself with a marriage of convenience." He shook his head. "You left one vital part out of the equation."

I narrowed my eyes. "What is that?"

"You." He stepped closer. "You have intelligence, beauty, a certain disregard for modern sensibilities — any man of sense would be won over by such a woman eventually."

I stared into his eyes, light against the shadowed sky. "This is why you came? To be won over?"

"No. I came to keep Northam from getting to you. He would have destroyed you."

I lifted one side of my mouth in an attempt at a smile. "One cannot destroy what is already broken."

"You're not broken. You are a woman of passion and belief, not afraid to fight for what you want." Gregory — there was no other way to think of him with that look in his eye — stepped closer still, too close for propriety. I put a hand on his chest to keep him from moving closer, but my fingers curled around the flap of his coat instead.

"The problem is," Gregory said quietly, "you want the wrong thing."

"What should I want?"

His gaze bore into mine. "Me. I would never hurt you as he did."

I longed for the promise in his voice to be real, for the meaning of his words to be true. I scrambled to find an objection to his reasoning. "This isn't right. You shouldn't be engaged to save me from the very thing I desire. You should be free to marry whomever you wish, as should I."

Gregory brought his hand to my face and his thumb brushed my cheek, leaving a warm trail in its wake. "I am marrying who I wish."

For a moment, the determination in his eyes made me forget. Both the impending storm in the sky and the storm raging inside me disappeared. There was no cold, no wind, no time. I had no need to even breathe. All I needed was to feel this, to feel wanted, to feel secure. I relished the gentleness of his touch, the promise of protection in his expression.

But even as my heart cried out with longing, my mind screamed a warning. I was not safe with him. I would never be safe with him; he had confessed that very thing the first night we met. He wanted love, romance. He believed he could make a woman love him simply through sheer willpower.

And he had shown I was susceptible. Gregory was exactly the sort of man I needed to avoid.

My hand flattened against his chest, becoming the barrier it was supposed to have been from the first. "But I do not wish to marry you. And continuing to insist on this marriage makes you exactly like him."

Gregory's thumb stilled. His gaze fell to my lips, and my traitorous heart began pounding. Then he stepped back and dropped his hand.

The first drops of rain splattered on our heads and faces. It wasn't the warm rain Alice had hoped for. The drops were cold and harsh, pounding against our skin and onto the surface of the lake where ever larger ripples marched outward until there were so many circles the whole surface was at war. A cold wind blew through the trees, and not even Gregory's proximity held off the shiver that coursed through me.

"We should return," he said abruptly.

I nodded and slid away from the boulder, away from him. I had just turned toward the path when he draped his coat across me, his hands lingering on my shoulders.

His tender touch stopped me. Edward had never given me his coat. If he had been with me, caught in the rain like this, he would have yanked my hand and run, unconcerned that he pulled too hard or ran too fast for me to keep up. Not Gregory. He lingered, letting himself get wet while the warmth of his nearness soaked through me, shielding me from the cold wind. Edward's touch had always felt forced, never as natural, as right, as Gregory's did. Edward had never smelled of mild cologne, saddle oil, and promises in such a perfect combination.

For a moment, I imagined Edward had never existed, that I had instead lost my heart to Gregory. I imagined myself leaning into him, resting my head against his chest, allowing his arms to wrap around me.

But there had been an Edward. And even if Gregory was not Edward, was nothing like Edward, I was still me. I had promised myself not to be taken in. I would stand by that promise. He would always be Lord Williams to me.

"Thank you," I said quietly, stepping away from his touch, back into the cold.

We walked in silence along the path and under the arch. The storm became worse with every passing minute. By the time we reached the lawn surrounding the house, my curls stuck to my face and neck. I pulled the coat tighter around me. Lord Williams looked much the same as he had after falling into the lake, except this time there was no smile on his face.

TWENTY

The door burst open at our approach. My mother blocked the entry, her gaze flicking over us, then flying over us again. "Where is Alice?" A hint of annoyance laced her otherwise calm question.

I glanced behind her. "We sent Alice back almost immediately. She should be here."

"She did not return."

I frowned. It wasn't like Alice to not return. "Perhaps she slipped into her room. She said she was studying history."

My mother shook her head and moved back into the house. "Colin!"

Lord Williams closed the door behind us.

"I'll fetch something to dry off with," I said, shrugging out of his coat. He took it with a nod. After retrieving some towels, I found him in the drawing room next to the fire.

My mother rushed into the room a moment later. "Margaret, I cannot find your sister anywhere. I have the servants searching the house, but she is gone."

My breath whooshed out of me in shock. "Gone? Where would she go?"

My father and brother raced into the room, both dripping water onto the floor.

"She isn't in the stables," Daniel said.

"Nor could I find her anywhere near the house," my father puffed.

"Father! You should not be out in this weather. You'll get ill." I quickly pulled his wet overcoat from him.

"What does it matter? Your sister is out there somewhere in this storm."

Lord Williams stepped forward. "Perhaps she got lost between the lake and here. I'll go search for her."

"I'll go with you," I said.

He shook his head. "You are already wet. You should stay here and get warm."

"You are just as wet as I am — more so, in fact, because I had your coat."

He looked down at his clothes, as though just remembering their dampness.

"Lord Williams, thank you for your offer," my mother interjected. "It would be a great comfort to know you are looking as well." I stared at her, shocked that she had agreed so easily. Only a deep concern for Alice's welfare would convince her to include a guest in family matters.

He nodded. "It was on my account that she was out in the first place."

"I insist on being included," I said.

Daniel shook his head. "Stay here. Get dry. We'll find her."

"I can at least search the garden."

"Do you really think she is there?" Lord Williams asked, looking at me doubtfully. "I will search there only as a precaution and retread the path back to the lake."

"I know the way best. You will need me. I could —"

He leaned close, pretending to adjust his coat. "Stay here. Please," he whispered. "I will concentrate better knowing that you are safe."

I looked up to search his expression. However, he looked away as though he hadn't said anything. His words warmed me better than any fire, but it was Alice who was lost out in the storm. Dear Alice. What if for some reason I was the only one who could find her? On the other hand, what if I wasn't here when she came home? I gritted my teeth and glanced around. My father and mother had to stay in as well. I could not pretend to care more for her than they did.

I sighed. "I will stay."

My father began struggling back into his coat. I placed a hand on his arm and said quietly, so that no one else heard, "Father, you cannot go back out. You will be no good to Alice or anyone if you become ill."

"What good am I sitting around?"

"If you fall ill, it will take attention away from Alice, who is sure to become ill herself from being out in this weather after so recently having a cold."

Pain flashed through my father's eyes before he bowed his head. "I am not much of a father when I cannot even go outside to search for my own daughter."

"Alice adores you. She could never doubt your love."

He met my gaze briefly before looking away. "I shall be in the study."

Daniel stepped next to me as our father slipped out the door. "Thank you. I didn't know how I was going to convince him to stay in."

"Just find her quickly. If anything happens to her —" I clasped his arm.

Placing a comforting hand over mine, he said, "We'll find her. Don't worry. My lord? If you're ready." Daniel and Lord Williams hurried out the door.

I left my mother in the parlor and went to ensure a large fire was burning in Alice's room and water was boiling in the kitchen for her bath before I changed into dry clothes. After that, there was nothing left for me to do except pace around the parlor and strain to see outside the window every time I passed it. My mother sat on the settee, staring at her sewing.

"Margaret, do be still," she said after a while.

"I can't. I should be out there looking for her."

"You should be doing no such thing." But my mother sounded as though she wished she were outside as well.

A few minutes later, she set down her sewing. "I will be in my room. Summon me the moment she is found."

"Of course."

After she left, I sat at the piano, but the thought of even attempting to distract myself reeked of treachery. I arose and searched out the windows for any sign of movement. The seconds turned to minutes, the minutes to quarter hours, then half hours. There was no movement except the rain splattering against the glass.

What if they failed to find her? What if something horrible had happened to her? I turned from the window and walked to the fire. I would not be able to bear life if anything happened to Alice. She was the ray of sunshine and happiness in our family. We would all be pitiful without her.

My thoughts darted back to the lake. Alice had been up to something then. I should have asked her what it was. I should have demanded we see her safely home.

And Lord Williams. . . . He'd stood so close to me, declared openly that it was him I should want. Arrogant man.

I smiled. Only he could be wholly arrogant and incredibly alluring at the same time.

Had he really thought about kissing me?

The idea made my cheeks hot and my lips tingle.

I frowned at my own foolishness. This was not good. I did *not* find Lord Williams alluring. Or any other complimentary descriptor.

Resuming my stance at the window, I peered into the dark. Enough time had passed for the grounds and gardens to be searched, and perhaps near the lake as well, yet the men had still not returned. I had no idea where they were, where they had gone to look. The storm worsened, the rain pounding against the window like thrown pebbles, the clatter dimmed only by the roaring wind.

Alice's favorite maid, Mary, entered the

room. "Any word? We're all so anxious."

"Nothing," I replied. "I shall be sure to inform you the moment I know anything. Alice's room is ready for her return?"

"Yes, miss."

"Thank you," I said. She curtsied and left.

I resumed pacing. Alice had to be safe. She had to be brought home. No other option was thinkable.

It was frustrating, this waiting. I wished I were with Daniel and Lord Williams and the male servants.

The clock chimed, marking two hours since the men had departed. I fell into a chair. It was the same chair Lord Williams preferred, the one he had begun to occupy every night after dinner. I rubbed my hands along its arms and thought of how my family adored him. Alice especially. She always blushed and smiled whenever he noticed her.

Where was she?

I went to the window once more, forcing my palm wide against the glass, allowing the cold to seep into my skin. There was a lull in the wind and though it was still dark from the storm, I could just make out the trees across the lawn. A boom of thunder made me jump. Then there — that was a light. A man cradling a bundle.

I grabbed one of the blankets that had been set near the fire to warm and ran to the portico.

Lord Williams appeared, Alice curled in his arms. He carried her into the house while I struggled to place the blanket around her.

"I found her huddled beside the boulder," he said quietly.

"The boulder? She's so wet. And her skin — it's so cold. Why was she there?"

He shook his head. "Where should I put her?"

"In her room. This way."

Alice's eyes fluttered open. "Margaret?"

"I'm here, Alice. You are going to be all right." I stroked her cheek, tucking a limp curl behind her ear.

"It didn't work," she said, her voice hoarse and shaking.

I placed my palm against the side of her face. We needed to get her warm. "Shh. Don't talk."

"I told him about Edward."

Why was she mentioning this now? "I know, Alice. It's all right."

She coughed, then said, "I thought he would leave, like you wanted."

Foreboding clamped in my chest. "Alice, honey, shh. Lord Williams is going to carry

231

you to your room. You shall soon be warm."

"He is going to take you away." Her eyes shimmered and tears mingled with rain slid down her cheeks.

Alice had told Lord Williams about Edward in an attempt to get him to leave — because this morning I had said that was exactly what I wanted. She was wet and shivering and would likely come down with another cold because of me.

"I will never leave you." I pressed a kiss to her forehead. She slowly closed her eyes again.

Guilt gnawed at me. Alice had waited to ensure her plan had worked rather than return to the house. And instead of seeing Lord Williams pull away, she'd seen him draw nearer. She'd seen him almost kiss me. What must she have thought?

"Her room is this way."

He followed me up the stairs to my sister's room. Mary was stoking the fire into a blaze. "Mary, Lord Williams has found Alice. Please inform my mother of her return." She nodded and raced out the door.

I glanced around. An empty tub was set near the fire, but it would take several minutes to fill it. And Alice would have to be undressed. "On the bed would be best."

Lord Williams laid her on the bed much

more tenderly than Daniel would have and stepped back but didn't leave. I worked to dry her hair and neck, ignoring his presence.

My mother ran into the room, followed closely by Mary.

"Oh, my darling girl." My mother fell to her knees next to the bedside and clasped Alice's hands, bringing them to her cheeks and then kissing them.

Alice opened her eyes. "Mama?"

"You're safe. Oh, thank heavens you are safe. Mary, help me get her things off." I reached for her dress, but my mother stopped me. "No, Margaret. Mary and I will attend to her."

I stepped back in understanding. My mother blamed this on me. Alice would never have been outside but for me. And though my mother didn't yet know it, Alice had stayed in the rain only because I'd made a scene this morning, so her blame was just.

My mother glanced at Lord Williams. "My lord, I can never thank you enough for rescuing my daughter. Margaret, see to Lord Williams. He will need something to eat and a chair by the fire."

"Yes, Mother." I turned and, without glancing at Lord Williams, walked into the hall, stopping at the top of the stairs near his door. "I am sure you wish to change. There will be a warm meal for you whenever you are ready."

"Thank you." He disappeared inside his room.

He had rescued Alice. He had saved her. I was in his debt, and the only repayment he seemed to desire was my consent to the marriage.

TWENTY-ONE

"Father, Lord Williams found Alice. She is
home," I said, peeking into the study.

My father placed his hand over his heart
and sighed. "Thank you."

"I am getting something for him from the
kitchen. Will you be eating as well?"

He shook his head. "Perhaps later. I want
to see my daughter."

I stepped out of the way as he passed. He
stopped and turned. "Margaret, Lord Williams is a good man."

Yes. And that was the problem.

I was in the dining room, using a poker to
stir the fire, when Lord Williams entered.
Did he know how his coat brought out the
blue of his eyes, even from across the room?
I quickly straightened and rang for a servant. "Your meal will be here in a moment."
The table was already set; it lacked only
food.

"Thank you."

He stood awkwardly, as though hesitant to be near me but having no other place to go. The fire felt overwhelmingly hot, so I stepped away. "You should warm yourself."

Walking forward, he stood a moment before the fire, hands at his side, before placing a hand on the mantel with a frown. He glanced at me, then straightened and turned to me.

"Miss Brinton, you have made your dislike both of me and of the prospect of marriage to me perfectly plain on more than one occasion. Therefore, I see no reason to continue as we are. I will speak to your father. If he is agreeable, let us end this engagement to which you are so averse."

End the engagement? Was he in earnest? I was to be set at liberty to keep my promise once again. "You would do this?"

He frowned. "Contrary to what you think of me, I *am* a man of conscience. Your sister's being lost was entirely my fault." He shook his head. "I should never have allowed this to continue for so long."

What did he mean? "Allowed what to continue?"

"You made your feelings for me quite clear at that unfortunate party. I should have known this would be impossible. One cannot convince a person who will not see reason." It was a reiteration of his words from the Hickmores', but this time he said it almost to himself, his tone sounding tired and a little sad. His frown deepened. "However, I again assert that my cousin is not for you. Choose someone else, someone with enough sense to support you comfortably but with a strong constitution to withstand your opinions, for you will be discontent otherwise."

He truly was releasing me. It was over.

The rush of relief I should have felt never came. Instead, the lingering warmth from the fire turned cold and an uncertainty that this wasn't what I really wanted needled at me. "It is not that I dislike you —"

He held up a hand, stopping me. "You needn't concern yourself with soothing my vanity. We have enjoyed being rather forthright with each other. I do not care to muddle it with false words and sentiments."

A kitchen maid entered with platters of food and set them on the table before leaving.

"My lord —"

He sighed but didn't protest my use of his title.

It was indeed over. "Thank you."

He nodded.

How awkward it was now to notice the

way his hair curled under the influence of the drying heat or how his coat didn't quite hide the muscular shape of his shoulders or the way his eyes, now distant and closed, still spoke of safety.

He truly was nearly as handsome as Mr. Northam, though in a different way. There was no darkness to his features, no alluring mystery about his character. There was no playful beckoning but a serious, honest openness to his expression. If one were seeking love, Lord Williams was definitely preferable to Mr. Northam.

I moved to his seat, straightened the utensils and platters, then stepped away. "Everything is ready for you."

He crossed toward me. "Are you not eating as well?"

I shook my head.

He seemed about to object, but stopped. "Won't you be seated, at least?"

It was a small request. Gentlemanly.

I nodded. He assisted me with my chair before taking his own.

I studied him as he dished potatoes and steak from the platter. Alice was safe. He'd found her, staying in the storm for hours until he did. My father was correct; Lord Williams was a good man.

He was also self-important and overbearing. He'd displayed a want of consideration for others on more than one occasion. Yet had I not done the same?

At that moment the thing I desired more than anything else was for there to have never been an Edward, for him to have never interfered in my life. I wished that I had met Lord Williams first, and that I'd had the chance to call him Gregory. Even if it had come to naught, at least we would have had a chance.

But of course such a wish could never come true. And there was no reason to think of it any longer. It was over. He would most likely leave in the morning. And I would never see him again.

The door burst open. Realizing that I had unintentionally shifted closer to Lord Williams, I scrambled out of my chair. Daniel stood in the doorway, drenched but with a smile covering his face. "You found her."

I clasped the back of the chair. "Yes. Lord Williams did. She's in her room. Mother is with her. And Mary. And Father." The words spilled forth uncontrollably in my effort to distance myself from the doubt within me. "Do you want something to eat? Here, you can have my chair."

I turned the chair, offering it to Daniel while at the same time placing it as a wall between Lord Williams and myself. I didn't dare look at him.

"Yes, food would be nice. I searched all the way to the Rosthorns'." He trudged to the table, a line of wet footprints evidence of his recent expedition.

I frowned, finally coming to my senses. "Daniel, you are dripping water and mud everywhere."

He shrugged and plopped into the chair. "I hardly think it matters tonight." He pulled dishes toward him and started piling food on a plate. "Why didn't she just come home?"

I glanced at Lord Williams. The smile was gone, a frown planted firmly in its place.

He blamed himself. But Alice's being out there was just as much my fault. More, really, because I was her sister. I should have known what she was about.

"I don't believe she thought it would rain quite so much, nor that it would be quite so cold," I said.

"She and I discussed it at breakfast, didn't we?" Daniel asked.

I didn't know; I hadn't eaten breakfast. This had all transpired because of the way I had acted before breakfast. "Earlier she'd hoped we could dance in it."

"Well, at least she's safe, thanks to you,

my lord."

Yes. Thanks to him.

I had to get away from him. Away from the way he made me wonder about breaking promises, about changing my mind. "Excuse me, please."

I left the room, walked out the front door, and leaned against the stone wall of the house. The cold rain fell a few feet from me, the wind blowing occasional drops onto my face and arms. The chill of the stones seeped past my dress and crawled along my skin. I pressed against the stone with more force, needing to feel its cold bite.

This was what I'd needed, this cold to clear my mind and allow me to focus on the reality of my situation. Which was actually quite simple.

Lord Williams would leave and everything would return to normal, just as though we'd never met.

TWENTY-TWO

A knock on my door awoke me. The room was dark except for the low fire. It must still be night.

The door pushed open. "Margaret?"

I rolled over. "Mother, yes, I am here. I'm awake." I rose to add more wood to the flames.

My mother closed the door with a soft click. "Your sister is unwell."

Poor Alice. "I shall take my turn at her side so you may rest." I grabbed my dressing gown off the back of the chair.

"Dr. Johnson is here."

"What?" I froze, one arm halfway through a sleeve. "Is it so serious?" A glance at the clock told me I had been asleep for several hours.

"It is a precaution. He says it is nothing more than a fever and a cough."

I hurried into my robe. "I should not have fallen asleep."

"Margaret, your father cannot stay. Not when there is fever in the house."

I paused in tying my gown. "You wish for me to speak with him?"

"Yes."

"Is he downstairs?"

"I believe so. And, Margaret, he should leave as soon as possible."

"But where will he go? We have no family for him to visit and he would never consent to staying in the village."

"Anywhere would be better than here. Convince him to go with Lord Williams — he is leaving this morning."

It was done, then. The engagement was off. And my father must have told my mother.

That she would still suggest such a destination was astonishing. "Mother, he cannot go to Lord Williams's."

She reopened the door. "I must return to your sister. I leave it to you to persuade your father of the necessity of his leaving and to come to some agreement of where he is to go." She swept out of my room.

Securing my dressing gown, I went in search of my father, discovering him sitting behind his desk in the firelit study. I knocked softly on the open door. "Father?"

He stood. "Margaret."

I stepped into the room. "I assume you know the doctor has come. Alice is ill."

He nodded, stepping around his desk to walk to me. "Yes. I sent John for him myself."

"Father, Dr. Johnson — and Mother — do not believe your continued residence here wise."

He took my arm as though to usher me out of the room. "I had heard, but I will not leave my home while my daughter is ill."

He couldn't stay. If he fell ill as well, he might never recover. None of us could bear to lose him. "Alice would not wish you to become ill because of her. It would make her worry, which will prolong her recovery. If she knew you were safe, she could concentrate on getting well."

My father hesitated. "Your mother put you up to this, didn't she? I appreciate your efforts and your argument in favor of my going. But I am resolved to stay." He glanced at a large chair facing the fire. "I am afraid, Lord Williams, that the end of your visit comes at a providential time."

Lord Williams stood. The room suddenly felt much too crowded.

I was still in my dressing gown. I flushed and quickly glanced away, searching for anything other than him upon which I could focus my attention.

"I'm sorry to leave your family in such distress."

He was really leaving. I would never see him again. It was for the best, for both of us, but that didn't prevent a pang of regret in my chest.

My father nodded. "I am afraid it cannot be avoided."

But part of the distress could be avoided. I had no desire to be the one to recommend my mother's suggestion, but I could not deny that it would be the easiest solution to the present dilemma. "My lord," I said, not looking directly at him. "You must have overheard our conversation. My father's health is somewhat delicate."

"Margaret," my father interrupted in a low voice of disapproval.

I ignored him. If I did not hurry, my courage would fail. "He was ill a while back. The doctor warned us that if he ever falls ill again, he is not likely to recover. He must be removed from the house while there is fever —"

My father, his hand still on my arm, urged me out the door. "Margaret, you cannot presume —"

I broke free of him and stood before Lord Williams. "We have no right to ask such a favor of you, but would you — given what has transpired, I should not think — could he accompany you? I am certain it will not be for long."

My father stepped forward, disapprobation in his voice. "Really, Margaret. I am amazed at you."

My neck and face flamed. But the idea was sound, even if my mentioning it was impertinent.

"Miss Brinton, I would be more than happy to have your father as a guest at my house for as long as needed."

I briefly met his gaze. "You would?" I could say nothing more, for the openness I had come to expect no longer appeared in his eyes, nor in any part of his expression. His face was as a mask of ice, cold and hard.

"Now see here," my father objected.

I quickly turned from Lord Williams. "Father, I could not bear it if you became sick as well. Please, go. If not for me and Mother, then for Alice. We will take such good care of her that you will return within the week."

He frowned, then shook his head. "Daughters are a joy and a curse, my lord. Do not forget that."

My father would go. Once Alice was well and he returned, it would be as though there had never been a Lord Williams. All would be as it should.

Ignoring the emptiness the thought poked into my chest, I said, "I will have John help me pack your things." Turning to leave the room, I glanced once more at Lord Williams. "Thank you, my lord." I paused, then whispered, "For everything."

After my father's trunk had been packed, I stole into Alice's room. Mary slept slumped in a chair near the fire. Alice also seemed to be asleep, but she moaned a little and fidgeted. I slipped onto her bed and placed a gentle hand on her head. She was burning.

"Alice, sit up. Take a drink." I helped her up and held the glass of water from the bedside table to her mouth.

She took a few sips. I set the glass back and tried to help her lay down, but she shook her head. Her voice was barely perceptible as she said, "It hurts."

"All right." I carefully shifted on the bed to lean her against me, pulling the blanket tight and stroking her hair. She coughed, a cough that hurt my throat and chest listening to it. Eventually, though, her breathing evened out. Kissing the top of her head, I whispered, "I'm sorry."

I held her until Mary woke with a start. She left the room with a promise to return quickly.

The door opened a few minutes later, revealing my mother. "Margaret, there you are. You are to go with your father."

I frowned. "Go with him?"

"Yes. To Lord Williams's. He will need someone to look after him."

She could not send me away. Especially not there. "But I can't leave. You will need me to help with Alice."

"Mary and I will manage. You'd best get dressed."

I couldn't go. I was just getting rid of him. And Alice — I wanted to be here for her.

Alice stirred with another cough. I gave her more water, helped her lay down, and tucked the bed cover around her. Then I followed my mother into the hall.

Did she not understand that, aside from the embarrassment of calling off the engagement, I was beginning to have feelings for Lord Williams? Going with him, spending more time with him — these were exactly the things I needed to avoid. "Mother, it is awkward enough for Father to go. But for me to force myself into his home — please do not ask this of me."

She acted as though I hadn't spoken.

"Mary is packing your trunk. You had best attend to it."

I studied her. "Are you very angry with me?"

She paused, then sighed. "No. I wish it were different, that you had behaved differently, but I understand. Your father may become ill even with our precautions. You must be there to look after him if such a thing occurs."

I would not be free from Lord Williams.

I would have to do what I'd promised him I would do in the first place: steel myself against him.

Twenty-Three

I slipped back into Alice's room half an hour later and laid my traveling cloak on the foot of her bed. My sister's only movement was the rise and fall of her chest, her only sound the coughs that came too often to allow her rest. She was still hot to the touch. Sitting on the bed next to her, I dipped a towel into the bowl, wrung it out, and draped it across her forehead.

"Alice," I whispered, not wishing to wake her but hoping she heard. "I am leaving." I was abandoning her. What would she say when she awoke and found me gone, when only hours ago I had told her I would never leave her? "I will write you." I took her hand in mine. It was curled in a fist as though clutching something. Moving her fingers to see what it was, I spied the lace handkerchief.

"Oh, Alice." I allowed her fingers to close around it again. There wasn't even a flutter of the eyelids.

I settled her hands in a more comfortable position and pulled the blanket tightly around her. "Please get better soon." I kissed her forehead and left the room before my emotion gave way to tears.

Everyone was assembled in the drawing room. I stood in the hall, smothering my feelings until I could smile. Then I entered and stood near Daniel. "Please tell Louisa I have gone and that I shall write."

"Of course."

John entered and announced that the carriage was ready. Outside, the clouds had blown away but the air was colder than ever. I pulled my cloak around me, though it seemed to do little to keep out the penetrating chill, and I hurried across the walk to the carriage.

Lord Williams offered his hand to assist me into his carriage. When I took it, his fingers didn't curl around mine as they had at the lake. I quickly lifted my hand from his once I was inside. He climbed in, taking a seat across from me, and I scooted into the corner to keep my legs far away from his. An accidental touch would only be awkward for us both.

My father said something to Daniel I didn't catch. Then he stood before my mother. "You must write me if there is a turn for the worse."

"She is going to be fine. And your own health —"

"Means nothing in the face of such an event. Eloise, I will not leave unless you promise."

She huffed. "It is only a little fever."

"In which case such a promise should be easy to make."

My mother hesitated. "I promise. Now go, Colin. I should return to Alice."

He embraced her, saying a few words into her ear before giving her a quick kiss. Such tenderness was what every girl dreamed of. I focused on the shadows out my window.

The carriage dipped under my father's weight and he settled on the seat next to me. It was too early to see anything but the outline of dark trees against an only slightly less dark sky. With Lord Williams's face being the only other place to look, I contented myself with the black view.

Once, when the sky was lightening to a morning blue, my knee brushed against his as the carriage swayed around a bend. He may have been asleep, but I couldn't risk looking at him; what if he was awake? Then we'd have to speak. I pressed my legs into the side of the carriage and closed my eyes, wishing sleep would come. Instead, I felt every jolt and rock of the carriage.

When the trees had definite form and the sky had become a pale blue, I risked a quick inspection of the carriage. Lord Williams had angled his legs so as to give me as much room as possible. If I had known, I would not have had to keep myself so cramped.

The sun was well into its morning rise when we crossed a bridge, the clear river beneath revealing its rock-strewn bottom, and drove between open gates.

I straightened. This was Lord Williams's estate. I tried to act disinterested as I surveyed the tree-covered land, but as the drive curved and I caught my first glimpse of the house, I gasped at its beauty. The large ivory-gray stone was capped by a dark roof, beautifully carved gables, and a procession of stone chimneys that lined the skyline. Large, rectangular windows surrounded each of the three levels and giant bow windows stood like elegant open pillars at the sides of the front of the house.

It was much grander than I had imagined.

The coachman pulled to a stop and our door was opened. After descending, I surveyed my surroundings in admiration. Most of the view was taken up by fields of green broken only by giant oaks, while the house was established on a small rise with a river running a short stroll away.

No wonder he wanted to drain the lake. He thought we should have a river instead, just like him.

"Welcome to Pettley Hall," Lord Williams said.

"Thank you," my father said. I took my father's arm and remained silent.

A butler arrived in the doorway. "My lord, welcome home. Your mother will be content now that you have returned."

Lord Williams strode forward. "Good morning, Sundson. She is in good health, I trust?"

"The same as when you left, my lord. She is in the breakfast room."

"Very good. This is Mr. Brinton and his daughter. They are here to stay for a few days. Please see that rooms are made ready for them."

"Immediately, my lord."

Once we passed through the door into the hall, I clasped tighter to my father's arm. Before us stretched an immaculate tiled floor. The walls of the hall were lined with paintings accented by stone molding frames, and the ceiling was delightfully high with light pouring in from the windows behind us. I had never witnessed a more picturesque and stately room.

We followed Lord Williams down a hall toward the left wing and into a large room made larger by one of the bow windows. Other windows, nearly floor to ceiling, overlooked the river. The feeling was one of comfort, more so than I'd thought possible in such a grand house.

A lady sitting at the table rose. She was of average height but her hair was cut uncharacteristically short, rendering her regal and commanding. She glided across the floor in the manner every young woman hoped to imitate. Her dress, the most exquisite lavender shade, barely rustled at the movement.

"Gregory. What a welcome vision you are. I had not expected you for some days yet."

"Good morning, Mother," Lord Williams bent to kiss her cheek. "Allow me to introduce Mr. Brinton and his eldest daughter, Miss Brinton. They will be staying with us while Mr. Brinton's youngest daughter is ill."

I curtsied. "It is a pleasure to meet you, your ladyship."

"You are both very welcome," Lady Williams said. "With the fatigue of so long a journey, and arriving here so early, you must be exhausted. Gregory, you have sent Sundson to prepare some rooms?" He nodded.

"Good. If you will follow me, I shall show you to them. I am certain you desire to freshen up, and I shall have some food sent to you there, if you would like."

"Thank you," my father replied.

I followed Lady Williams and my father to the door but paused and looked back. Lord Williams stood where we had left him, watching us, a frown on his face. He inclined his head, then turned and moved farther into the room. I hurried to catch up with my father.

TWENTY-FOUR

Lady Williams led us up a massive staircase near the entry hall. At the top of the first landing she directed us to a door on the right. "Mr. Brinton, this will be your room. Your daughter's room is next to yours."

My father nodded. "Thank you, your ladyship." He entered the room and closed the door.

"Miss Brinton, if you would follow me." She opened the door to the room directly above the breakfast room and stood aside to let me in. The ceiling was as high as it had been downstairs. Light blue ornate trim framed the pink walls and a writing desk stood in front of one of the windows that ran the length of the room. A wardrobe and vanity claimed the wall on either side of the burning fireplace and a large bed stood near the door, flanked by small tables. But the best aspect was the curved white bench situated in the alcove created by the bow window.

"Oh," I murmured in delight.

"I am glad that you like it." She scanned the room. "Your trunk is here, but I see it has not been unpacked. Perhaps your lady's maid was delayed in the kitchen."

I regarded my not-quite-old trunk. "I do not have a lady's maid, your ladyship. The maid who would normally have accompanied me was needed at home to tend to my sister's illness."

"Of course. I shall send my own lady in to help. Someone will be found to assist you before the day is over."

"Thank you. You are most kind."

She smiled. "Not at all. It is the greatest pleasure to have company."

Once she'd left, I sat on the bench. The whole of the front of the estate stretched before me, acres of grass and copses of trees.

A knock sounded at the door. For an instant, I thought Lord Williams had come to inquire after my comfort. Just as quickly, I dismissed the idea. "Come in."

The door opened to reveal a nicely dressed older lady and a young maid. "Excuse me, miss. I am Mrs. Field, Lady Williams's lady's maid."

"Of course. Please come in."

The other maid silently set a tray of food

on one of the tables and set about unpacking the trunk. Mrs. Field watched her until, seeming satisfied she would do a decent job, she turned back to me. "Would you like assistance out of your dress? You'll feel better after washing."

"Yes, thank you."

A basin was filled with warm water. After refreshing myself and changing out of my traveling gown, Mrs. Field and the other maid left and I sat in the alcove with my food, my back to the river, mesmerized by the view.

When I finished eating, I wrote letters to both Louisa and my mother, including a note for Alice, then opened the door and peeked out. No one was around. I knocked quietly on my father's door to see if he'd join me on a walk about the grounds, but there was no response; he was most probably napping. I made my way downstairs alone.

In the entry hall, I studied the paintings of people I didn't know, their eyes seeming to follow me as I moved about the room. There were busts of marble in each of the corners as well. I strolled slowly, stopping to study each one.

"The statues are Roman, from the first and second century."

Lord Williams's voice startled me into stepping away from the statue I'd been close to touching. "They're beautiful."

"I hope your room is to your satisfaction."

"It is. Especially the view from the alcove."

He nodded. "Is there anything else you need?" His tone was formal, a host checking on his guest.

"No. I was just. . . . My father is asleep but I am not tired."

"My housekeeper will give you a tour to acquaint you with the estate."

He didn't offer to give me the tour himself. Perhaps he had pressing business that couldn't wait. Or perhaps he no longer wanted anything to do with me. I couldn't blame him for either. "A tour would be most welcome."

Lord Williams rang, and within a few moments his housekeeper appeared.

"Mrs. Duval, please provide Miss Brinton with a tour of the house." Then he left. There was no lingering glance, no smile, no parting word.

I ignored the sense of loss stirring within me. I had not wanted him when he offered for me. I had begged for him to release me. So why was I feeling as though I had fallen from the wall and had the wind knocked out of me?

260

Mrs. Duval smiled. "Since we are here, it seems a good place to begin. The main portions of the house were first constructed during the reign of the Tudors. . . ."

I followed her to the front of the room.

After showing me the entry hall and the wood-paneled dining room, she led me down the right wing containing the antechamber and drawing room, all the while explaining about Jacobean wings, which had been added more recently and changed the original square house into a *U* shape.

Mrs. Duval paused before the last door of the wing. "Since you have already seen the breakfast room and his lordship is occupying the study next to it, this is the last room of consequence on this floor." She opened the door to a good-sized room with a large piano commandeering its far corner. "This is the music room, constructed within the last few hundred years. It contains the piano you see there, along with a harp, a violin, and a flute."

I stepped past her. "Is it much used?"

"Her ladyship played every day before the passing of the late Lord Williams. The current Lord Williams enjoys the room when there is company."

For all the time we had spent together, I could not say if Lord Williams enjoyed hosting house parties. It seemed one should know if a man preferred a large gathering or the intimacy of a few close friends. I walked to the piano and ran my finger along its polished wood. "Is there often company?"

"Often enough." Mrs. Duval's clipped tone suggested she would reveal no more about the family than she saw prudent. "This room is at your disposal for the duration of your stay."

I touched the keys longingly. Alice would love this room. She might even be more amenable to practicing if she could do so on such a fine instrument.

"When you are ready, I will escort you upstairs."

We made our way up the large staircase. Instead of heading to the right, which would have brought us to my bedchamber, Mrs. Duval opened the door to the room directly in front of us. "The ballroom," she said, stepping aside.

I cautiously made my way in. Light poured through windows facing the front and side of the estate. Tall mirrors lined the wall of the pink- and white-trimmed room, reflecting the light and brightening the entire area. An empty fireplace topped by an exquisitely ornate molding took up the center of the wall and promised heat on the cold nights when this room was filled with music and laughter. An alcove, twin to the one in my room, beckoned from the far corner.

"It's perfect."

"It is usually a favorite with the younger ladies."

The glamour of the room dimmed. How cliché I was, to love a ballroom best. "Yes, I am sure it is." I strode back through the door. "Is there anything else to be seen?"

"The house boasts over one hundred rooms, with a long gallery on the floor above us. There are also the grounds. If you are not too fatigued, they are worth beholding."

The excitement I should have felt at the prospect of seeing more failed to arise. I shook my head. "I am a little tired. I think I shall rest for dinner."

She nodded. "Of course."

I trudged back to my room, wishing for all the world I was home.

I spent the next hours with my head against the window, watching the estate grounds until a maid entered and assisted dressing me for dinner. When I entered the ante-chamber, where Mrs. Duval had informed me everyone would assemble, the conversation halted.

"Ah, there you are, Margaret," my father said with a smile.

"Am I late? I apologize if I am."

"Not at all, my dear," Lady Williams said.

Lord Williams held his arm out to me. "Miss Brinton?"

I hesitated, then placed my hand lightly on his arm and allowed him to lead me toward the dining room.

"I hope you enjoyed the tour of the house?"

"Yes," I replied. "Very much."

"And the grounds?"

"I haven't yet ventured outside." Lord Williams didn't comment, so I filled the silence by explaining, "Your housekeeper suggested I should, but I found myself a little fatigued."

"Of course."

His comment was polite yet dismissive.

"Miss Brinton," Lady Williams asked as we took our seats. "I understand you are quite musical."

A little warily, I replied, "I enjoy music very much, your ladyship."

"I am glad to hear it. This house always feels more full when there is music in it. Will you play for us after dinner?"

It was the last thing I wished to do. I should be at home, tending Alice, planning a marriage with no danger of affection, no danger of being hurt, and looking forward to a life of solitude. "I should be delighted."

Lord Williams raised his brows but said nothing.

When we entered the music room an hour later, Lady Williams indicated a small table next to the piano. "We keep all our music there."

Thanking her, I trooped to the table and shuffled through the papers, passing over most of the songs I had in my own collection. When I came across the one Lord Williams had asked me to play, though, I paused. What was it about this song in particular that appealed to both him and Mr. Northam? My body warmed at the memory of Lord Williams's hand on my back, at his whisper about my performance at the Hickmores'. I glanced up to find his gaze on me, but he turned casually and said something to his mother. I turned the sheet over and continued my perusal.

In the end I discovered a dozen or so pieces that were unfamiliar. I removed a few and studied them with interest, then set them aside to work on when I found some time to myself. Retrieving a sonata I had memorized, I laid the sheets out on the piano before me, not trusting myself to play from memory on an unfamiliar instrument while an audience looked on. Even with the music I made two mistakes, but Lady Williams was gracious in her praise.

Lord Williams, however, said nothing. His comments certainly weren't required. But anything would have been better than his detached silence.

It was obvious he had no wish for me to be here.

I should never have thrust my father and, inadvertently, myself upon him. And while I certainly didn't expect him to be as attentive as he'd been before, I hadn't expected this coldness.

It was for the best, but it still stung.

Lady Williams requested another song, but I couldn't. "I'm afraid I am more tired than I thought. Would you be offended if I retired early?"

"Of course not, my dear," she replied.

My father rose quickly to his feet. "You are not ill, are you, Margaret?"

"No. Just weary from the day." I slid from the room and leaned against the wall outside the door.

"I hope she is not becoming ill," I heard Lady Williams say.

"She has had a long day, mother," Lord

266

Williams replied, his tone dismissive.
I slunk to my room and fell onto my bed.

TWENTY-FIVE

The next morning I paused at the top of the staircase and peeked over the railing. Nothing moved except the morning light slowly brightening the hall below. I straightened myself and walked elegantly down the stairs in case a servant walked by.

The entry demanded reverence, so I kept my pace slow and my footsteps quiet against the tile. When I finally escaped the house, shutting the front door securely behind me, I inhaled a deep breath of relief.

The river moved in a constant hurry. There was nothing peaceful about it, no sounds of quiet lapping, no stillness to reflect the trees and clouds. Instead, the current tugged at the branch of a nearby tree, unsuccessfully straining to tear it free.

I sat on a bench and tossed stones into the water until the sun broke above the trees and lit my face. At least its warmth felt familiar. I leaned back and tilted my face upward. With my eyes closed, I could almost imagine I was home.

There was no path near the river, but I walked its bank anyway, taking care to step on the grass and avoid the mud. My explorations took me around the back of the house, where I found a garden in the courtyard created by the towering walls of the house's two wings. A stone path ran down the middle of the garden, stretching into the shadowed courtyard and ending at a door. Little shrubs, half a dozen inches high, created rectangular walls around flowerbeds lining either side of the path, and ivy climbed a short distance up the sides of the house, forming arches over the windows.

It was so much more formal than our own garden, the one Lord Williams had been so opposed to. He must have been mocking me that morning we'd walked together. I strolled the paths, missing the naturalness of my own place. When the church bell struck the hour, I returned to the front of the house and let myself in, startling a footman in the entry.

During breakfast I took the opportunity to assess my father's health. He appeared rested and eager to spend the day in the library, confirming that my accompanying him to Lord Williams's had been unnecessary. And, based on Lord Williams's taciturn responses, unwanted.

As the meal ended, Lady Williams said, "You are most welcome to join me this morning, Miss Brinton. I believe one of our neighbors is planning to call."

Feeling rather obliged, I agreed.

She led me into one of the parlors, and within a few minutes, a woman near her age with high, arched brows, white hair, and a commanding presence entered. Lady Williams smiled. "Miss Brinton, allow me to introduce my friend Mrs. Hargreaves. Mrs. Hargreaves, Miss Brinton will be staying with us a few days."

"Will she? How wonderful." Mrs. Hargreaves spoke with a slight accent I couldn't place and took a seat next to Lady Williams. She eyed me. "No need to ask you why you are here."

Though her tone wasn't unkind, there was no mistaking the insinuation in her words. "I am afraid you are mistaken," Lady Williams intervened. "Miss Brinton's father has come to view Gregory's handling of the estate. Miss Brinton was pressured into the trip as company for him."

I started at her words. She could only have known I didn't wish to be here if Lord Williams had told her. Which meant he knew as well. Was this why he'd been so formal and distant?

Or perhaps he was formal and distant because there was no longer a reason to be any other way.

Mrs. Hargreaves looked over me. "Hm." Then she smiled. "She will do."

"Unfortunately for us all, I believe it is out of the question," Lady Williams said.

"Never give up, Clarice. *Der Hunger kommt beim Essen.*"

I glanced between the ladies, not understanding the German, though at least now I could place the accent.

"You must excuse my friend, Miss Brinton," Lady Williams said. "She forgets we are not all fluent in her native tongue. What she means is that everything must start with a little step, though you must excuse her in this as well. She is unused to young ladies visiting without aims at my son."

"I never understood why the English do not learn my language," Mrs. Hargreaves said. "It's ofttimes more apt at expressing a sentiment than this stilted language of yours."

"Yes, yes. You have said as much before," Lady Williams replied.

Sundson entered. "Lady Cox and Miss Perrin."

Mrs. Hargreaves rolled her eyes and leaned toward me. "Lady Cox is the wife of a knight, but she thinks she should be queen! Miss Perrin, her daughter from her first marriage, is not a bad sort of person, though. Rather timid." She shrugged.

A lady taller than Sundson entered, followed by a younger woman, obviously her daughter. They had the same dark brown hair, the same heavy brows and round chins. But where Lady Cox's smile formed into a pinched frown when she noticed Mrs. Hargreaves, Miss Perrin smiled a dazzling, albeit somewhat blank, smile. Lady Cox surveyed Mrs. Hargreaves and sniffed loudly, then turned her focus to me. Her eyes instantly narrowed.

"Lady Cox, Miss Perrin," Lady Williams said. "How good it is to see you. It has been over a week."

Lady Cox's eyes never left me. "I see you have company. We do not wish to intrude."

Mrs. Hargreaves snorted, and Lady Cox's attention leapt back to her. "Good morning, Mrs. Hargreaves. You are the same as always, I see. Is this girl some relation of yours?"

Mrs. Hargreaves produced a condescending smile of her own. "Where is the benefit of change when one is practically perfect?"

272

Lady Cox ignored her question. "Would you do us the honor, Lady Williams, of introducing us to your pretty young guest?"

Lady Williams sent me a genial smile. "This is Miss Brinton. She and her father have come to visit for a few days."

"How pleasant." Lady Cox's tone led me to understand there was nothing pleasant about my visit in her opinion. No doubt she also believed I was here to capture Lord Williams. I wondered what she would think if she knew of the days he and I had just passed together.

Determined to remain unaffected by her hostility, I smiled. "It is a pleasure to make your acquaintance, Lady Cox. Miss Perrin, would you like to sit here?" I indicated the place next to me.

"I'd be delighted."

I scooted over on the cushion. She plopped beside me, the jolt bouncing me into the air. At that moment Lord Williams entered the room.

I struggled to right the skirts of my dress, but Miss Perrin shot out of her seat, unsettling me on the cushion once again.

"Oh, your lordship!" she exclaimed.

He strode into the room with a wide smile. "Lady Cox, Miss Perrin, Mrs. Hargreaves. It is wonderful to find you all here." He kissed each lady's hand in turn.

Lady Cox's surliness disappeared. "We are so pleased you have returned. I admit I was surprised by your continued absence. We had thought you would not be away more than two days."

Ignoring me completely, Lord Williams stood next to Miss Perrin. Rather close. Close enough that it appeared his hand brushed hers. My chest tightened.

"I apologize for staying away so long," he replied. "I encountered business that detained me from returning."

Business? I was business? He was acting more like the Lord Williams from the Hickmores' and less like the man I'd come to believe him to be.

Perhaps I had been correct all along. If so, it was a hollow victory.

"Business is so odious." Lady Cox proceeded to relate some tale regarding something she had done the day before.

"I am so glad you've returned," Miss Perrin whispered to Lord Williams.

"As am I," he replied with a rather intimate smile.

This couldn't be happening. He had professed his desire for my hand only two days before, yet his regard for Miss Perrin was unmistakable. He acted as though I weren't even there.

Perhaps he was exactly like Edward, courting me as *business* while retaining a true regard for someone else.

Yet was this not exactly what I had set myself up for in seeking Mr. Northam's hand? I myself had declared that I wouldn't seek to change Mr. Northam's wandering ways. If what Lord Williams had implied was to be believed, Mr. Northam might even be so brash as to bring a mistress into the very house his wife occupied.

But there was still a difference. There would never be pretended affection between me and Mr. Northam, while Lord Williams had led me to believe —

Chagrin rippled within me. Lord Williams had told me that if Mr. Northam had wanted to make me love him, he could. And while I'd sworn it wouldn't happen, Lord Williams had shown it was possible. It didn't matter that the engagement had been called off; in the end, he had still broken through my barriers. I didn't love him, but he'd certainly changed how I felt about him. He'd proved what a fool I was.

This must have been what he'd meant when he'd said he shouldn't have allowed it to continue for so long. He'd not only intended to keep me from his cousin, but he'd also intended to show how foolish my plan was. He'd thought to make me care for him as a way of proving he'd been right.

Did he know he'd succeeded? That I'd begun to care for him?

And now that the game was given up, he'd decided to return to his normal life. One that didn't involve me, my plans, and my —

Not my heart; that hadn't been affected. But certainly my regard.

Curse the circumstances that had placed me next to him that night at the Hickmores'. If only I could disappear and never hear the name Williams again.

I might not be able to leave his estate, but there was no reason why I must remain in the room with him now. I stood. "Please excuse me." I dropped a quick curtsy. "It was a pleasure to meet you all, but I have just recollected a matter I wish to discuss with my father."

"I believe you will find him in the library," Lord Williams said. The lack of formality in his tone caught my attention. His eyes were not as cold as I had expected, but neither were they as inviting as they had been. His agreeableness must have been a result of Miss Perrin's presence.

"Thank you."

Instead of searching for my father, I

walked to the music room and shut the door. What I needed was my lake. Or at least to be outside. But outside held nothing but a garden too formal to enjoy and a gurgling river that was more annoying than peaceful.

I had to get away. From Lord Williams, from his mother, from his house, and his life.

Yet would this not be my life if I answered Mr. Northam's letter? Hours spent with my head against a window, with no one for conversation but the servants unless Mr. Northam or a kind neighbor came for a visit? I would be isolated and alone.

While Edward's actions had left me feeling abandoned, I had never truly been alone. I had always had Daniel and Alice for entertainment and Louisa for confidences.

Yet if not Mr. Northam, then who? What other choice did I have if I wished to be free from the deception, from Lord Williams, from my own foolishness — free from of all of this?

Grabbing one of the songs I had set aside, I sat at the piano and worked my way through the scales and arpeggios, aching to bury the reality of my situation.

An hour later, the door opened. "Margaret?"

I stopped playing. "Father."

"Lord Williams mentioned I might find you here. Did you wish to speak with me? Is everything all right?"

I almost said yes. It would have been so easy to pretend with a false smile and a nod that I was fine. But if I was to leave, I could not pretend for my father. "I cannot stay here. It is too awkward, too embarrassing, too —" I couldn't say painful or dangerous. My father wouldn't understand. "Please, isn't there any other place we can go?"

He walked up and put his arms around me. "We cannot leave so soon after arriving. What would Lord Williams think of us?"

"It no longer matters what he thinks of us. Besides, he cannot regard me with any less esteem than he already does."

He sighed. "Perhaps you are right. But we must await word from your mother. Tomorrow would be sufficient time for Alice to be well again. Then we can simply return home."

If the post came early, by tomorrow night I could be home. Home to my lake. Home to my family.

But I would still have to determine what to do about my future.

TWENTY-SIX

Lady Williams again invited me to join her the next morning, insisting that Mrs. Hargreaves would be her only visitor and that she had taken such a delight in my company yesterday.

Mrs. Hargreaves's delight undoubtedly had more to do with my not being related to Lady Cox than with any merit I could claim of my own. But as the post had not yet arrived, I would be in the best position to receive any news if I remained near Lady Williams. And I could escape Lord Williams. "Yes, of course."

We retired to the same room as the day before. Within moments Mrs. Hargreaves was announced.

"Ah, Miss Brinton. I am so glad you decided to join us again this morning." She sat where she had before, but leaned toward me so that we were quite close. "You mustn't pay any heed to Miss Perrin."

"Mrs. Hargreaves," I replied, determined to put an end to whatever ideas she held regarding Lord Williams and me. "I thank you for your concern, but as I expect our stay will be of very short duration, I do not believe I need be concerned with Miss Perrin at all."

"You are leaving soon?" Mrs. Hargreaves asked with a frown.

"We await only news of my sister's recovery. It was never our intent to visit, except my sister became ill and we found it necessary to be away for the sake of my father's health. Lord Williams graciously offered his home."

"Of course he did. I know all about it," Mrs. Hargreaves said, patting my hand.

She couldn't know all the details. Not how Lord Williams had almost caused me to regret my decision. Nor how similar he was to Edward. And especially not how I ached for word from home, how empty I felt wandering the large house and grounds.

"Perhaps," Lady Williams said, "you had not heard that the Browns have decided to vacation in Bath this year. Such a long, expensive journey for a clergyman. But his lady's health has been on the decline ever since winter."

"I had heard," Mrs. Hargreaves said. "It is

old news, Clarice. But I catch your intent, and so shall leave off teasing Miss Brinton."

"I doubt you'll do any such thing," replied Lady Williams.

"I hope you are not teasing Miss Brinton," Lord Williams spoke from the doorway, hat in hand. "Though if it is a matter of some humor, I should like to hear it."

Did the man turn up every morning for his mother's visitors?

Sundson followed him into the room. "The post, your ladyship."

I sat forward.

"Thank you, Sundson," Lady Williams said as he held out a silver tray with three or four letters on it. She picked up each letter individually. At the last one, she hesitated, glanced at Mrs. Hargreaves, then said to me, "There's something for you, dear."

I jumped up. "Thank you."

The letter was from Louisa. Taking the letter a little distance away, I opened it and glanced over it quickly, then paused and read over it again.

"I hope it is not bad news?" Lord Williams asked.

"I — Alice still has a fever but seems to be getting better."

"That is good news," Lady Williams said.

"What else does it say?" Lord Williams

281

asked quietly.

What did it matter to him? What did it matter to me if he knew? He may have caught me off guard, but I was not deceived in him any longer. I would not be hurt by him. Let him see that for all his effort, he'd failed.

I handed him the paper and saw the moment he read the words in the way he stilled. *Mr. Northam called. I can see why you like him, though Daniel is furious. He refused to tell Mr. Northam where you were. Do you think he'll come looking for you there?*

Lord Williams handed the paper back, his gaze meeting mine. "I am glad your sister is recovering."

"And the other news?" I asked, my voice low to keep our conversation private.

"You already know my thoughts on that subject." His voice was as quiet as mine, but his tone was dismissive.

"Yes." I refolded the letter. I had meant to be strong in letting him read it, to show him that the past week had meant nothing. But it had meant something. Just not to him. My words came out barely above a whisper. "I do know your thoughts."

His brow furrowed.

"Gregory," Lady Williams said, "are you joining us again this morning?"

Sundson reentered. "Lady Cox and Miss Perrin." Lady Cox bustled in, Miss Perrin following in her wake. I took the opportunity to step away from Lord Williams.

"Ah, I see everyone is here," Lady Cox said.

Lord Williams bowed his head. "Unfortunately I was just leaving. I have some business on the northern corner of the estate. Mr. Brinton is riding out with me. We shall be away until dinner."

"You will be showing him the garden?" Lady Williams asked.

"Of course," Lord Williams replied.

Lady Williams nodded. "Miss Brinton, have you seen the garden yet? It is one of my favorite places on the estate."

"If Miss Brinton has been out of the house at all," Lord Williams said, "I am certain she has discovered it. It would not surprise me if she has been out each morning to enjoy a walk before the rest of us have even opened our eyes."

I didn't allow myself to be flattered by his insight into my habits; I was just business, after all. "I have seen the garden. It is quite formal, but it fits the estate perfectly."

Lord Williams eyed me.

"Oh, there is another garden," Miss Perrin said. "Walled and filled with roses. It's quite wild."

"Elisa," Lady Cox said, shaking her head. Miss Perrin fell silent.

My father entered and, after introductions were made, small talk ensued. I walked to him. "Father, I received a letter from Louisa. Alice still has a fever but seems to be improving."

His brow furrowed with concern. "She still has a fever? Can I see the letter?"

"Oh." I slid the letter behind my back. "Louisa had things to say of a private nature."

"Of course." My father nodded.

"Take care of yourself today. With Alice getting better, it wouldn't do for you to fall ill."

Lord Williams stepped beside me. "Mr. Brinton? Are you ready?"

Saddle oil and cologne floated to me on the air, the smells of what might have been had we both been different people. The scents of what would never be. "You are welcome to accompany us, Miss Brinton," he offered.

I glanced at the party behind him and found Lady Cox glaring at me. "I thank you, my lord, but I doubt Lady Cox and Miss Perrin would like it. I do not wish my presence to inconvenience you more than it already has."

"Your thoughtfulness knows no bounds," he muttered before turning toward the others. "Good day, ladies." With a nod to his mother, he and my father left the room.

"He is such a handsome man," sighed Lady Cox, suddenly next to me.

"Hm," I responded noncommittally.

"Do you disagree, Miss Brinton?"

I shrugged. "I do not think it matters what I think of Lord Williams."

Lady Cox smiled in the most cat-like way. "Yes, I believe you are correct. You do know that he and my daughter are practically engaged?"

He was exactly like Edward. I was lucky to have escaped. "I offer you my congratulations."

"Nothing is official, but I hope the matter will be resolved quickly."

As did I. "There is nothing as bothersome as waiting."

"Very true." Lady Cox moved next to her daughter and spoke a few low words to her before turning her attention to Lady Williams and Mrs. Hargreaves.

Miss Perrin approached. "I am so glad you are here, Miss Brinton. There are not many ladies in the neighborhood with whom I can associate in good conscience. Lord Williams is most attentive, to be sure, but one does miss the companionship of another female, does one not?"

"Quite true."

"But you must have many good friends at home, I suppose."

"I have one friend with whom I am very close. We have known each other all our lives and I hope soon to call her sister. But life would be very dull if there were room for only one friend."

She graced me with one of her dazzling smiles. "Oh, yes. You said it perfectly."

We stood in silence, listening to the older ladies' chatter. Everyone seemed to fit so naturally together. Even Mrs. Hargreaves and Lady Cox had their own routine of insults and rebuffs. I had no place in their small circle.

But it was possible we would be here for at least a few more days. It would be prudent to make some effort. "Have you always resided in the neighborhood?" I asked Miss Perrin.

"No. We moved here only a month ago, when Mama married Sir Timothy."

She and Lord Williams had formed an attachment quickly, then.

Of course, they had no doubt spent more time together than he and I had, and he had drawn me in easily enough. "Are you pleased with the area?"

"I suppose one could call it charming, but to own the truth I find it a little oppressive. If not for Lord Williams, I might have returned to live with my sister near Portsmouth. Sometimes I think I shall die if I don't feel a sea breeze on my face. But, of course, that is just an exaggeration, for I have not passed on yet."

I nodded and, as casually as I could, asked, "Are you very attached to Lord Williams?"

"Oh, yes. He is the very best of men. One could do much worse than Lord Williams, but I don't believe one could do much better, even if he is only a baron."

Although she did not speak of him as a woman in love might, her response left no doubt that when he asked, she would accept.

Let him find the love he'd so argued for at the party. I would certainly not stand in the way. "It is not my place to do so," I said, "but I wonder if we can prevail upon Lady Williams to invite you to dinner. Perhaps your mother. . . ."

Miss Perrin beamed. "That is a wonderful idea. We have no engagements tonight. Then you can perform for us. I myself am not very musical, though I have one song Lord Williams gifted me a few weeks past. Oh, it is not learned as it ought to be. I hope he does not request I sing it for him."

Lord Williams had given her music? No wonder Lady Cox was in expectation of a union. "How kind of him."

"He is the soul of generosity. Mama, Miss Brinton has thought up a wonderful idea." She left me to go to her mother.

TWENTY-SEVEN

A few hours later, I headed away from the river to a lane of trees at the end of which stood a small gate. Once I reached the gate, I pushed it open and stopped under an arbor of white roses. This, then, was the garden Miss Perrin had been speaking of. Blooms of pink, red, white, yellow, and variegated strains stretched down the path before me, their nodding heads beckoning for someone to smell and admire them.

My garden had never looked like this. It's how it should have looked, though.

Moving down the path, I strolled past trellises and along twisting lanes, the roses making way for mums, asters, lilies, and some flowers I had never seen before. I touched the overhanging leaves of maples and vines as I passed under them. Everything was vibrant without being overwhelmingly so.

This is where I should have been spending my days. I imagined walking in the garden early in the morning when the smell of dew mingled with the aroma of the flowers, when the garden awakened under the first rays of the morning sun.

"Miss Brinton."

I started up from where I'd bent to inspect a flower, its textured petals soft and delicate. Lord Williams strode down the path toward me.

"You are supposed to be gone all day." I glanced behind him, but he was alone. Father. Something had happened. "My father —"

"Your father is fine. We decided to divide the estate into two days, as he wished to spend extra time examining farming strategies."

"Oh." This did not bode well for my lake. "He has liked what he's seen, then?"

"He seemed to, though you would get a better idea of his true thoughts by asking him."

"I see." Even now, I felt a pull toward him, a certain delight that he had sought me out. I had been right to disregard him that first evening at the Hickmores' party. Why was I still so drawn to him? "I will go ask him."

He held up a hand. "Miss Brinton, I had hoped we could speak for a moment."

"Do we have something to speak about?"

"I believe so." He gestured down the path I had already been traversing.

"You must excuse me. I should attend to my father."

"He requested time to learn more of my farming methods. I left him in the study with a large stack of books. There is no reason to disturb him." He stepped forward, blocking my escape. "Please."

Whatever he had to say could not take long. I nodded and we began our stroll.

"I hope the garden meets with your approval."

"Yes. It is quite magical." An uncomfortable silence settled between us. He should be the one to speak. It was he who asked for this conversation, after all. Yet when the silence became overbearing, I asked, "Does your estate hold any other secrets? A hidden lake, perhaps?"

"Though the estate boasts a fair-sized wood with excellent hunting and a few hills that provide quite remarkable views, I am afraid I cannot claim a lake as one of my assets."

"Do you gather a large party for your hunts?"

"We do hold an annual hunt on the grounds, but I prefer an expedition with only a few friends for company." He stopped and turned to me. "Let me be frank. Are you still determined to unite yourself with my cousin?"

Better Mr. Northam than him. "I do not believe it proper for us to converse about such things."

"We have always spoken rather boldly with each other, have we not? It suits both our temperaments, and has from the very first. Do not turn reticent now."

He had taken measure of my character so easily that first night, had known a direct conversation was my preference, had seen through my defenses and spied my weaknesses. I had not been so wise. "Yet one may speak boldly without being open about one's intents."

"You do not wish to tell me?"

"I wasn't speaking of my own character."

"You think I have not been open?"

I shrugged. "I think you have done exactly as you wanted."

"And what is that?"

I didn't hesitate. "To illustrate how wrong I was."

He frowned. "How have I done that?"

Did he hope I had not recognized what he'd been about? "Did you not assure me that if your cousin wished to make me care for him he would succeed?"

"He would. Because he would stop at nothing to get whatever he desired."

I gestured to him. "It seems to be a family trait, at least where the male line is concerned."

"You think I am like him?" he asked incredulously.

"Aside from ensuring that your cousin and I could never be together, as you have confessed, was it not also your intent to prove the folly of my assertion that your cousin could never win my heart and make me love him?"

He stood a moment, confusion in his expression, before it was replaced with disbelief. "You think I set out to make you love me to prove a point?" He paused. "Did I succeed?"

Arrogant, hateful man. "In making your point? Yes."

His gaze grew more intense. "Then you care for me."

Was I mistaken in thinking he didn't care? That look in his eyes. . . . But, no. It was only the look of someone determined to get his way. "Of course not."

"And my having no effect on you is why you are twisting your fingers like you wish to wring them off?"

I stilled my hands. "Must I confess admiration for you to end your insistent pestering? At least there is no deception where your cousin is concerned, whereas with you . . . I have no one to blame but myself." I stepped past him and hurried toward the gate.

"Margaret, wait —"

I spun back around. "I never gave you leave to use my name. But that doesn't matter, does it, because your title allows you to do what you want? You speak of your cousin taking what he wants and how you despise him for it, but how have your actions been any different?"

He stepped toward me. "I did what I did because it was the right thing to do."

"According to you."

"I was protecting you."

"I did not ask for your protection. I do not want it. Surely I am not the first woman to set my sights on Mr. Northam. Yet you cannot have gone ensnaring all those who have come before. Unless. . . ." Had he? Perhaps I was not the first woman he had engaged himself to.

"Of course not. It was nothing like that."

"Then I can only assume you singled me out because I would not pay heed to your advice."

He frowned. "I admit I thought you would see reason given time."

I had been correct. All of this — everything — it had all been to prove himself correct, to feed his conceit, to purposefully mislead and hurt me. "I congratulate you on your superior judgment; you seem to understand my character better than even I do. Your efforts were not in vain; you have proved your point well. If there is nothing else, I will return inside."

I didn't wait for his response.

I found my father in the study precisely as Lord Williams had said. "How did you find the estate?" I asked, moving toward him.

"Lord Williams is a most attentive landlord. Not one of his tenants wants for necessities and comfort."

"I am glad to hear he cares."

My father frowned. "Is something the matter?"

"Being here, that is all. I'll be in the music room. There were a few songs there I have not seen before." And it was the only place other than my bedchamber where Lord Williams did not seem to bother me.

I worked my way through one song a few times, but my mind was only partially concentrating on the notes. How long must

I stay here and face the humiliation of my own weaknesses? How long before my mother wrote, requesting our return? Alice had to get better soon. My mother's letter would give us a better idea of Alice's expected recovery than Louisa's, since Louisa most certainly received her updates from Daniel.

I stopped the piece without finishing and began to softly play my mother's favorite song, hoping like a child that the song would somehow carry to her and persuade her to write. It didn't seem to be enough, though. My heart still ached for home. So I began to hum and finally to sing.

I sat after, my hands silent on the keys. Though I was no less alone than before, I felt as though she'd heard, as though she were just in the other room listening.

How I wished to be home.

I rose to retrieve a different song when low voices sounded in the hall, almost as though in an argument. The next moment, Lady Williams walked into the room. "That was beautiful, Miss Brinton. You don't mind if I sit and listen, do you? It has been such a long time since we have enjoyed such superb music in this home."

I set the piece I'd picked up back down. "Not at all." It was her house, after all.

"Did you hear that, Gregory? For goodness' sake, come in and sit down. There's no point lurking in the hallway."

Lord Williams walked in, his face a mask of disapproval. "I can't stay. I was passing, that is all."

"Nonsense, dear. You've been lingering for the past ten minutes. We Williamses never could resist music, could we?"

His frown deepened. "Excuse me, I have some business to attend to."

"It can wait. Miss Brinton was about to sing us a new song."

He sat in the chair his mother had indicated without looking at me. Embarrassed by his obvious reluctance to stay, I stepped away from the music. "In all honesty, I had not meant to be heard."

"But you have such a lovely voice," Lady Williams said. "What if Gregory joined you in a duet? It has been too long since I've heard him."

I looked at him in surprise. He sang?

A movement outside the window drew my attention, but when I looked, nothing was there. I refocused on Lord Williams. Why couldn't he be the man he'd pretended to be? Why must he be the distant and cold baron who must always be proved right? "I am not up to the task, I'm afraid. But

297

perhaps his lordship would like to play something instead?"

His eyes met mine. "No one said I played, Miss Brinton."

With as fine a room as this and an ability to sing, he must have some note-reading ability. "Do you not?" I challenged.

Lady Williams chuckled. "Oh, he plays. Not as well as you, but well enough."

I gestured to the piano. "Will you do us the honor?"

Something moved just outside the window again. This time I was sure of it. I frowned and walked to the window.

"Is anything the matter?" Lord Williams asked, rising from his seat.

"I thought I saw —" A face flashed in the window. I screamed and jumped back, bumping into Lord Williams with such force that we both stumbled. His arm flew around me, keeping me from falling. But even the safety of his arms could not protect me from the shock of what lay outside.

Mr. Lundall's grin turned to a frown. He stood from the bushes where he'd been hiding and placed his hands on his hips. He gestured to us and muttered something, then turned and stomped toward the front of the house, disappearing from view.

Lord Williams's embrace loosened, but he

still held me against him. "He seems to have gone. I assure you, you are quite safe. That man shall be apprehended at once."

I slid out of his arms and mumbled, "He is harmless."

Lord Williams placed a hand on my arm and turned me to face him. "You know him?"

I nodded. "We are acquainted."

"My dear," Lady Williams said, putting an arm around me.

There was some commotion in the hall. Sundson's angry voice reverberated into the room. Mr. Lundall's quieter voice responded. Their voices grew louder until they burst into the room, Sundson in the lead, a footman holding Mr. Lundall firmly by the arm. Lord Williams stepped in front of his mother and me as though to protect us.

"Excuse me, my lord, but this *gentleman,*" Sundson said, "demands an audience with the young lady."

"Miss Brinton," Mr. Lundall said, wrenching his arm from the footman's grasp. He yanked on his red waistcoat and straightened his sleeve, shooting a look of disgust at the footman.

There was nothing to do but introduce them. I cleared my throat and stepped from behind Lord Williams. "Lord Williams, Lady Williams — Mr. Lundall."

TWENTY-EIGHT

My father stepped into the room. "I heard some commotion and came to see — Mr. Lundall?" My father glanced at me, then back at Mr. Lundall, his eyes narrowing.

Mr. Lundall turned to my father. "Yes, Mr. Brinton. It is I."

"Why have you come?" my father demanded. But then he seemed to think better of his question. "A word, if you wouldn't mind."

"Not at all." Mr. Lundall refocused his attention on me and smiled.

"In private, sir," my father said with annoyance.

"Of course. A private audience with you is one of the purposes for my visit. But first —" He glided across the room, appearing beside me before I registered his intention. Lord Williams straightened and stepped closer. My hand tensed, ready to plug my nose. But the need to ward off the stench never came. Surprised, I stared at Mr. Lundall. He looked exactly the same as ever. But there was no smell.

"You look radiant this afternoon, Miss Brinton," Mr. Lundall exclaimed, grabbing my hand and kissing it.

"So you have informed me each time we have met." I slipped my hand out of his grasp and hid it in the folds of my dress.

He nodded. "It will always be true. You are my sun, shining brightly any time of day."

"Then I would that it were night," I muttered.

"Mr. Lundall?" my father commanded.

"I shall return presently." Mr. Lundall bowed and strode back to my father.

"You always do." I sighed.

Lord Williams watched Mr. Lundall's retreat. "Perhaps I should join them."

My hand shot to his arm. I couldn't have him in the interview between Mr. Lundall and my father. What would he think? Not that it mattered, of course.

He glanced at my hand and I quickly removed it from his arm. "I apologize," I stammered, "but I believe there is no need to trouble yourself. My father will show Mr. Lundall out."

"Miss Brinton, that gentleman was scampering about my grounds. Please excuse me." He marched out of the room. Sundson followed.

"Well," Lady Williams said, "this has proved a most exciting afternoon, don't you think?"

"It has certainly been very unexpected."

"I believe I shall ask Sundson to set an extra place for dinner," she continued.

I shook my head in disbelief. "Lady Williams, I have the greatest hope Mr. Lundall will not be present for dinner."

She smiled subtly. "I have the greatest hope that he will. I would hate to be disappointed." She, too, left the room.

I stared at the door until a noise in the hallway recalled me to my surroundings. If Lady Williams got her way, this room would be the first place Mr. Lundall came looking for me. I hurried out of the room and up the stairs, shutting my bedroom door securely behind me.

When I walked into the antechamber for dinner, Mr. Lundall rushed forward, offering me his arm. It seemed Lady Williams had gotten her wish.

I hesitated.

"Miss Brinton." He held his elbow closer to me.

"Mr. Lundall," I said, "this is hardly necessary."

"I insist on being allowed to escort you in."

"But Lady Cox and her daughter have not yet arrived. I am in no need of an escort as of yet."

Sundson entered. "Lady Cox, Miss Perrin, Mr. Hargreaves, and Mrs. Hargreaves." Lady Cox swept into the room followed by Miss Perrin, Mrs. Hargreaves, and a thin, balding man with a small nose and no chin.

An unexpected surge of relief ran through me. I had not known Lady Williams had invited Mr. and Mrs. Hargreaves as well. At least I'd have someone sympathetic to speak with.

Introductions were made, Lady Cox provided an excuse for Sir Timothy's absence, and dinner was announced.

Mr. Lundall practically elbowed me in my ribs. But the uneven numbers and Miss Perrin being of higher status than I provided my excuse, "You should escort Miss Perrin, Mr. Lundall. I shall come behind," I said.

He frowned.

Lord Williams offered his arm to Lady Cox, but she pushed her daughter into her place. "Oh, please don't stand on ceremony on my account. Elisa would provide much better company for you."

Mrs. Hargreaves muttered something to her husband, who nodded.

In the end, I walked in alone. Miss Perrin sat in the seat I usually occupied while I sat across from her, at Lord Williams's left. Mr. Lundall ignored Miss Perrin's invitation to sit next to her, instead taking the place on my other side. My only comfort was that Lady Cox seemed displeased by having to sit in a seat lacking honor, wedged between her daughter and my father.

After the first course was served and conversation filled the room, I tilted my head toward Mr. Lundall. I wanted to ask after his surprising lack of stench, but not even I could be that rude. "Why is it that you are here, sir?"

"It pains me that you should think I have any intent other than to see you."

"You must have had some other reason to come into the area. Else how would you know where to find me?"

"My dear Miss Brinton, I could find you faster than a hound could find a fox or a hawk his mouse. I merely followed my heart. It will always lead to you."

His declaration was not the quiet hush of private conversation. Lady Cox must have assumed his volume invited her comment.

"What beautiful words, sir. Miss Brinton must be enraptured by your esteem of her. And to have you come all this way just to seek her out. Why, any woman with sense would see what a catch you are."

I was not about to allow Lady Cox the pleasure of cornering me. "Yes, Mr. Lundall is quite the catch. And such an exquisite dancer. Miss Perrin, do you enjoy dancing? If so, I recommend that you not miss an opportunity to dance with Mr. Lundall, should such an opportunity arise."

To my surprise, Miss Perrin's cheeks pinked and she dropped her gaze to study her plate. "I should be honored. Of course."

Lady Cox frowned. "Lord Williams is also a fine dancer, is he not, Elisa? I believe you said you had never before danced with anyone so skilled."

Miss Perrin's face reddened to an unbecoming shade.

"Though I mean no disrespect," Mr. Lundall replied, fluffing the ruffled cuff of his sleeve, "I assure you that my skill on the dance floor quite surpasses most."

"While I am sure it does," replied Lady Cox with a huff, "you must concede that a baron would simply have more opportunity to perfect such a talent than. . . ." She waved her hand through the air as though the comment was not worth the effort of finishing.

"I shall concede no such thing," Mr. Lundall stated, "and if Miss Perrin will provide me with the opportunity, I promise that she shall soon agree with me."

Lady Cox looked appalled. "I did not mean to encourage you to seek out my daughter's hand, sir."

"I would consider it an honor."

"I believe Mr. Lundall would make an exceptional dance partner," my father interjected, laughter in his eyes.

"I dare say," Mrs. Hargreaves broke in, "it would be a fine thing to see the young people dance. Perhaps we should provide them with the opportunity after dinner?"

Lady Cox looked as though she wished to smash her food in Mrs. Hargreaves's face. "I think that is hardly necessary."

"A dance sounds delightful," Lady Williams agreed. "It has been too long since we have enjoyed one here. What do you think, Gregory?"

He seemed amused. "I have no objection to it, if Miss Perrin and Miss Brinton do not oppose."

The humor of the situation evaporated. I did not wish to dance with either gentleman.

Mr. Lundall smiled at me. "Miss Brinton

is a superb dancer. I have never known her equal. This meal cannot end soon enough for me."

Lady Cox snorted, and my mind seized on a way to extricate myself from the activity. "You flatter me, sir. However, I must decline. It would be selfish of me to accept when I have, on a previous occasion, had the pleasure of dancing with you. As this may be Lady Cox's only opportunity for such an experience, I shall relinquish my spot to her and relegate myself to the position of spectator."

My father tilted his head in approval of my argument.

"I did not mean to give the impression that I wished to dance," Lady Cox sputtered.

"Are you refusing to dance with his lordship's guest, Lady Cox?" Mrs. Hargreaves asked.

"Of course not." She glared at Mrs. Hargreaves. "I shall consent to a dance, though I think one will be more than adequate."

"Then it is settled. Miss Brinton can take your place when you have finished," Lady Williams concluded.

It was not quite the outcome I'd hoped for, as it did not release me completely from the obligation.

After we had withdrawn to the music room, Lady Williams said, "Miss Brinton, perhaps you will do us the honor of playing?"

It was just the excuse I needed. I sat at the piano and played the opening measures. When I checked to see if the couples were ready, I tried not to let the discomfort of seeing Miss Perrin standing opposite Lord Williams outweigh the gratification of observing Lady Cox standing opposite Mr. Lundall.

After the song had finished, Lady Williams rose from her seat. "I shall take Miss Brinton's place so that she may dance."

I rose and slowly made my way to the position across from Lord Williams. Miss Perrin had, with some alacrity, assumed her position across from Mr. Lundall with a rather determined air.

"Elisa, do not fatigue yourself," Lady Cox called out sharply. "Come rest next to me." She patted the settee.

"But Miss Brinton will not be able to dance if I do not," Miss Perrin objected.

"Oh," I said quickly, "I do not mind."

"Are you certain, Miss Brinton?" Mrs. Hargreaves said. "It doesn't seem fair that you should not enjoy —"

"Yes, quite sure."

Lady Williams's brows knitted together in concern, but she said, "Tea, then. And cards." The group walked out of the room toward the drawing room, Miss Perrin quickly securing Mr. Lundall's arm. Lady Cox scowled at him. Mr. Lundall glanced at me, but I smiled encouragingly and he turned his attention to Miss Perrin.

"I am sorry to miss the opportunity of dancing with you," Lord Williams said quietly, walking beside me into the drawing room.

We paused just inside the room. "But you enjoyed your dance with Miss Perrin, did you not?" I asked.

"Of course."

"Miss Brinton." Mr. Lundall indicated an empty chair at his side. I sighed and walked over to it, annoyed at feeling disappointed that it wasn't Lord Williams offering me a seat next to him.

Mr. Lundall immediately leaned toward me, though his gaze rested on Lady Cox. "I cannot abide an interfering parent." He eyed her a moment before shifting his attention to me. "In all your magnanimity, you are too polite to mention the changes I have made to my person since we last met. I do not wish to embarrass you by bringing them up, only to illustrate that I am not above recognizing my mistakes and changing the presentation of the person I put forth."

He must be referring to his lack of smell. "It does offer quite a different presentation."

Lord Williams traded his seat for one near us. "Mr. Lundall, you seem a man of solid sense and good taste. Miss Brinton and I were in conversation earlier and could not arrive at an agreement. Do tell us, what means would you go to in order to protect someone you knew to be in danger?"

His wording made him seem wholly benevolent. I glared at him. "Mr. Lundall, please pay no heed to his lordship."

Mr. Lundall leaned toward me again and loudly whispered, "Though it pains me to do anything you do not wish, I cannot singly ignore his lordship when he has so graciously accepted me into his home." He straightened. "Do you speak of mortal danger or a more philosophical danger?"

"I apologize," Lord Williams said. "Danger of making a choice the person would rue for the rest of his or her life."

"That is not accurate," I said. "It is a choice others might think would make the person unhappy, but that person is certain

311

is perfect." Although I wasn't so certain anymore. But no one, especially not Lord Williams, needed to know that.

"In that case, I would endeavor to help this person see the error of his or her choice," Mr. Lundall advised.

"It is not an error," I said.

Lord Williams spoke over me. "And if the person did not heed your counsel?"

He would not be the only voice in this conversation. I turned to Mr. Lundall. "Would you, for instance, take measures to force the person to make a different choice, one that might inadvertently be worse?"

"Worse?" Lord Williams gestured around the room. "This is worse?"

"It isn't about the location," I muttered.

"If it were a person I cared for," Mr. Lundall said quietly, "I would ensure the person's safety and then hope to be granted enough time for each of us to understand the reasons behind the choices of the other."

His sincere response was so out of character that it gave me pause. "I think that a very good plan," I said tentatively.

"Yes. I wholly agree." Lord Williams's eyes met mine. "I am glad we are in agreement that the safety of the one in question is of paramount import."

He viewed his engagement to me as securing my safety? "Rash actions are never safe decisions," I replied.

Lord Williams leaned forward. "Mr. Lundall, as a man of experience who has obviously seen much of the world, what would you do to win the good opinion of someone you cared for?"

I shook my head. "This seems an irrelevant question."

"Does it?" Again Lord Williams's gaze met mine. What was he about now? Had he decided on some new venture to prove me wrong? Or had he decided that he had not succeeded in fully proving his point of the weakness in my plan and wished to pursue the matter more?

"Of what are you speaking?" Lady Cox called from the card table. "It seems to have Miss Brinton in something of a flushed state."

I felt my cheeks. They were a little warm. "We are speaking of winning hearts, your ladyship. I would dearly love to know what you suggest for a man to win a woman's affection."

"Flowers. Gifts. Those are the most obvious," she said. Those were the same things Lord Williams had listed. My gaze leapt to him. He made a small kissing motion with his lips.

Abominable conceit.

"But it is important to consider the person's temperament," Mr. Lundall broke in. "An overabundance of such things, when the person is not inclined to enjoy them, can have an opposite effect of the one desired."

This was a lesson Mr. Lundall had so kindly taught us both.

Lady Cox scoffed. "What woman does not enjoy flowers and gifts?"

"I very much enjoy both," Lady Williams agreed. "But it also depends on the giver. If there isn't foundational attachment, no amount of gifts will change that."

Mrs. Hargreaves nodded. *"Den Nagel auf den Kopf trefft."*

"Oh, really," Lady Cox said with exasperation.

"I believe," Mrs. Hargreaves said, "that this is also a saying in your language? Lady Williams has rather hit the nail on the head?"

Lady Cox turned away from her. "Lord Williams is rather talented at selecting gifts fit for the recipient, is he not, Elisa?"

"Oh, yes," Miss Perrin stuttered, glancing between Lord Williams and me.

"Has he ever given you a gift, Miss Brinton?" Lady Cox asked.

"Only the gift of his opinions and counsel," I assured her. "Though I have no doubt that whatever gifts he gives, he does so with impeccable ability, as his taste is rather refined." I shot him a smile.

"It seems I have been remiss in my duty as host," Lord Williams replied. "I usually ensure each of my guests receives a gift. However, it is quite fortuitous that I waited, is it not? Else you might have found yourself with something quite disagreeable."

I narrowed my eyes, recognizing his words as the ones I had spoken to him. "No doubt you have a talent for selecting quite the perfect thing."

"You shall have to be the judge, though I believe my talents in the matter rather compare to those I have developed for lawn bowls."

His demeanor appeared unaffected, but I thought I caught a hint of laughter in his eyes. I pretended indifference with a shrug. "Seeing as how you lost at lawn bowls, perhaps I would rather not receive a gift."

Mr. Lundall leaned forward. "One man to another, Miss Brinton has a strong dislike of donkeys."

Lord Williams glanced at me, eyes wide, and mouthed, *"Donkeys?"*

I shook my head, trying to indicate that it

was not a subject that needed discussing.

"Thank you, Mr. Lundall," Lord Williams said. "I shall take her aversion to donkeys under consideration."

Lady Cox smirked. "Miss Brinton, do you sing?"

Startled at the change in subject, I replied, "A little."

"That is all? What a shame. Elisa is such an accomplished vocalist. I do believe she was looking forward to a duet. Lord Williams, perhaps you would do us the honor of joining her?"

"I think a duet would be a delightful thing," Lady Williams said. "Could we persuade you to join your daughter, Lady Cox?"

"Me? I admit I have not so fine a voice as Elisa's. It is one of my greatest regrets that I was not trained as she has been."

"I needn't sing, Mama," Miss Perrin said, obviously embarrassed. I felt sorry for her. My mother had never put me on display the way hers did.

I would sing with her, if only to spare her further discomfort.

Lord Williams stood before I could. "It has been some time since I have sung before company, but I would very much enjoy a duet with you, Miss Perrin."

Miss Perrin flashed him a smile of obvious gratitude.

When Lord Williams's voice filled the room, pleasure seeped through me. I tried to ignore my response but found I was as unsuccessful as a child trying to block a river by building a dam of sand.

TWENTY-NINE

Sitting on a bench near the river the next morning, I frowned at the way the water continuously tugged at the branch of the tree. The branch would eventually give way, breaking off from the power of the river's flow. There was something to admire in the tree's effort to stand its ground, but losing the branch was inevitable. So why struggle so desperately to retain it?

"My cousin and I used to race boats made of old newspapers out here. It was the only time I ever beat Northam at anything."

Lord Williams stood a few steps away, a shoulder resting against a tree, newspaper tucked under his arm. He looked relaxed, at home. This was the place that showed him to greatest advantage, here beside the river, his face without any of the frowning arrogance it had carried for so long. If women saw him like this, they'd be swarming the estate for his attention. I returned my focus to the water. "Surely not the only time."

He squatted beside the bench, picked up a stone, and threw it into the water. "The only time. He always gets what he wants." He turned and caught my gaze. "Even when he doesn't actually want it."

The resignation in his eyes stole my breath. "And here I thought you were this talented man," I said quietly.

His lips turned into a small smile. "I apologize for last night. I'm afraid I wasn't my best self."

Forget the blue dinner coat. That smile could make a woman wish things — the look in his eyes, and his lips curved just so.

If he asked me at that moment to refer to him as Gregory, I don't think I could have resisted. The title of Lord Williams no longer seemed to fit.

I turned back to the river. "Neither of us seems to make the other perform to our best selves."

"And yet what we have together works, does it not?"

"Does it?"

Gregory sighed. "I did not set out to prove a point, though perhaps I should have. It would have avoided all of this."

"All of what?"

"Whatever we have going on between us.

You cannot deny that there is something, even though you want to."

I might not deny it, but neither did I have to admit it. "If not to prove me wrong, what did you set out to do?"

"Is it so hard to believe I truly did not want Northam to have you?"

"Yes." There were other ways to ensure marriages didn't happen. There was more to his story than he was telling me.

But merely convincing me how wrong I was also didn't seem a strong enough motivation to engage himself to me any-more. The conceited baron from before would have done so at all costs, but this man before me who shared memories and smiles?

So then, why?

Gregory stood. "I know you must miss your brother and — how did you phrase it? All the little irritants he provides? So . . ." He held up the paper. "How about a race?"

I shook my head. "I don't think that's a good idea."

"Why not?"

I couldn't tell him that it was because I couldn't spend time with him, because whenever we spent time together I felt more drawn to him, felt as though I wanted to always be with him. "We'll be late for breakfast."

He shrugged. "As the master of this estate, I think I can put off breakfast by a few minutes. Besides, we both know that's just an excuse."

"I don't know how."

"Ah." Gregory grinned. "I finally found something at which I have a chance at besting you." He handed me a sheet of the newsprint. "A boat is only as good as its folds, so pay careful attention."

I tried to hand the paper back. "Why don't you fold it for me?"

He frowned in mock sternness. "If I folded both boats, then I would merely be racing against myself. There is no entertainment in that, let me assure you."

I looked down at the paper. *A little competition to ease my anxiety.* That's what Daniel would say.

I did miss him. And Alice and Mother and my lake.

Perhaps this diversion was exactly what I needed.

"Fine, oh talented one. Please instruct me on the intricacies of building a boat."

"Your wish is my command." Gregory sat on the other side of the bench and set his paper between us. "Fold it over like this and make a good crease." He showed me how to first make a hat from the paper, then continued to make a boat. I followed his instructions until the final step of tugging the sides apart. "Won't I rip it?"

"Would you like some help?"

I nodded and, using both hands so it didn't unfold, held my boat up for him. Instead of taking it, Gregory placed his hands over mine on the paper. My eyes flew to his. His gaze held mine as he slowly drew the corners apart. "As long as you're gentle, it will turn out perfectly." He hands lingered on mine a moment before I realized I shouldn't be looking at him, shouldn't be touching him.

I stood. "So, that's all, then?"

"Yes. You are an excellent student."

"That's the first time I've heard that." I lifted my boat for examination while I tried to still the pounding of my heart.

He eyed me as though he wanted to offer a rejoinder, but then stood as well. We walked up the river until we'd passed the back of the house before moving to the water and bending down.

"On my mark," he said. "One, two, three." We both dropped our boats into the water. He'd pushed his so that it careened out into the current. Mine floated hopelessly at the side.

"You need a stick." He searched the ground a moment before straightening with a long stick. "I should thank the grounds-keepers for overlooking this." He held it out to me.

"I just push it off?"

He nodded.

I set the stick against the boat and started to push.

"Wait," he said, grabbing my hand. "You have to push from the bottom or you'll capsize it." With his hand on mine, Gregory guided the stick to the bottom of the boat and helped me push it off into the current, where it chased after his. When we straightened, my back brushed his chest.

I wanted to stay just like this, with him close, his hand still over mine, no worries about intent or the future or the past marring the moment.

"Should we follow?" he whispered, his thumb sliding over my fingers.

We should. But I couldn't bring myself to move. Not yet. If only I could know the real reason as to why he insisted on keeping me and Mr. Northam apart, I might be able to finally let go and allow myself to lean against him, to accept him. To be happy with him. "What happened at the Hickmores' that made you care so much about keeping your cousin and me apart that you would throw away your own life to stop it?"

His thumb stilled a moment before resuming its caress. "Most of the women Northam attracts are ridiculous creatures who try to entrap him by beating him at his own game. They're hollow shells of respectability, pretty faces, for the most part, but not much more. He allows them to flatter him for a few days before disposing of them. But you were different. And —" He stopped, his hand tightening around mine as he shifted subtly closer. "Once Northam realized what he had, he would never have let you go."

Gregory's words tugged at me, evoking emotions I had promised never to feel again, a hope that things could be different — that my future didn't have to be one of loneliness and shame.

Yet his explanation still wasn't complete. I turned so I could gauge the truth of his words in his eyes. "Even that, though, isn't enough for what you did. You're a man of title, fortune, good looks, and sense, yet you engaged yourself to a woman you didn't know, who openly confessed she wasn't interested in you."

He stared at me, a frown of indecision momentarily tugging at his features. "I did.

But the reasons with which I set forth are no longer the reasons that keep me continuing to seek out your company."

"Then why not tell me what they were?"

"Why not ask what they are now?" he asked quietly.

Yes, that is what I should be asking. Because that was what really mattered, wasn't it? Wasn't the past just the past?

And yet, the past mattered. It made us who we were. And the present, whatever was going on between us — I couldn't trust it unless I knew the past.

This dance between us, the back and forth, the looks and silences — I couldn't do it. Not when heartache was the only outcome. I dropped the stick and his hand fell away from mine.

"Perhaps we should return," he said after a few moments of silence.

We turned and headed toward the formal garden at the back of the house. We'd made it halfway to the door when he stopped. "Please do not throw yourself away on my cousin."

I ran my fingers across a white flower. "You cannot truly wish to unite yourself with me. I bring you no advantages."

"And you cannot truly wish to live a life of misery. Northam will only hurt you further."

I lifted my gaze to his. "And you're promising me you won't?"

"I can promise to try not to." He stepped nearer. "Don't give up on something because of someone else's deception. Not all men are like Mr. Rosthorn."

No. Some men were like Gregory, nonsensical and able to capture a woman's heart against her will. "How am I to believe this when you won't tell me why this began?"

He plucked a rose off a bush and twirled it in his fingers. "I admit my actions could be considered drastic." He sighed before focusing on me as though to assess my reaction. "It was the only way to finally put an end to Northam's games."

This was not the response I had expected. "How does your engagement to me have anything to do with your cousin's habits?"

Gregory hesitated, then shook his head. "It doesn't matter."

"It matters to me."

We searched each other's expressions for a moment before he said, "Margaret, I —" He cut himself off and shook his head. "I apologize, Miss Brinton. You were right to correct me. I should never have taken such liberties in addressing you so casually." He held the flower out to me. When I reached to take it, his fingers wrapped around mine. He stepped closer. "Only, I cannot bear to call you anything so formal. I don't want to be distant and formal with you."

We stood, inches apart, and I felt that even if all in the world turned wrong, as long as he had me I would be safe.

"Ah, Miss Brinton, Lord Williams." Mr. Lundall's all-too-familiar voice cut through the moment. I instinctively stepped closer to Gregory, realizing too late that I was leaning against his chest. I stepped away, yet Mr. Lundall frowned as he made his way toward us; he had obviously observed us.

"I hope I am not too late to join in your morning walk," he said.

"Unfortunately, we were just returning to the house," Gregory said. He rubbed his thumb over my fingers again. I yanked my hand out of his grasp.

Mr. Lundall's eyes narrowed at Gregory. "Miss Brinton, I was hoping to enjoy a quick, *private* word with you."

Not again. "I apologize, Mr. Lundall, but I wouldn't wish to be late for breakfast. Perhaps at a later time?"

"It will only take a minute."

"Yes, but the air is uncomfortably chilled. After breakfast the air will have warmed."

He didn't look convinced but held his arm

out to me anyway. "Very well. Please allow me to escort you in."

I resisted the temptation to look at Gregory. "There is really no need for such formality."

"I would consider it a great honor, Miss Brinton." Mr. Lundall bounced his elbow up and down, emphasizing its presence.

I sighed and took his proffered arm. "Thank you."

As Gregory passed my seat to take his own at the table, he placed the flower next to my plate. My gaze wandered to it more than I would have liked. Everything Gregory had said felt like the truth, yet he was still hiding something, and it seemed important. But how important was it? Was it worth sacrificing whatever attraction lay between us, whatever future lay before us, simply because he wouldn't tell me? What if I were to set aside my misgivings and just see where allowing myself to care for him led?

Gregory and my father left the breakfast table and I tried not to watch Gregory as they disappeared out the door. When Lady Williams rose, I glanced around. It would be only Mr. Lundall and me left at the table. I would not be cornered in the breakfast room with the servants listening to Mr.

Lundall propose yet again. I hurried after Lady Williams, leaving Gregory's flower on the table.

Mr. Lundall rushed up to me. "Our walk? We have little time, for I have requested my chaise to be at the door at noon."

"Of course."

I dragged my feet through the entry. As we exited the front door, we came upon Gregory speaking with Miss Perrin. A servant arranged an easel a few feet away, and a lady who must have been Miss Perrin's chaperone sat on a bench near the house, a book in her lap.

Gregory and Miss Perrin turned at our approach.

"Miss Perrin, how good to see you again," I said.

"And you." Her cheeks colored. "Mr. Lundall, I did not know you were still here."

Mr. Lundall bowed and kissed her hand. "I am leaving in half an hour."

"So soon?"

"I'm afraid so." He turned to me. "Shall we?"

I sighed. "Very well."

"Just a moment, Miss Brinton," Gregory said. "Miss Perrin has come to paint a scene of the river. Would you be interested in joining her?"

"Oh." Of course Miss Perrin was an accomplished artist. And of course I was not. "Um. . . ."

"Miss Brinton," Mr. Lundall interrupted, "I did not know you were an artist. Which is a shame, because I am a vast lover of art."

"Perhaps you will stay and attend to our progress?" Miss Perrin suggested rather hopefully.

The servant appeared with another easel, and Mr. Lundall straightened his shoulders. "I say, man, put that right here." The servant set the easel in the appointed place.

"No, not there." Mr. Lundall took a few steps to the side. "Here."

The man did as he was bid.

Mr. Lundall surveyed the location, then shook his head. "Over here, I think." He strode thirty feet away. "Yes, here. This is perfect."

The man glanced at Gregory, who nodded, so the easel was once more placed where Mr. Lundall had indicated. Mr. Lundall shifted from side to side before nodding his head. "Yes, this is the perfect spot."

"Oh, I have never painted from that location," Miss Perrin exclaimed. Turning to me, she asked, "Would you mind?"

"Not at all," I replied.

She smiled and hurried to Mr. Lundall.

"It appears Mr. Lundall has an admirer," Gregory said.

She certainly did seem to enjoy Mr. Lundall's company. And Gregory certainly did not seem to be interested in her, not when he was holding my hand and proclaiming that he did not wish to be formal with me. Yet there was a kind of familiarity between them. And Lady Cox believed an engagement imminent.

"I have been led to believe — and I am not the only one — that there is perhaps an expectation between the two of you." I glanced at him to gauge his reaction.

Gregory's brows rose in disbelief. "I assure you, Miss Brinton, that despite whatever expectations Lady Cox has, I have no plans regarding Miss Perrin other than allowing her to escape now and then from her mother and stepfather."

I turned quickly to hide the silly grin covering my face. Gregory was not interested in Miss Perrin. He was not like Edward after all.

Yet I shouldn't be feeling this rush of elation. It shouldn't matter to me what his plans were.

A canvas of stretched paper had been placed on the easel before me. Beside it, a small table held a box containing twelve watercolor blocks, an assortment of brushes, and a dish of water. I picked up a brush with a small handle and pretended to study it, though my mind was racing. If Gregory didn't seek an alliance with Miss Perrin, if he was indeed not like Edward, and if it was not his intent to seek my hand only to teach me a lesson, then perhaps he was exactly as he seemed.

This was bad. If he was what he seemed, and I allowed that whatever had initially spurred him to ask for my hand was unimportant, then there was nothing to keep my arguments against him from floating away like the boats we'd sailed down the river.

Except there was. I could not deem that reason as unimportant. He might not be hiding a mistress, but he was still hiding something. And what of my promise? Allowing myself to care for Gregory would lead only to heartache.

I set the brush down and picked up a thicker one, dipped it into the water, then paused to study the landscape before me. It was probably best to start with the lines of the bank of the river. But with watercolor, did one work from dark colors to light or light colors to dark? I couldn't remember. If I chose wrong, the painting would be spoiled. Perhaps if I first practiced on the branches of a tree. Surely no one would notice if I practiced a little in the upper corner of the painting. Just to get my bearings.

I slid my brush across a dark brown block. Glancing once more at the shore, I lifted the brush to the top of the canvas where I thought the branches should go. The canvas was perfectly clean. There wasn't even a dirty fingerprint on it.

It was ridiculous to pretend I could paint. I would humiliate myself by even attempting the endeavor. Better to save the paper and paint for Miss Perrin or some other young woman who set her sights on Gregory.

I spun around to confess my lack of talent. Gregory had stooped down directly behind me as though to see the painting from my angle and, in so doing, became my unintended canvas as my brush stroked his face. He flinched and stood, but too late. A thick brown line streaked his cheek.

I stepped back. And bumped into the easel, sending it toppling into the table of paints. The whole setup crashed to the ground.

"Oh, my goodness. I'm so sorry." I should have rushed to pick up the canvas and rescue the paints, but I couldn't take my eyes off Gregory. His hand rose to his face, his finger swiping at the mark, smearing it.

The servant appeared next to us and I again apologized as he began cleaning up my mess. When the easel was righted, I placed the brush on its lip and turned back to Gregory. He had a handkerchief to his face but instead of cleaning the mark off he had smeared it some more.

"I didn't realize you were directly behind me. Here. Let me help." I held out my hand for the fabric.

"It's all right."

"You're only smearing it. Please, stop."

He hesitated, uncertain. I snatched the handkerchief from his fingers and dipped it into the now-righted water, which contained only drops. I hoped it was enough.

I reached back for his face. He flinched away. "I'm not going to hurt you," I exclaimed.

"Really, it's all right. I'll just step inside —"

"Gregory, just hold still. It will only take a moment."

He stilled, and I realized I'd called him by his name. Out loud.

How had I let that happen? Without meeting his gaze, I quickly rose onto my tiptoes and, with a few gentle swipes, cleaned the paint from his face. "There. It's gone." My next breath was filled with him — his light cologne, the faint saddle oil. I hadn't realized we'd moved so close. Nor had I realized that my other hand cupped his face, steadying it while I cleaned his cheek. Our faces were mere inches from each other. If I leaned forward ever so slightly, our lips would touch. I raised my gaze from his mouth to his eyes and my breath caught as truth flooded over me.

All my precautions, all my objections, all my arguments — they were for naught.

I was in love with Gregory.

THIRTY

I reeled back, remembering too late that the easel had been set up again. Again it crashed to the ground.

"Sorry," I said distractedly as the servant set about righting it.

I couldn't be in love with Gregory. It was impossible. It was merely loneliness and worry for Alice that had me thinking such ridiculous thoughts.

I shoved the handkerchief at Gregory, staring at it to avoid looking at his face.

He seemed to take forever in reaching for it. His fingers brushed my hand, lingering long enough to send a tingle up my arm. A tingle that I rather enjoyed and that left me longing for more.

I flinched away. "To own the truth, my lord, I do not paint. Please, excuse me." I walked toward the house, hoping my pace didn't reveal my retreat for what it was — flight away from him. How had I let this happen? I had promised never to allow my heart to fall in love again.

I had to get away. Far away.

"Miss Brinton," Mr. Lundall called. "Wait."

I stopped. I had forgotten all about Mr. Lundall and his desire to speak to me. It would provide a needed distraction until I could regain control of my wayward emotions.

He rushed to my side as a chaise was brought around front. Mr. Lundall frowned and looked at his timepiece. "It is time already. We are too late for our walk." He dug into his pocket and retrieved a letter. "Here. This is from your brother. He commissioned me to bring it to you."

I took the note, imagining a scenario where Mr. Lundall pestered Daniel for my whereabouts and Daniel, thinking it would be good humor, not only told him where I was but gave him a note as an excuse for Mr. Lundall to visit. He had probably been laughing ever since Mr. Lundall had left to come find me.

"But, if you've spoken with Daniel, you must know about Alice."

"I regret that I did not know she was ill, so I did not ask after her. Your brother provided no information. I hope the letter answers all your questions to your satisfaction."

"Why did you not give this to me yesterday?" I broke the seal in my eagerness to know the letter's content.

"Mr. Lundall," Miss Perrin said, joining us, her presence forcing me to put the perusal of my letter on hold. "Would you think me terribly unrefined if I begged a ride home? The light isn't ideal for painting just now, and I believe Miss Bowen is bored." I glanced at Miss Perrin's companion; she appeared completely content to sit on that bench until she'd finished her book.

"I have only this chaise," Mr. Lundall explained.

"It is not very far, I assure you. And we are not overly large women." She smiled her dazzling smile.

"It will be uncomfortable, but if you do not mind —"

"Not at all."

"Very well."

My father and Lady Williams walked out of the house, and Lady Williams smiled with delight. "Miss Perrin, how good to see you. Won't you come inside?"

Miss Perrin shook her head. "You must excuse me, your ladyship, but Mr. Lundall has been so good as to offer me a ride home."

"You are leaving, Mr. Lundall?" my father asked.

"Yes, I am afraid so. The man attending me this morning told me it is to rain tomorrow, so my departure must be today."

"It has been such a pleasure to make your acquaintance," Lady Williams said.

"The pleasure has been all mine." Mr. Lundall kissed her hand.

Miss Perrin also said farewell, not seeming at all sorry to go, and Mr. Lundall handed her up. Miss Bowen, disgruntled to have her reading interrupted, was handed up on the other side of the chaise by Gregory.

After Miss Perrin and Miss Bowen were settled, Mr. Lundall bid me farewell. "I shall see you upon your return. I hope it will be soon."

I nodded, also hoping my return would be soon, though I was not eager for him to renew his attentions.

"Mr. Lundall," Gregory said, "if you ever find yourself in the neighborhood, you must come visit."

"Very kind," Mr. Lundall replied. He made one more round of goodbyes, then hopped into the chaise and took the reins from the waiting servant.

The moment Mr. Lundall clicked the horses to a walk, I unfolded the paper. *The bearer of this letter is entitled to as many private words with Margaret as needed. P.S. She's not any better.*

I handed the letter to my father with disgust. Daniel had told us less than Louisa.

"It is not bad news, I hope," Lady Williams said.

My father answered. "My son has an overdeveloped sense of humor. And I am afraid he reported less news than the letter yesterday."

"Well, you must stay as long as needed."

He nodded his thanks and faced Gregory. "I am ready to finish our tour, if now is agreeable to you."

"Of course." Gregory turned to me. "You are welcome to join us, Miss Brinton."

I shook my head, avoiding looking at him by focusing instead on the lawn beyond the house. "No, thank you. I think I shall go explore the garden some more."

"Ah, so you have discovered it," Lady Williams said. "Is it not the gem of the estate? I would join you, only I am afraid I must be from home to visit some neighbors who shall be very much offended if I do not call on them this morning. But it does not do to leave you alone. Gregory, will you not postpone your outing and attend to Miss Brinton?"

Walk with Gregory? That could not happen. "Oh, please do not change your plans on my account. I will be most content in the garden, I assure you."

"You will not be too lonely?" Lady Williams asked.

I shook my head. "Not at all."

"I do not mind postponing the tour until tomorrow," Gregory said.

"But it is supposed to rain," I pointed out, still avoiding his gaze. "It seems as though we must all go our separate ways today so as to enjoy this last bit of sunshine. For who knows how much longer we will be able to enjoy our stay here before we are called home again? And Father is so much interested in the estate."

"Are you certain?" Gregory asked in a low voice.

"Yes." I glanced up and our eyes met.

I was really, truly in love with him.

I tore my gaze away. "I am very certain."

Sundson emerged from the door. "Your ladyship, your carriage is ready."

"Oh, thank you. Well, I daresay we shall at least each have stories to share at dinner this evening."

Not me. I would never share this story.

As I strolled the garden a few minutes later, my mind returned to the conversation of that morning. Gregory did not want to be formal with me. He did not want to be distant.

And I was in love with him.

What if I did let it go? What if I could actually marry for love?

When I retired to my room that evening, I discovered a large vase of flowers from the walled garden had been placed on the desk. Next to them was my favorite book of poetry.

Perhaps Gregory had talents for gift-giving after all.

THIRTY-ONE

I awoke the next morning to the plinking of rain against the windows. Dragging myself out of bed, I trudged to the alcove and pressed my forehead against the cold glass. Heavy drops plopped into the river, the little rippling circles sweeping downstream and out of sight.

I traced a droplet sliding down the window. A day inside. A whole day of Gregory's company.

I turned from the windows, struggling against the delight rising within me.

Perhaps he was busy. Perhaps he was from home.

But perhaps he wasn't.

After dressing, I made my way downstairs. A clock sounding through the halls indicated I still had three quarters of an hour before breakfast. I wasn't ready to face Gregory and the turmoil he created within me. I turned to the music room, rifled through the paper, and chose a few songs that fit the mood of a rainy morning. Near the end of a particularly beautiful song that I was certain Alice would enjoy, someone entered. Grappling against my excitement at Gregory's presence, I finished the last measure then glanced up and gasped, my hands slamming onto the keys of the piano as I struggled to rise.

"Mr. Northam," I squeaked. My throat constricted and my stomach twisted into a tight knot. I had forgotten how handsome he was. The images in my mind had not done him justice. Although his clothes were dry, his dark hair was wet, long strands matted onto his chiseled face. It curled over his heavy brows. His dark eyes turned from astonishment to sultry delight.

"Miss Brinton. What a pleasant surprise. I am so much happier it is raining now that I know you are here." He stepped farther into the room. "I thought an angel was in here playing and came to investigate. It appears I was correct."

"I am certain it isn't anything you have not heard before."

He moved to my side. "Only once. And on that occasion the music was interrupted." He stood close, close enough that I could see the drops of water running down his face. Close enough that I caught the lingering scent of expensive cologne.

"What are you doing here?" I asked, somewhat breathlessly.

"I might ask you the same thing."

My mind scrambled for an explanation. "My father came to tour the estate. I accompanied him."

"I was under the impression you thought Williams the worst of men."

"He was."

"And now he is not?"

"I had no choice in coming here."

"Then perhaps it is fortuitous that I came to end your misery. Though you did not write." His voice was quiet, no more than a murmur.

"It was impossible for me to write you."

He took my hand and slowly raised it to his lips. "There is always a way."

A week ago this was exactly what I had wanted: him, like this, as we played our little games. I should still want him. A part of me — the rational part, the part that knew what was best — still did.

But the other part was fighting, screaming that there was no love where Mr. Northam was concerned, that my days would be lonely, that my life would be unhappy. I didn't want to be unhappy.

I just didn't want to be hurt again.

"Perhaps, Miss Brinton," he continued, still holding my hand, "you will play away the gloom of this rainy day."

His eyes were perfect. His tone was perfect. He was who I should choose.

"Northam!"

Gregory's voice resounded around the room. I wrenched my hand out of Mr. Northam's grasp and spun to face the door. Gregory's blue eyes seared me with their chill.

"Ah, Williams. You should have told me you were entertaining such a lovely guest. I would have come sooner."

Gregory's expression squashed the warmth of Mr. Northam's words. "Why have you come now?" he demanded.

Mr. Northam shrugged. "I came to see what you were about. And now I am ever so glad I did. Do tell me, am I in time for breakfast? I'm dreadfully hungry."

His tone was flippantly light, as though he took no notice of Gregory's dark expression. Perhaps Mr. Northam was used to it. But I was not. Each second under that glare rendered me more uneasy.

"Excuse me," I muttered, curtsying to Mr. Northam. His answering look, intimate and promising, made my face flame with embarrassment knowing that Gregory watched. I dropped my gaze and moved toward the door. "Good morning," I mumbled, offering Gregory a curtsy as well. His look was as disapproving as it had ever been at the Hickmores'. I quickly slipped out of the room.

Pausing just outside the door, my hand on the wall for orientation, I closed my eyes. Mr. Northam was here. What was I going to do?

"What are you up to, Williams? What is she doing here?" Mr. Northam's curious tone drifted into the hall. Would Mr. Northam say something about our time together at the Hickmores'? Would he reveal how close I'd come to kissing him?

I straightened, my fingers splayed against the wall. What if Gregory mentioned our engagement to Mr. Northam? What would Mr. Northam do?

Gregory's voice, close and cold, replied, "Northam, I do not want you here."

Mr. Northam's laughter, mocking instead of jovial, echoed into the hall. "You never did have a good poker face."

How had this happened? I was not fool enough to ignore that I had been given another chance to protect my heart. I could still be safe from Gregory. But I no longer wanted to be safe from Gregory. I wanted to be safe *with* him.

Was that even possible?

I had to get away from their conversation until I could reason this out.

I went to the breakfast parlor. Lady Williams stood in the middle of the room, facing the window, watching the rain fall outside, but she turned at my entrance.

"Good morning, Miss Brinton."

I curtsied. "Your ladyship. I did not mean to disturb you." I glanced over my shoulder. No one seemed to be coming yet.

She smiled kindly. "I have not yet seen your father or my son, my dear. But you are welcome to wait for them here, if you would like."

I could not face those two men again on my own. Mr. Northam had control of my mind, while Gregory had control of my heart. Which one should I trust? "Yes, thank you, I would like that very much."

"It is a shame your short stay should be marred by such gloomy weather." Lady Williams turned back to the window.

"The river did look lovely this morning with the rain falling on it."

"That *is* quite a beautiful sight, isn't it?" She glanced at me.

I nodded. "There is something majestic

about the rain."

Lady Williams smiled. "My dear, you are quite correct. I believe my son was very wise —"

Quick, heavy steps sounded in the hall. I froze. When there was no doubt they were headed toward us, I fled across the room, pausing only when I was safe near the window, my body mostly hidden from the doorway by a surprised Lady Williams.

Gregory stormed into the room, his boots smacking against the floor in an angry mutter. Lady Williams turned her astonished face from me to her son. "Why, Gregory, whatever is —" She cut herself off when Mr. Northam entered. "Ahh," she murmured quietly.

"My dear aunt, how are you on this rainy morning?" Mr. Northam walked to her and bent slightly to kiss her hand. His eyes flitted to me and he smirked.

"Very well, thank you, my dear Fredrick," Lady Williams responded. "And what an unexpected surprise this visit is. We were just about to sit to breakfast. Won't you join us?"

How could she be so calm? Of course, she could not realize the predicament caused by inviting her nephew to eat with us. Although with how she'd reacted to Mr. Lundall's arrival, it may not have made a difference.

My attention darted to Gregory. His expression was hard, his jaw muscle jumping. He stood at the head of the table, his hands gripping the back of his chair, his knuckles white. His gaze turned to me as though he felt me watching him.

I glanced away and focused back on Lady Williams, refusing to look at anyone else, hoping her steady character would still the agitation within me. My father appeared. Lady Williams glanced at her son, but his refusal to make introductions was obvious in his blackened expression.

She sighed. "Mr. Brinton, allow me to introduce my nephew, Mr. Fredrick Northam." My father's brows rose. "Fredrick, this is Mr. Brinton. And perhaps you have not yet met his daughter, Miss Brinton?"

Mr. Northam eyed me with a meaningful grin. "Oh, yes, I am already acquainted with Miss Brinton, thank you, Aunt." Embarrassed at his open flirtation, my face heated despite my struggle against it. He turned to my father and bowed. "It is a great pleasure to meet you, sir."

My father returned the bow, but his lips drew into a thin line. His gaze turned to me and I wondered if the panic I felt was visible in my expression. Clenching my jaw, I forced a smile. I would have to get through this, though at the moment I coveted the convenient ability of some women to faint at will.

Lady Williams moved to the table. Forcing my feet forward, I mimicked her actions of scooting the chair out and sitting, even claiming some toast though I had no wish to eat. I spent a great deal of attention on buttering it.

"Of course," Mr. Northam said, his tone cutting through my concentration, "your daughter and I became acquainted at a recent house gathering." He raised his glass in my direction.

My gaze flew to Gregory. His jaw muscle jumped, though he didn't look up from his plate. I looked back to Mr. Northam. He continued relaying different events of our time together at the Hickmores'.

My father paid close attention to his every word. What did he think of Mr. Northam now that they had actually met?

As breakfast drew to a close and we stood, a small smile curved Mr. Northam's lips. "Miss Brinton, perhaps now I could have that song?"

I bit my lip, waiting, but Gregory said nothing. He wasn't going to rescue me.

Mr. Northam offered me his arm.

This was the way it was supposed to be. It was always supposed to be me and Mr. Northam.

And yet, I couldn't quite squelch the hope that things would be different.

THIRTY-TWO

A few hours later, I peeked into the study. Gregory sat behind a desk covered in neat stacks of paper, a ledger open in front of him. Perhaps if I could just have a moment alone with him, I could understand what future would be best.

This plan had to work.

I knocked on the door.

Gregory glanced up, then stood. "Miss Brinton. May I assist you with something?"

Stepping inside, I said, "I was only wondering if you could help me with a passage from this book. It's . . . difficult . . . to make out."

The request was silly. I didn't need help with the passage. I needed help knowing what to do. What his true feelings were. What mine were. And if they should matter.

"What book is that?"

"It's this book of poetry." His brows lifted. He probably thought me completely idiotic.

353

I lowered the book. "Or perhaps you had a novel you could recommend?" His resulting frown made me wish I'd never come seeking him. "Or a sermon on conduct?" I lifted my brows in challenge.

Gregory glanced to the side of the room. Mr. Northam sat in a large chair, a different ledger open in his lap, a look of contemplation on his face as he studied me.

"Oh, Mr. Northam. I did not know you were here."

"And now that you do?" He set aside his ledger. "May I assist you in your selection?"

I stepped back. "I hadn't meant to interrupt. It is clear you are both about business matters." I stole a glance at Gregory. He bore an odd, detached expression, as though my presence were indeed an interruption. "I will seek out my father's recommendation."

"I would like to assist, if you will allow it," Mr. Northam said, rising. "I was simply obliging Williams in reviewing estate matters."

"Oh. But those are important, are they not?"

Mr. Northam smiled his dazzling smile, the one he used to draw people in, the one that failed to evoke any emotion within me. It was the smile that guaranteed I was safe

354

with him because I would never fall for him, especially not now that I had his cousin to compare him with.

"My cousin has developed shrewd methods for establishing what is his," Mr. Northam said. "It is simply his follow-through that needs assistance — skills to retain what he gains. But those can be taught later; you are definitely of more import. Let's leave my cousin to his work, shall we?" He gestured toward the door.

I glanced at Gregory and his disinterested expression. "Yes, thank you." I preceded Mr. Northam out of the room.

Dressed for dinner in a violet evening dress, I fiddled with a hair pin while a maid spent extra time on my hair.

Mr. Northam had escorted me to the drawing room, where we discovered Lady Williams was already reading. We spent the afternoon together companionably with him reading to us for quite a while; he had a magnificent voice and was definitely a man of much talent. He'd been all attentiveness, but that would fade the moment I was secured. I could count on that. And there was no affection, no attraction between us.

With Gregory, there was definite affection and attraction, and he was honest and direct. But he was also refusing to share something with me.

I did not want to be the cast-aside woman, the one people scorned or pitied, as was my future with Mr. Northam.

Neither did I want to be misled like before.

Which would lead to the least pain later?

The answer was no longer clear.

"I've finished, miss."

I blinked at my reflection in the mirror. The maid had put my hair up exquisitely except for one, thick curl at the back, which she draped over my shoulder.

"Thank you."

She curtsied. "Is there anything else you need?"

I needed advice, someone to tell me what to do, someone who understood enough to help. But that wasn't what she had in mind. "No, thank you."

Having a few minutes before we were to assemble for dinner, I made my way to the ballroom. All the curtains were closed, the room dim. I wrenched open the soft but heavy curtains to every window. I needed space and light and options.

The rainclouds had cleared and the low sun streamed through the west windows, dancing across the wood floor. Following its example, I spun slowly once, twice, before pausing in the alcove to survey the grounds. With a start I realized that I loved this place, the grounds and the view. I loved this house. Everything spoke of Gregory's good management and intelligent hand. I had not seen one disgruntled servant, one aspect of the estate in disrepair.

He was the perfect landholder, the perfect gentleman.

Mr. Northam's estate was probably just as spectacular. I would probably love it just as much.

I turned and walked down the stairs.

Low voices greeted me when I neared the antechamber. Hearing my name, I paused.

"Is there an understanding between you?" Mr. Northam asked.

"Whatever exists between us is none of your business," Gregory replied.

"Would you care to wager on that?"

"Northam, leave her alone."

"A little late for that, don't you think, *my lord*?" Mr. Northam's tone was derisive.

I bit my lip and closed my eyes. I didn't want to be married to such a man. What was the good of protecting my heart when it would quickly fill with disdain? But marriage to him provided safety, protection, a chance to forget the past. I still needed that.

Setting aside my indecision, I strode through the door.

Gregory sat settled in a chair at the far end of the room, while Mr. Northam stood near him, his back to me.

Gregory noticed me first. He shot out of his chair, a mixture of surprise and admiration on his face. Then Mr. Northam turned and stepped in front of him, blocking him from view.

"Miss Brinton."

"Mr. Northam."

He had changed for dinner and looked more handsome than I had ever seen him. He was soon by my side, smelling of that expensive cologne. He took my hand in his. "You look lovely."

The feeling behind the words seemed genuine. "Thank you."

Glancing over Mr. Northam's shoulder, my eyes locked with Gregory's. And suddenly, more than anything in the world, I wanted it to be him holding my hand, telling me I looked beautiful.

My father and Lady Williams entered, followed by Sundson announcing dinner. Mr. Northam placed my hand on his arm. I had no choice but to allow him to lead me into the dining room. He took the chair next to mine and doted on me throughout the meal, offering me dishes, speaking with me almost to the point of ignoring everyone else. Gregory, meanwhile, said hardly a word.

As Lady Williams and I made our way to the drawing room afterward, she said, "Well, my dear. You've certainly made quite an impression on my nephew. I've never seen him so attentive."

"To be honest, it unsettles me."

Lady Williams laughed quietly. "I have been impressed with your intelligence this week. I'm glad to see it extends into the realm of men."

Between Edward, Gregory, and Mr. Northam, it didn't seem to even exist. "I'm afraid my intelligence doesn't extend too far into that realm."

She smiled knowingly. "Don't underestimate yourself, dear."

That certainly wasn't a problem. What I had done was overestimate myself. I had overestimated my ability to remain aloof. I had overestimated my desire in securing the man I'd thought I'd wanted. The only thing I had underestimated was how wrong I always seemed to be.

It didn't take long for the gentlemen to join us. My father's eyes focused on me briefly when he entered, something of interest and amusement in them. Gregory headed straight for the window. Mr. Northam approached me. "Should we play cards this evening?"

The suggestion was a welcome diversion from the music that had been requested so often. I immediately agreed. "Lord Williams, will you join us?"

"Oh, Williams never plays cards," Mr. Northam remarked disdainfully.

That wasn't true. Gregory had played cards with Daniel at my own house.

I was about to say as much, but Mr. Northam continued, "Besides, we already have four players." Casting one last look at Gregory standing alone at the side of the room, I took the seat between Mr. Northam and my father.

Halfway through our game, Gregory had the folding doors between the drawing room and the music room opened and began playing the piano. The first song was a plaintive one that had Lady Williams lifting her eyebrows and glancing at him. But, as my father played the last trick and won the game, Gregory began a new song. It took only a few notes to identify the music as the piece I'd played at the Hickmores'.

The vein in Mr. Northam's neck stood out. "Shall we play another round?" His light tone did not quite disguise the clenching of his teeth.

It was something to do with the song. But whatever battle was raging between these two men, I wanted no part in it. It seemed too dangerous a place to be.

I stood. "Thank you, Mr. Northam, but I'd rather not. As you have witnessed, I am not much of a card player. Perhaps his lordship will take my place."

Moving to a chair in the corner of the room, I picked up the book lying on the table. Once I was settled, I opened it to the middle and realized it was a farming almanac. I would look ridiculous pretending to read a farming almanac. The book under it, however, was the novel Mr. Northam had picked out.

What was I going to do? What choice should I make? Security with almost certain misery? Or heartache with a chance at love? I needed to make the decision, and I needed to make it now.

Was Gregory even still a choice? I looked up, hoping something in his expression would let me know, but only a disapproving frown greeted me.

What about how he'd held my hand? How he'd told me he didn't want to be formal with me? Was that only when we were alone? Was it some sort of game to him, one he wasn't willing to play when others were around?

Mr. Northam took the chair beside me and a new thought struck me: if I married Mr. Northam, how would I ever be able to face Gregory again?

I couldn't. We would be forever lost to each other.

Yet our families would have to meet; we would have to endure each other's presence. I would have to become acquainted with his wife.

No. That wasn't what I wanted. I would never be strong enough for that.

Mr. Northam leaned close. "It is a shame, Miss Brinton, that we are always surrounded by others. Small gatherings do not afford the possibility of escape that larger ones do."

"You are quite correct, Mr. Northam."

"I had hoped to find a moment alone with you today. An uninterrupted moment."

I flushed at the memory of our almost kiss, embarrassed by what I had been willing to settle for, mortified that I had remained in a room with him alone. What would have happened if Daniel hadn't appeared?

A slow smile of pleasure grew on his face. Perhaps he believed I longed for another such moment. Maybe I should. But I couldn't.

I didn't want him.

Even if Gregory no longer wanted me, even if the appearance of his cousin had made him change his mind as his actions of the day seemed to imply, I still didn't want Mr. Northam, or the security he offered me.

"Perhaps tomorrow will prove more fortuitous." I kept my eyes locked on Mr. Northam, though my whole being wanted to look at Gregory.

"Then tomorrow can't come soon enough."

It was the escape I needed. I stood. "I couldn't agree more. If you will excuse me, I am feeling overly tired."

"Of course," he replied, rising and taking my hand to kiss it.

THIRTY-THREE

I excused myself from the room. Gregory didn't heed me, and as I made my way up the stairs, I despaired that Mr. Northam's appearance had washed away any chance that had remained with Gregory.

Not that I'd wanted another chance.

Except now, I did.

When I neared the top, heavy steps sounded on the stairs, sending me scrambling into the shadows of the now-dark ballroom with a pounding heart. What would I say to Mr. Northam? Could he really not have waited for morning?

Gregory appeared in the doorway, his face hidden in shadow, his body outlined by the light spilling into the room from the hall behind him.

Had he come after me? Or had he come for some other purpose and didn't know I was in the room? "My lord?" I moved into the soft glow of moonlight streaming

364

through one of the windows.

He stepped into the room, leaving the door open. "I'm sorry if I startled you."

I shrugged, but realized he probably couldn't see my gesture. "Is there something you needed?"

His quiet laugh sounded scornful.

I waited a moment after the laughter died. "If there is nothing, I should go."

He stalked forward. "I was given to understand that you have no fear of being alone with men in ballrooms."

A gasp at his rudeness escaped me. Perhaps I had been correct in refusing him after all.

I stepped back. "On the contrary, it appears that men have no scruples about cornering me in ballrooms when what I wish for is solitude."

"Is that what you wish for now?"

Did he have to ask a question that I couldn't answer honestly? "Perhaps if I knew why you were here, I could better answer your question."

His hand reached up as though to touch my cheek but then hesitated and fell back down. "I thought it would have been obvious."

Disappointment flooded me at the lack of contact. "I assure you, nothing about this day has been obvious."

"Has it not?"

"No."

"Not even my cousin's attentions to you?"

"That obviously has more to do with you than with me."

"Yet you encourage him."

No response formed in my mind. He was correct. I had encouraged Mr. Northam.

"He relayed to me all that transpired at the Hickmores' after I left," Gregory said.

"You mean after you walked out in the middle of my performance, humiliating me." My rebuke rang around the room.

"I am sorry for that."

"Why did you do it?"

"I needed to leave."

"And your departure could not have waited a few minutes more?"

He didn't reply.

With a huff, I turned and walked into the alcove.

His footsteps quietly followed me.

This ballroom felt so different from the Hickmores'. There, if Mr. Northam had asked me to marry him, I would have said yes. I would have even danced with him.

But I didn't want him to ask me now. And it wasn't him I wished to dance with now, either. "Did your cousin relay to you that he offered to teach me to waltz?"

Gregory stirred and took a step forward. "And you accepted?"

"No, I —" I stopped. Taking a deep breath, I stepped up to him. His expression was easier to see up close. "Would you teach me?" I whispered.

I held my breath, waiting for an answer, and took in as many of his features as the dim light would allow. His hair that curled when wet, his handsome face, so open when he genuinely smiled, his eyes that expressed so much of his emotion. He was strong and ethical and good. My lungs burned in my chest. Still I didn't breathe. But not a muscle moved in his face, nor anywhere in his body.

I exhaled. That was my answer then. "I will prevail upon someone else to teach me. Excuse me, Lord Williams." I stepped around him.

His hand grabbed mine. Startled, I spun back around.

"Margaret," he whispered, suddenly close. His hand rose again, this time without hesitation, and cupped my face, his thumb gently tracing my cheek. I tilted my head into his touch. This was all that I had ever wanted. The gentle touch, the whisper of my name from a man I adored.

He leaned forward, his breath warm on my cheek. "I can't. It wouldn't be proper."

Of course it wouldn't be proper. I'd been caught up in the moment, caught up in the way I wanted to be with him, with only him. And unlike his cousin, he was too honorable to risk a scandal.

"Unless. . . ." he said, shifting closer, his other hand rising to cup my face.

"Unless?" I asked, my voice barely audible, hope tinged with trepidation swelling within me.

His forehead came to rest against mine. "Margaret, choose me." The raw emotion in his plea tore at me.

He still wanted me. He still cared for me. The appearance of his cousin hadn't changed that.

My elation was dampened only by my own questions. Could I do it? Could I choose him and break my promise? This man was better than any I had ever known. My father and Daniel both wanted me to marry him. Louisa and my mother would congratulate me. Even Alice would have welcomed him as a brother if I had not been so against him.

Gregory could not offer me safety. Not as long as I cared for him. But I loved him. Did that not count for something?

Slipping my hand up his neck and into his hair, I finally touched that lock that curled above his ear. His breath hitched and he pulled away ever so slightly. His eyes, full of desire, searched mine.

I wanted to be with him. I couldn't deny it. My mind screamed in protest, warning me of danger, but I no longer wished to deny that Gregory was who I wanted.

His gaze dropped to my lips. I swallowed, anticipation building in my chest. He leaned closer. His breath brushed my mouth, making my lips tingle. His head tilted. I closed my eyes.

"Thank you for informing me of this," my father said, his voice suddenly sounding just outside the door.

I tore away from Gregory and stumbled back a few steps, my heart pounding in my chest, my breath agonizingly loud as I focused on the hall outside the door and watched as my father strode past. I couldn't be caught alone with Gregory. What would my father think?

But then I realized what I'd done and my gaze shifted back to Gregory. What did it matter if I was caught? Hadn't I just determined that Gregory was the person I wanted to be with, and hadn't he revealed as much to me?

I stepped toward Gregory, wanting him to know that I wasn't ashamed to be with him. That *he* was my choice.

Mr. Northam's voice stopped me. "I hope I did the right thing in telling you." He said something else, but it was too muffled to make out.

Gregory glanced toward the door then motioned me toward the alcove as he shifted, blocking my view of the door and, I realized, blocking me from being seen.

There was no reason to hide anymore, though, was there? We'd proclaimed our feelings for each other. What did it matter if his cousin discovered us? Confused, I retreated to the shadows of the alcove just as Mr. Northam appeared in the doorway. "Ah, Williams. There you are."

I pressed myself farther into the shadows as Gregory turned toward his cousin. "What do you want, Northam?" he asked icily.

Mr. Northam stepped into the room. "I didn't know you enjoyed this room so much. Or perhaps you're hoping for success where I failed?" He peered around Gregory as though searching the room.

My gaze jumped between Gregory and Mr. Northam. Success where Mr. Northam had failed? What did Mr. Northam mean?

Gregory's voice turned colder. "Did you

want something in particular?"

"I want you to offer me a drink in a more comfortable location. We have matters to discuss."

It seemed to take a full minute for Gregory to move. "Of course," he growled as he finally strode out the door.

Mr. Northam made a pretense of following him, but paused at the door and turned back. He surveyed the room with a slow turn of his head, stopping a moment on my location. I pressed against the wall, holding my breath, trying not to move.

Then he left, closing the door behind him, plunging me into darkness.

Thirty-Four

The next morning I walked down the stairs with resolve. There was no longer reason to hesitate. I wanted to be with Gregory, if he'd have me. He was worth the risk to my heart. I would not back down, nor would I pull away again.

Ignoring the small twinge of uncertainty that last night had produced, I located him seated at his desk, studying a ledger. And this time he was alone.

I stepped inside. "My lord?"

"Miss Brinton." He didn't look up from his ledger.

I frowned. This wasn't the reception I'd hoped for. In an act of boldness, I strode to the desk. "About last night. . . ."

He finally looked up, sitting back in his chair and folding his arms with a casual disinterest in his expression.

My uncertainty grew. Was he really so unmoved by what had happened last night?

Wasn't he going to say anything? I'd come into the room, seeking him, even giving him a topic upon which to converse. So he should say *something* about last night. Or anything at all.

He just sat in his chair and waited.

All right, I would start. I was, after all, the one who had initiated the conversation.

How did I begin? Did I tell him that I'd changed my mind? That my heart was truly his? Or did I bring up the dancing and how I was ready to agree to his suggestion of "unless"? And would he please kiss me, because I was desperate to feel the touch of his lips against mine? That had to be in there somewhere. Maybe I should bring that up first. No, second. Because first should be my asking if he would mind it so very much if I didn't release him from the engagement after all because I'd realized I didn't want to be without him.

It all seemed ridiculous now that I was standing before him with him showing no interest in me whatsoever. "Never mind."

I turned to leave, then turned back, unable to leave his presence so soon. "Only I wanted to say thank you. For the flowers. And the book."

"Those weren't delivered last night."

"No. But there never seemed to be an opportunity yesterday to bring it up."

"Because of my cousin?"

"Well, yes. But also because you hardly spoke to me. That made it difficult."

"Did you want me to speak to you?"

I ran my hand along the spines of books on the desk. I wanted so much more than for him to speak to me. "I think I'll go see if the post has arrived."

"It hasn't come yet, Miss Brinton."

"Oh." I picked up the top book, turned it over in my hands, and set it down. I was making a fool of myself. I should just leave. "The rain has stopped." I waited, but he said nothing. Had I ever been so ridiculous? "Well, goodbye." I stepped toward the doorway.

Gregory lurched out of his chair, grabbed my hand, and slowly pulled me back toward him. "Why are you really here?"

I could barely think with him being so close. Yet there was mirth in his eyes. "Are you — laughing — at me?"

"It seems you've become a little confused, Miss Brinton. I assure you, this is not the sound of laughter."

"I have not become confused. I have become. . . ." My gaze dropped to his lips and I lost any desire to speak.

"Do you know what I've become?" He

374

stepped toward me and I backed against the wall. When he leaned closer, I realized I was trapped. Not that I had any desire to escape.

"What have you become?" I asked, my voice little more than a whisper.

He leaned even closer. How could he get closer and still not touch me? "I have become a man haunted by your smile, by the music of your voice. I'm filled with a need to see you, to be close to you. Even when I should be away seeing to my responsibilities, I find myself unable to be parted from you."

My hesitation evaporated and all my uncertainties drained away. He wanted me as much as I wanted him.

I lifted my brows in mock innocence, struggling to appear unaffected. "Should you be seeing to responsibilities now? I'm sorry to be keeping you. I'd hate to be blamed for the estate falling apart."

He straightened. "You're right. Where is my hat?" He turned away, and this time I grabbed his hand.

"Gregory." I slid my fingers between his.

He was again instantly before me. "Margaret." His voice sounded almost pained. He leaned an arm against the wall above me, his face close to mine. "I couldn't leave you, even in jest." His gaze swept to my forehead, my lips, and back to my eyes. "You have captured my heart completely. I surrender to you."

There was no verbal response I could give. I reached up and slid my thumb along his cheek.

He closed his eyes. A small groan escaped his throat. "Are you deliberately torturing me?"

My thumb traced down his cheek to his bottom lip. A lip I desperately wanted to feel against my own. His eyes popped open and his arm flew around my waist, drawing me against him. "I knew I was in trouble the moment Mrs. Hickmore introduced you."

"Oh, come Williams. Love at first sight?" Mr. Northam's voice cut through the haze surrounding me. "Even you can do better than that."

The compromising situation I found myself in made me flinch, and Gregory's grip around me loosened, his expression changing to one of hopelessness. But I didn't move out of his arms.

"I don't think your father would approve of such an embrace, Miss Brinton. Not even I was so scandalous."

It was indeed scandalous, but there was

no question of what would follow a kiss this time; Gregory was no Mr. Northam. We had declared our feelings to each other. All we needed was to make it official.

Gregory, though, dropped his arm from me completely. He stepped back and leaned against the wall, his head against a fist, jaw clenched and eyes closed.

I placed a hand on his arm. Mr. Northam could have no doubt about my decision. "What do you want, Mr. Northam?"

Mr. Northam smiled and leaned casually against the door frame. "I want to tell you a story. The same one I told your father last night. It goes something like this: boy meets girl, boy falls for girl, boy's cousin reveals the truth to girl. . . ."

"Get out, Northam," Gregory growled.

"And miss watching this unfold? I think not."

It took me a moment to register what Mr. Northam had said. "Boy's cousin reveals the truth to girl?" My touch on Gregory's arm became uncertain.

Mr. Northam smiled. "Didn't you ever wonder why a baron was so interested in an untitled and only moderately wealthy woman?"

Gregory pushed off the wall and faced his cousin. "Shut up, Northam."

"He's already told me everything," I said. But that wasn't true, and Gregory and I both knew it.

"Did he tell you about the wager?"

A wager? My hand dropped from Gregory's arm. Mr. Northam's smile grew.

"Northam, leave. Now." Gregory's voice was hard with anger.

I placed my hand back on Gregory's arm, only this time it was to keep him from interrupting. "What wager?" I asked quietly.

Mr. Northam's gaze held mine. "When Old Lord Williams was dying, his last wish was that Williams here persuade me to change my dissolute ways. And Williams promised to do whatever it took."

"I promised my father, yes, but I did not agree to your terms."

Mr. Northam's smile held condescension. "You're too far in to go back now."

I glanced between them. Gregory's fists were clenched at his side, his jaw muscle working rapidly. Mr. Northam looked completely at ease. He seemed to be enjoying every second of Gregory's discomfort.

"You remember I mentioned our disagreement, don't you, Miss Brinton? Where *my lord* believes women would choose him over me, title or no? Well, I promised that if he could win a kiss honorably from any woman of our joint choosing before I obtained that kiss through my own means, I would reform. You are the lucky woman he agreed to."

I stared at Mr. Northam, too shocked to speak.

Mr. Northam pushed off the wall and walked to me. "Don't take it to heart. It really has nothing to do with you at all. Just your lips."

"That's not true," Gregory said, taking my hand. My mind churned but didn't seem to be processing what had been said.

"No?" Mr. Northam asked, smirking at him. "Then why did you race to her house and demand an engagement from her father when you realized you were going to lose?"

"A wager?" I asked, unable to believe it. Yet Mr. Northam's expression exuded truth. Gregory had said himself that he'd chosen me to end Mr. Northam's games. I focused on Gregory. His expression was earnest, his eyes asking me not to believe it. Yet within them was the confession — what Mr. Northam said was the truth.

There had been all those times when Gregory had first arrived and I'd felt as though I was pure entertainment, that my life had been a game to him.

I'd been correct. He hadn't been interested in me. He'd been trying to win a kiss.

My stomach knotted.

Pulling my hand from Gregory's, I staggered a step away from both men.

Mr. Northam smiled. "Was he that convincing? Congratulations, Williams. Your skills must be improving. Have you been practicing behind my back? Leaving a trail of broken hearts wherever you go?" He laughed. "You know, if I hadn't interrupted you just now, you might have won. Of course, it only seemed fair to interrupt, since a similar inconvenience occurred when I was just as close."

I had almost let Mr. Northam kiss me. I had wanted him to. And Gregory. . . .

I felt unsteady, lightheaded. "This was all a joke to you. To both of you. I was a joke."

Gregory shook his head. "No, Margaret. It was never like that."

"Margaret?" Mr. Northam looked at me with interest. "I underestimated you, Williams. Tell me, *Margaret,* do you address my cousin as Gregory?"

The heat of embarrassment crept up my neck. What a fool I was.

Mr. Northam stepped in front of me. In a lowered voice, he said, "You blush beautifully."

Gregory was between us before I'd opened

my mouth to reply. "Get out, Northam. You are no longer welcome here."

Mr. Northam laughed. "I will. But not before I win."

He shoved Gregory aside, grabbed me, and kissed me, hard.

I pushed against him but couldn't back away until he let me go. I ran my arm over my mouth in an effort to wipe away the taste and the feel of his lips on mine, though I couldn't wipe away how Mr. Northam's eyes gleamed with victory and amusement. "How does it feel to be kissed by a real man, *Margaret*?" He started humming the song he'd requested I play for him at the Hickmores'. The one Gregory had played last night.

I finally understood. That song was some sort of victory song for them. And I hadn't even been the prize. I'd been the paper they'd used to make their boats, neither of them caring that I would eventually become waterlogged and sink.

Gregory's fist connected with Mr. Northam's smile. Mr. Northam hit a chair before falling to the ground.

"What is going on here?" my father roared from the doorway, his anger more severe than I'd ever seen. When his gaze found mine, though, the pain in his eyes stopped my heart.

"Father?"

"Margaret, an express has arrived. We are leaving."

An express. The room emptied of air. "Alice has —" A lump formed in my throat and I couldn't speak past it.

"No. Not yet. But there is not much hope. We must return home as soon as possible."

Not Alice. My father must be mistaken. But the deadly reality showed in the sagging creases of his frown and the rounding of his shoulders.

"Margaret." Gregory was beside me, an arm around me.

This was what I'd wanted. I'd wanted him.

But Alice was dying because of this wager. And I —

I had been duped again.

"Let me go," I whispered.

"The wager may have played a part in the beginning, but I promise, all I've said is true."

I shoved out of his arms. "My sister is dying because of you."

Even now, though, I wanted to be enfolded in his arms.

Naive, fickle heart.

My father stepped forward and put a hand on my shoulder, turning his back to Gregory. "I am sorry for all that has happened. But we must be strong." His eyes glistened with threatening tears. His hand, instead of comforting, felt cold and heavy and final.

Was there ever a time when I did not have to be strong? A lake of exhaustion settled on me. I lifted my chin and forced a smile, but I had to swallow before I could say, "Of course, Father."

He offered me his arm. I slid under it, settling it on my shoulder and wrapping my arm around his middle. He squeezed me to him. "Let's go home."

THIRTY-FIVE

My father stood in the door to my room while I collected my traveling cloak and ensured my trunk was packed. As we descended the stairs, thoughts of Mr. Northam and Gregory threatened at the back of my mind like hounds ready to tear me apart.

Struggling to focus entirely on Alice, I allowed my anxiety for her to fill my mind, my ache for her to flood my chest and bury the confusion and pain hovering there.

Gregory and Lady Williams awaited us as we exited the house. Lady Williams stepped forward first. "I am so sorry you have to go. You do not know how much I have enjoyed your visit."

I studied her, wondering if she had been in on the charade. But her eyes held real disappointment. "You have been so kind. Thank you."

She took my hand and gave it a squeeze. "I do hope you find the situation at home better than the express has led us to believe."

I bit my trembling lip. "Thank you, your ladyship."

Gregory stepped forward.

I curtsied before he could say anything. "My lord." Then I turned and walked a few steps toward the river. Its constant movement eased a bit of the disquiet within me, its gentle shushing prodding me to be at peace.

"Please don't leave like this," Gregory whispered behind me.

"How am I supposed to leave?"

He hesitated, then laid a gentle hand on my back. "I don't know. I just know it shouldn't be like this."

Even now I craved his touch, his presence.

"My lord," my father said. Gregory's hand fell away as he turned to address my father.

Something fluttered in the water. I walked a few steps toward it before realizing what it was: one of the boats had gotten stuck on the branch of the tree. It would never go anywhere, never be free. It would struggle until the river rose or the branch broke. Then it would sink.

I turned and made my way to the carriage, where a footman waited to assist me. When I held out my hand, though, Gregory clasped it.

Caught off guard, I looked up.

His face had become so familiar it was a wonder we had ever been strangers. That we would return to being strangers.

"Margaret. I'm sorry."

I forced a smile. "At least our time together has been diverting." My voice broke and I turned away. I couldn't bear to look into his eyes, not when they were filled with the warmth and desire I had grown to love.

I moved to step into the carriage, but had only placed my foot on the step when he raised my hand and brought it to his lips.

I loved the feel of my hand in his, loved the way he looked at me still. And I couldn't help it — I longed to be with him. Longed to find a way to make everything that had happened matter, for it not to have been only for a wager.

But I knew the truth. I had been duped again.

I had known from the first that he wasn't for me. I should never have allowed myself to think of him as Gregory. He should have been, and now forever would be, Lord Williams.

I just had to convince my heart of it.

"Goodbye, Lord Williams," I said softly, tugging my gloved hand out of his. Before evidence of my despair made me look more the fool, I scooted to the far corner of the carriage.

My father entered directly after. Lord Williams stepped to the carriage door once it was secured.

"Mr. Brinton. Miss Brinton."

He lingered a second, his gaze on me, before stepping back. With a nod from him, the carriage jerked forward.

Resisting the urge to look through the window for one last glimpse of the man I loved, I asked, "What does the letter say, father?"

"It begs us to come home, to say our goodbyes."

Goodbyes? How did I say goodbye to someone who was such a part of me, such a part of each of us? Considering my experiences, I should have been quite proficient. Yet the hole in my heart that seemed to grow the farther we drove from Lord Williams proved I had not yet mastered the task.

My father cleared his throat. "Margaret, is what Mr. Northam told me last night true?"

The pieces of my heart that were still intact crumbled and disappeared, swept away by unshed tears. "I don't think it matters anymore." I closed my eyes to shut out the world, forcing an image of Alice sick in bed to fill my mind, demanding she take her proper place of most import.

My father didn't speak again, but after we had passed through the gate marking our exit from Lord Williams's estate, he took my hand and held it for a long time.

My mother rushed out of the house as the carriage stopped at the door, white apron covering her green day dress. When my father stepped down, she fell into his arms. "I am so glad you have come."

"Are we too late?" His voice was quiet.

She shook her head.

He let out a heavy sigh of relief. "And Parson Andrews?"

"He came this morning. We did not know when you would be home."

"Will she last the night?" My father's hushed words sent a chill through me.

"I don't — I. . . ." My mother buried her head in my father's chest.

"Come."

She covered her face with her hands and allowed my father to lead her into the house.

I'd still held out hope that it wasn't as bad as the letter had said, that things had seemed exaggerated in print. But now, there was no doubt.

Following them inside, head bowed, I shed my bonnet, gloves, and coat, trying not to notice how small our hall felt nor how low the ceiling. Daniel intercepted me as I made my way to the stairs.

"Margaret, how did you find Lord Williams's estate?"

I frowned. "It was fine."

"What else?"

I watched my parents walk up the stairs. "What else is there? It is a lovely place. If you ever have the opportunity to visit, I suggest you take it." My parents disappeared and I finally looked at Daniel. His expression was curious, but it was too earnest for casual conversation. Being home all this time, unable to leave in case he was needed, must have made him feel trapped; would that we had traded places and he had gone instead of me. Although it was quite likely that he was merely upset not to know how his joke had played out. "Or perhaps you were referring to Mr. Lundall's visit? Even that was not as objectionable as you likely intended, though it was a shock at first. I do not begrudge you your laugh."

"I was not referring to Mr. Lundall. I am referring to the estate. Did you approve of it?"

"It was fine, Daniel. I don't know what

more you want me to say. I'd like to see Alice."

"And Lord Williams? Am I soon to welcome him into the family or did you really ruin your chances with him?"

Alice. I needed to focus on Alice. And pretend that none of what had occurred at Lord Williams's mattered to me. I could do this. I would be strong. "Neither Lord Williams nor Mr. Northam had any true interest in me, so there was nothing to ruin."

"Northam found you?" Daniel's tone filled with anger and disgust.

I would explain this once, and then hopefully it would never come up again. "The only interest either of them ever held toward me was the winning of a long-standing wager." My voice caught and I had to take a breath before I could continue. "That is why Mr. Northam showed interest in me at the Hickmores'. That is why Lord Williams concocted this scheme of an engagement. I turned out to be a way to best his cousin." As I said the words, my chest felt as though it would cave inward. I had trusted Lord Williams, had broken my promise by loving him. I loved him still. And yet it was all over. Again.

"That cannot be true. You must be mistaken."

Did he think I was making it all up? Could he not see I was struggling to stay afloat as it was?

No — I would not sink. I rolled my shoulders back. Edward had not ruined my life. Neither would Lord Williams. Mr. Northam and Lord Williams had wished for nothing more than a few weeks' entertainment. I was not going to mourn at being their tossed-over plaything. I had a sister to attend to.

"It is true. Lord Williams confessed to it himself."

"Did he?" Daniel paused, then tilted his head with curiosity. "What did they want from you?"

Such a simple thing. A small thing. Too small for all that had happened, for all they'd gone through, and all I'd gone through, and Alice — "A kiss."

He smirked. "Who won?"

I gaped at him a moment, then swung my hand up and slapped him. "How dare you make a mock of it, of me? Our sister lies dying and you're laughing over how two men used me, used all of us. Yet for all that has happened, Lord Williams is more to be admired than you. At least he pursued what he wanted. You are nothing but a coward, laughing at the misfortunes of others while petrified at the thought of experiencing your own. You are not willing to risk even the smallest amount of gossip to do what honor dictates, nor to obtain what you want. You do not deserve Louisa, though for your sake, I hope she never realizes it."

Pushing past him, I strode up the stairs. And though my mind told me I'd done right, instead of feeling victorious I felt more despondent than ever.

THIRTY-SIX

The curtains were drawn and, though the fire was large, the room was dim. Alice lay with the covers encasing her, paler than I had ever seen. I waited just inside the door while my father examined her, kissed her, held her hand.

"Colin, you shouldn't linger," my mother said.

Laying Alice's hand back down, he stood and turned to her. "When was the last time you slept?"

She shook her head. "I will not leave her."

"Margaret will stay with her. You need rest."

"But what if I am absent when she — when it —" She hid her tears with her hands.

"Margaret will fetch you if Alice so much as twitches."

Stepping forward, I said, "I will, Mother. I promise. I should never have left in the first place."

"I cannot leave."

"Eloise." My father's voice took on a sternness I had never heard him use with her before. She dropped her hands in surprise as he continued. "You will come with me and you will rest."

He took her hand and pulled her into his arms, his voice turning tender. "Only for a little while. You shall need your strength for what is to come." She nodded into his shoulder and finally allowed him to lead her from the room. As they passed, my father placed a hand on my shoulder. "Come find me if anything changes."

I nodded my understanding. He wanted to be summoned first so he could assist my mother with whatever took place.

After shutting the door behind them, I sat in the chair next to Alice's bed.

She didn't stir. The arm closest to me lay on top of the sheets, covered with a white linen bandage from the bloodletting. The bedside table held small apothecary bottles lined in a row along the edge. Reaching past them, I grabbed a towel that lay in a bowl of water. After wringing it out, I wiped Alice's face, dampened the cloth once more, and laid it on her forehead.

I sat by her, alternating between holding

her hand and placing wet towels on her forehead. When Mary came in with new water and clean cloths, I helped her remove the old. Later, she came in with supper for me and broth for Alice.

"She won't take any, but Cook insists on sending it anyway. Your mother's been trying any way she can to get a few drops in."

"Thank you, Mary."

She curtsied and left. I took a spoon full of the broth, but it would never make it unspilled to Alice's mouth. So I dipped the corner of a clean cloth in the broth, pulled back Alice's lips, and squeezed in a few drops. She didn't swallow.

I took her hand again. This was all my fault. If I hadn't been so stubborn, if I'd just accepted my plight like I should have, agreed to the match and pretended to be happy about it, Alice would be laughing in the drawing room. She'd be begging to play cards or wanting to show off how much she'd progressed on her song.

But that wasn't the whole truth. It wasn't all my fault. It was as much Lord Williams's fault as mine. His and Mr. Northam's and that stupid wager.

I stood and walked to the window, pulling back the drapes just enough to see out. The sun was setting, casting brilliant colors across the cloud-laden sky, as though waving a farewell for the night. Or as though saying goodbye.

Was Lord Williams standing in his breakfast room, eyes on the sky? Or standing by the river, a frown on his face? Or had he decided to attend a different party, try again with a different woman, over and over until he finally won his wager and kept his promise to his father?

I dropped the drapes and returned to my vigil, again taking up Alice's hand. If I could just feel sorry enough, could just regret enough, could just be strong enough, perhaps I could change back the clock and make it so none of this had happened. I could heal her, put color back into her face, infuse her with laughter and love and everything she'd been before.

But no amount of hand pressing nor soft cajoling seemed to make any difference.

Eventually Mary retrieved the dinner tray. I picked up the book on Alice's nightstand, the one we'd been reading together at night before I'd left for the Hickmores', and, flipping back a few chapters, began to read. When I'd read to the point she'd marked, I closed the book and sat on her bed, telling her of the changing colors of the leaves, of Daniel's idiocy, of what she and I would do once she regained health, all in the hopes that something — a touch, a word, a feeling — would sink past her sickness and bring her comfort.

When I'd run out of things to say, I returned to the chair and rested my head against her hand. I must have dozed, for a pounding on the front door startled me upright. The pounding sounded again, then went quiet, voices replacing the noise. Who had come? Was it Lord Williams?

I stood. Heavy footsteps led across the hall and up the stairs. Father pushed the door open but remained in the hall.

"Margaret, a doctor from London has arrived."

"London?" I looked past him to the unfamiliar face of a middle-aged man. Not Lord Williams. I stepped aside.

The man came in, cast me a dismissive glance, and sat in the chair I'd just vacated. "You say your country doctor has been attending to her?"

"Dr. Johnson. Yes," my father replied.

The man nodded. He examined Alice, opening her eyelids, her mouth, feeling her throat, inspecting the wound from the letting. Then he inspected the different bottles on the side table. "He seems to have been thorough, though that letting wound doesn't look deep enough. Aside from another letting, I am not certain there is more I can do. I'd like to discuss what he's done with him before I arrive at anything definitive."

"Of course. We shall send for him immediately." My father gestured back out of the room, shutting the door again as the heavy steps retreated.

I sank back into the chair and glanced around the small and now quiet room. My father must have sent for the doctor shortly after we'd returned home. Or perhaps even before we'd left Lord Williams's.

And I'd thought Lord Williams had come. To what? Sit with me? Mumble apologies?

Hold me and tell me it would all be well?

What a fool I was. What a fool my heart was.

I shifted Alice into what I hoped was a more comfortable position, rewet the cloth, and placed it back on her forehead.

An hour later, both doctors visited again, letting more blood. Afterward, the house fell into silence.

When the large house clock struck one in the morning, I resettled into the chair and took Alice's hand in mine. "Alice, I'm so sorry. I would trade all my pride, all my promises, my very heart if need be, for you to live." I could have prevented it, if I'd only known. No harm would have come from letting either of the men steal a kiss. Well, only another mark on my reputation, but I had dealt with that before. It wasn't right that my family was suffering — that Alice was dying — because of Lord Williams and Mr. Northam. How would we ever be happy again?

Anger, fiercer than I had ever experienced, rushed over me. "Alice. Wake up. You have slept long enough. Do not give those men the satisfaction of seeing that their actions affect us. Be strong. Alice!"

She didn't stir, didn't give any sign that she had heard me. I pressed her hand with my own. "Alice, please wake up. You are being incredibly selfish. You have always been given everything you want. It is time to give something back. Wake up!"

Nothing.

This wasn't right. It wasn't fair. This wasn't the way things were supposed to have turned out. I clenched my teeth. "You cannot go. You cannot leave us. I will not let you!"

But where was the authority of an empty threat shouted into the night? I had no power: no power over my past, no power over my future, and no power over Alice's life. My words were as meaningless as Lord

Williams's had been when he'd stated he would never allow love to die.

My throat closed and my eyes stung. There was no one to see the pain now. There was no reason to be strong any longer.

I laid my head next to hers. "I love you," I whispered. "I'm sorry. So very sorry. I was wrong to not hide my emotions. I was wrong to be so openly defiant of Mother and Father. Please don't die. You mustn't leave us. We need you. I need you."

Intertwining my fingers with hers, I gently squeezed. "Please, Alice. If you get better, I promise — I don't know what I promise. I'll do anything. Only, please, get better."

THIRTY-SEVEN

I awoke and glanced around, disoriented. The room was completely dark except for the glowing embers in the fireplace.

The fire. The closed curtains. The body next to me.

Alice.

Nothing indicated whether it was still night or early morning. I shifted, wanting to move farther from Alice so I could rise without disturbing her. But as I moved, a freezing fear seeped through me.

Alice's hand was cold.

I sat up and stared at her. There was no movement in her chest, no trace of color in her face.

She had died while I had slept. I hadn't even noticed.

Anguish wrenched a convulsive sob from my chest. I gently untangled my fingers from hers.

She didn't look at peace, as I had been

told people looked once they passed. Her arms lay unnaturally straight by her side. Clasping her hands, I crossed them over her chest. Then I pressed my lips to her face.

Her forehead wasn't cold. Her face was as hot as it had been the night before. Hope exploded in my chest. I turned my head so my cheek rested near her mouth and waited.

A small, almost undetectable breath brushed my cheek.

Alice was alive. She had lived through the night.

I quickly rubbed her arms and hands, blowing on them as I did, trying to warm them. Then I tucked them beneath the bedclothes and hurried to build up the fire. Opening the door to go in search of Mary, I paused as my mother appeared at the top of the stairs, looking rested and guilty. She must have slept through all that had happened last night.

She froze when she saw me. My throat constricted at her pained expression. "She's alive," I rasped past the burn in my throat.

Relief softened her features. "Thank you," she whispered, her voice shaking. I stepped out of her way as she entered the room, then retreated to my own room to wash and change.

There was no trunk near the bed; Mary

402

must have already unpacked for me and had the trunk returned to the attic. It was as though I had never left.

I opened my drapes and leaned my forehead against the window. There was no river glistening below me. No stretch of fields and oaks. Just the small, formal garden off to the side and the path leading down to the lake.

How was I ever to enjoy that garden again?

But my lake. I needed my lake. At least Lord Williams hadn't ruined that for me.

There was no way to visit it this morning; I couldn't leave the house when I might be needed at any moment. Yet being alone with my thoughts when they constantly found their way back to Lord Williams was torture.

I left my room and made my way down the stairs, meeting my father on his way up. "She's alive."

He nodded. "I heard. Thank you for staying with her. Though she would deny it, I think your mother was very grateful for a respite."

"It is what I should have been doing all along." If I had stayed home instead of going with my father, my mother would not have been so worn out in the first place.

But if I had stayed, would I have regretted driving Lord Williams away? I would never

403

have known about the wager. Except if Mr. Northam should have come after all, determined to capture the winning kiss.

No matter what way the situation was inspected, I lost.

Alice lasted through the day with no change. Dr. Johnson and the London doctor came and left, warning us she could pass at any moment.

Assembled in the drawing room later with my father and Daniel, a clattering on the stairs silenced our movements. It had finally happened. I braced myself as Mary burst into the room.

"She spoke!" Mary exclaimed.

My father shot out of his chair. "What?"

Daniel and I glanced at each other, eyes wide.

"It's Miss Alice, sir. She spoke!"

"What did she say?" my father demanded.

Mary's excitement dimmed. "Well, she didn't actually say anything. She just mumbled a bit, you see."

"But," Daniel interjected, "that must be a good sign, when she hasn't shown a hint of life in days."

Mary nodded, her smile brightening again. "Yes, that's what the missus thinks. She bade me come and tell you all the news."

"I want to see her." My father strode from the room.

I slumped in my chair, powerless against the relief washing over me. "Thank you, Mary."

She curtsied and left.

"She's going to recover," Daniel said, his tone light. "I haven't been out of the house in days." He stood.

A sudden thought struck me. "Do you think she's still going to — I mean, have you heard that sometimes people, right before they pass, appear to revive a little?"

"I'm going for Dr. Johnson." Daniel threw his book on the table and ran out.

I bit my lip and struggled out of my seat, making my way back to Alice's room.

"I believe she has made it through the worst of it," Dr. Johnson declared an hour later before turning to the doctor from London as though awaiting the final word.

"Yes," the man said. "I believe she has. What she needs now is rest."

Dr. Johnson put his things back into his bag. He stood, glanced at Alice, then shook his head. "I'm unsure if I have ever seen a case so hopeless turn around. I am very happy it has."

"As are we," my father replied, walking

both doctors out of the room.

"Margaret, did you hear? She's going to live." My mother fell into the chair next to Alice's bed and cradled her hand.

Daniel cleared his throat. "I've — um. There's something I need to see to. Excuse me."

I followed Daniel into the hall. "Where are you going?"

He stopped, but avoided my eyes. "I've a matter that needs my attention." He took the stairs two at a time.

An hour and a half later, Daniel returned. I'd finally left Alice's room for the study, hoping that now that the danger for Alice was over, I might lose myself in a novel or two. I avoided the one Mr. Northam had read to me and chose one recently acquired, something Lord Williams could not yet have read and so could not have yet determined to be worthwhile or not; I didn't want to spend my whole day wondering if he would have approved of my choice. My father sat in his chair behind the desk, though he didn't seem to be doing much more than relaxing in the knowledge that Alice would be fine.

Daniel stepped into the room. "Father, may I speak to you?"

"Where did you go?" I asked.

Daniel glanced at me. "In private."

I walked out and Daniel closed the door. Something was up. I leaned my ear against the door, hoping I could hear something of the conversation and discover what Daniel was about, but the voices were too low. When they emerged, Daniel requested everyone to gather in the drawing room. Once our mother arrived, Daniel cleared his throat. "Mother, Margaret, I have asked Louisa to marry me. She has consented. The banns will be read beginning Sunday."

He'd done it. He'd finally made it official.

"Oh, Daniel." My mother looked ready to weep. "I'm so happy for you. For both of you."

"What made you decide to ask now?" I asked.

Daniel met my gaze briefly before looking away. He didn't respond, but he didn't have to; that look had said everything. He'd finally asked Louisa because he didn't want to end up like me, alone, in love with someone he'd never be able to have.

Something shifted inside me. The place that had been filled with worry for Alice filled instead with the dark, murky waters of jealousy. Daniel was marrying while I, once again, was without the man I had grown to love.

If I couldn't feel happy for him, I should at least feel happy for Louisa. I forced a smile and hoped it didn't look like a grimace.

"When is the wedding to be?" my mother asked.

"As soon as possible. We see no reason to wait longer than it takes for the banns to be read."

She frowned. "Daniel, we will need more than a few weeks. Alice will not be fit to attend, and her health is my first priority at this point. I shan't be able to assist in the preparations at all. What will Sir Edward and Lady Rosthorn think?"

"It was they who suggested it."

At my mother's doubtful look, Daniel continued, "It isn't as though this is a surprise. I believe Lady Rosthorn has been preparing for the wedding for at least half a year."

"She's probably in such a rush because she's afraid you'll put it off longer," I said.

"Margaret!" my mother chided, but my father chuckled.

Daniel glared at me, and I shrugged. "You said yourself Lady Rosthorn is already prepared. How fortunate you could love someone for so long and have everything work out perfectly."

"Margaret, really," my mother said.

"Excuse me." I stood. "I really am happy for you, Daniel. More so for Louisa, that she doesn't have to wait any longer. I'm going to check on Alice."

As I left the room, Daniel muttered, "She could have at least acted happy."

"Don't judge her too harshly, Daniel. Not now," my father responded quietly.

THIRTY-EIGHT

As the sun rose the next morning, I passed under the arbor and surveyed the small garden before me. Every bloom seemed tired, heads hanging, wearied from the long summer as though they, too, had felt the burden of the past week. I moved toward the bench, but stopped at spotting the bare spots of rough wood where the paint had flaked off. Even the paths felt more narrow and confined, as though the garden had shrunk in the days I'd been away.

I sat on the bench in defiance. Nothing had actually changed. Everything was just as it ought to have been.

Only the last time I'd sat on this bench had been because Lord Williams had pushed me onto it when he'd thought I was ill. It seemed so long ago, as if the memory belonged to someone else.

He couldn't have thought I was actually ill. He must have been teasing, just a part of his attempt to win me over. It must also be why he'd asked me to call him by his first name.

Such an intimate thing, someone's name. The way it embodied the whole of a person, the way *Gregory* conjured memories with just a word: a river, a rose garden, a smile inviting me to draw nearer, inviting me to focus on those lips, to hope for things that could never be.

Foolish names. I stood and strode out of the garden, down the path to the lake. Plucking a leaf from one of the trees that stood unmoving in the windless morning, I walked out onto the few rocks jutting into the lake, realizing that even the birds sang in hushed tones. Yet there, on the water, was the reflection I had so missed, the one the river could never provide. I was home.

But as I stared at the water's mirror of the trees and the clouds and the sky, I realized the clouds appeared brown instead of the white they were in reality. The sky, too, was tinted a shade of green.

The murkiness of the water distorted the colors, making things appear different than they were.

I tossed the leaf into the lake. It sat unmoving, not even taking on enough water to sink.

The lack of movement mocked me. Had the lake always been so lifeless? So unchanging? And that smell — it wasn't the freshness of water in the sun but the stink of decay and stagnation.

No. It couldn't be. It was just today, just this moment — it was because there was no wind, because I'd been away, because of everything that had happened. Soon the lake would be what it had always been.

I left the rocks and continued my walk. But the more I walked, the more unsettled I felt. Perhaps some fish in the lake would be a good thing; it would add movement and life, at least.

When I returned, my mother was waiting for me. "You missed breakfast."

"My apologies."

She sighed. "There is some toast on the sideboard for you. Please hurry. I am going to pay a congratulatory visit to Louisa and her mother, and I suggest you accompany me. You have not seen Louisa since Alice fell ill."

I missed Louisa. But I could not visit her. She would inquire about what had occurred at Lord Williams's, and I couldn't yet trust myself to recount all that had taken place without showing how it had affected me.

"Will I be welcomed?" I hadn't been there since discovering Edward's infidelity, although admittedly my continued absence was more my doing than any formal exclusion from the Rosthorns.

"Of course you shall. They are to be family now. Besides, I request your attendance. And I expect you to exhibit more excitement for your friend than you did for your brother. We would not wish them to think we are in any way displeased with the union."

"But she will want to know what occurred with Lord Williams."

"We all wish to know that. However, we shall not stay long. And with talk revolving around the upcoming wedding, I doubt there will be enough time for the conversation to center on you."

Chastened, I nodded.

As the carriage drew along the drive to the Rosthorn estate, I was astonished at how little had changed. A stand of trees had been removed off to the side and a bench swing stood in its place, while an area that had once been pastureland was now planted over in trees. But on the whole, it was as though the past years and all the hurt and confusion that had occurred within them had never taken place.

Would I one day feel this way about what had occurred with Lord Williams? It didn't seem possible. I didn't remember losing Edward hurting this much.

The carriage stopped in front of Sir Edward's tan, stone home, larger than our own and more classical in style, and I paused. The grounds smelled of childhood and laughter, insignificant secrets and petty hurts. There were new sounds — a water fountain trickling in the garden and the calls of foreign birds that must have belonged to the aviary Sir Edward had constructed the previous year. But even with these changes, the essence of the estate had stayed the same.

We climbed the steps to the house, and the butler, Mr. Brands, opened the door.

"Mrs. Brinton. Miss Brinton." He inclined his head.

I smiled into his familiar face, now creased with a few extra lines but still as foreboding as ever. "Brands. You've grown shorter."

He scowled, but the glint of laughter in his eyes betrayed him. "I see you have not changed."

Mrs. Hargreaves's words came to mind, and I quietly replied, "Where is the benefit of change when one is practically perfect?"

"If Lady Rosthorn is receiving callers,"

my mother cut in, casting me a look of exasperation, "we wish to pay our respects."

"Yes, mum. Mr. Brinton and Miss Rosthorn are with her in the morning parlor. Might I offer my congratulations for a felicitous match?"

"Thank you, Brands," my mother said, inclining her head.

He gestured toward the entry. "If you would follow me."

I glanced about me at the light walls of the large hall as we climbed the stairs and turned left toward the morning parlor. The door was open, allowing me to see into the room. The drapes covering the long rectangular windows on the far wall had been changed from deep crimson to primrose, which suited the room much better, but the new drapes appeared to be the only change. The couch Louisa and her mother sat on, with Daniel standing hunched over its back peering at some papers Louisa and Lady Rosthorn held between them, was the same one we'd turned over and used as a fort when younger. The side chairs had been our shields, the table our castle walls.

"Mrs. Brinton and Miss Brinton," Brands announced. The three occupants looked up.

"Eloise. Margaret," Lady Rosthorn said with a smile. "How good of you to call.

Please, do come in."

As we walked into the room, Daniel turned over the papers that they had been looking at. What was on them that he didn't want me to see?

I walked to Louisa and took her hands. "I am so happy for you, though I'm certain you could have done better."

Daniel scowled, but Louisa shook her head, dismissing my words with a smile. "We were just going over the guest list for the engagement ball."

Why hadn't Daniel wished me to see the guest list?

My mother looked surprised. "Will there be time before the wedding?"

Lady Rosthorn gestured for us to sit. "We have decided to postpone the wedding for two months in the hopes that Alice will be well enough to attend."

A lump formed in my throat at their consideration. My mother smiled. "That is very kind. Alice would hate to miss the wedding."

"When is the ball?" I asked.

"One week." Louisa beamed.

"We would like to assist you in whatever way possible," my mother said.

"Thank you," Lady Rosthorn replied. "We know you are busy nursing your daughter, and that, of course, should take priority. However, perhaps you would be so good as to provide a list of guests you would like to attend."

My mother nodded and inquired further into the details. Daniel stood behind Louisa, a hand resting on her shoulder, and she continually glanced up at him to smile. I realized that with their engagement, I no longer possessed the greater claim to Louisa's affection. Our relationship would be altered forever. I had lost my best friend.

After a few moments, my mother signaled to me and we both rose. "We will send over a few names."

I hugged Louisa. "I am truly very happy for you."

"Thank you," she replied. "You will come early, will you not?"

"I will be there to ensure not a hair nor ruffle is out of place."

Once back in the carriage, my mother said, "You lacked the enthusiasm I requested, but I do not think they noticed. It is a good match, and I will feel much easier once it is over. I only wish I could see you as happily settled. You will have to have a new gown. I was thinking green."

"Blue. I want it to be blue."

My mother frowned. "Are you certain?"

I nodded silently, trying not to wonder what it would be like to plan a wedding with Lady Williams while Lord Williams stood behind me.

Before Edward, all I had ever wanted was to be cherished as I knew Daniel would cherish Louisa. As I had thought Lord Williams would have cherished me.

What an utterly ridiculous desire.

THIRTY-NINE

My father came into drawing room later that afternoon, halting my scales. "You have a caller."

My hopes leapt. "Who is it?"

"Mr. Lundall."

Would my foolishness at wishing to see Lord Williams never end?

"Would you like me to send him away?"

I hesitated. "Mr. Lundall came to the door? Like a regular caller?"

"Yes."

This was something he had never done before. Perhaps something was wrong. "It is all right. I will see him."

Mr. Lundall soon entered, hat in hand.

I stood. "Good afternoon, Mr. Lundall."

He shifted his hat. "I hope I am not intruding."

He had never worried about intruding before. "Not at all. Won't you sit down?" I motioned toward a chair and took a seat near it. He sat and unconsciously fluffed the frilly white cuffs of his shirt, ensuring they created even circles around his wrists. With his red waistcoat and light blue coat, he looked almost normal.

"Your sister is recovering. I am very glad to hear it."

"Thank you."

He seemed in no hurry to continue the conversation. "Is there something I can do for you?" I asked.

Mr. Lundall nodded.

I waited. When he said no more, I prodded, "I would very much like to know what it is."

He seemed to inhale a giant breath. "Miss Brinton, I have made no pretense of my desire for your hand. I am here to ask you one final time, please make me the happiest of men and be my wife."

I should not have been surprised. And yet his manner was so different, so much less affected than normal, that I was taken off guard.

He continued, "I know I am not your first choice, that your heart belongs with another. Yet, here I am. I cannot promise you a title, for I do not possess one to offer. But you'll be treated with all the courtesy and admiration you deserve."

I scrutinized him. He seemed in earnest. Yet why would any man persist in pursuing a woman so determined to reject him? "If I may be so bold as to ask, why do you continue to court me when I have never encouraged you?"

"I thought it was obvious." He flicked an imaginary speck from his glove.

"You have declared your attraction to me, but I do not flatter myself that it is strong enough to overcome every other obstacle."

He frowned. "Your radiant appearance is merely an added benefit to the match. But, no, that is not the reason I seek your hand."

"Then why, sir?"

"You are a damsel in distress, are you not? I saw it the moment I laid eyes on you. The anguish written into your every movement convinced me that I was the man to change that."

He could not be serious. "You have pursued me all this time because I was unhappy when we first met?"

"My dear Miss Brinton, you were not merely unhappy. It was as though you would never smile again. I shall never forget; you were wandering the garden area of the park, and when I inquired after you it was related that your engagement some months before had ended in the most egregious manner. I instantly set about to rescue you from your despair."

I gaped at him. This man did not care anything for me. All this time his only wish had been to become someone's knight in shining armor. He, not Mr. Northam, had been my perfect choice all along. My heart would be safe with him and, it would seem, he would never expect love in return. Only contentment.

Could I be content with him? No matter how sweet his words nor how tender his touch, he would never move my heart the way Lord Williams had. I would be entirely safe with him.

Yet I ached for the way Lord Williams's presence had filled me. With Mr. Lundall, I would always be empty.

But that is what I had wanted. What I had promised to secure.

Could I do it?

I stood and faced the window. "You still wish to marry me, though there will never be love between us?"

He stood and stepped toward me, though it took a moment for him to respond. "Yes."

I turned and took in his determined smile and the trace of hope in his eyes. There was no mistaking that he was a kind man. A woman could do much worse in life than choosing him for a companion, even if it meant altering her ways to conform to those of a dandy. A patient woman might curb his flair. In time he would most likely become the best of companions. He would always be good looking.

For one brief moment, I allowed myself to imagine what marriage to him would be like. He would never mistreat me, of that I was certain. And I would have some measure of freedom with him, probably more than most women obtained from their husbands. I might even grow to be content.

I would do it. I would tell him yes and let him rescue me from my foolishness and my selfishness and my longing for Lord Williams. I would accept his offer, and he would take me away from the past, away from this place, away from my memories of hurtful love.

Away to some place different, yes. But not away from who I was.

I would merely be changing one place of stagnation for another. I wouldn't really be changing anything except location and marital status. I wouldn't be free.

Neither would he.

What good was the future if it contained only the prison of the past?

"Mr. Lundall." I hesitated, then placed

my hand lightly on his arm. "I wish you to know that I appreciate your attentions and your offer. If I were a wiser woman, I am certain I would accept you. But I do not love you. I am afraid I cannot marry without that love."

"I do not need your love." His eyes pleaded for it to be true though his voice betrayed his doubt.

I dropped my hand. "You may not, but I need to love the man I marry. And I expect love in return. Marriage would become no more than a prison for us both."

After a moment of quiet, he asked, "You are certain?"

No. I wasn't certain. He might be the last man to ever offer for me. And then what would become of me?

But I was certain that remaining as I was would not free me.

I wanted to be free. "Yes," I replied.

Mr. Lundall's smile was sad and resigned. "Very well." He put his hat on. "I bid you a good day." Then he turned and walked out of the room.

FORTY

I settled myself at the piano after dinner a few days later with a collection of music before me. Daniel approached a short while later. "Leave off playing, Margaret. Come join me for a game of chess."

"No, thank you."

"How about cards, then? I'll persuade mother and father to join us."

"Mother never plays cards. Besides, I do not feel like a game tonight."

"I suppose this has nothing to do with a certain someone? Is it safe to say his name?"

I stopped playing. "I cannot think who you mean."

"This is so much worse than after Edward. These morose songs on the piano, the lack of a proper display of character — even Louisa commented on it."

It *was* worse than with Edward. So much worse, in fact, that I began to doubt I'd even been in love with Edward. Perhaps I'd only ever been in love with the idea of him. Because I had never felt this empty before, as though everything within me had been washed away and all that was left was this pain that made it difficult to breathe.

Last time, everyone had expected me to mourn. It had been acceptable to show my grief. This time, however, it wasn't. And it appeared I hadn't been doing a good enough job at hiding it. I'd do better. Be better.

I would not let this drag me under.

Standing, I said, "Not in front of her mother, I hope." I admired Lady Rosthorn, but in her desire to show compassion she would certainly tell Mrs. Johnson, and then the whole town would know.

"Louisa is not in the habit of keeping confidences from her mother. Besides, I thought you didn't even like him."

"I didn't. I don't."

"Yes. I can see you don't. How foolish of me to deduce otherwise."

Declaring my intention to retire for the evening, I bid my parents a good night with the intent of checking on Alice before going to bed. Daniel followed me into the hall.

"The lake is being drained tomorrow."

I spun around. "What? Are you sure about this decision, Daniel? Lord Williams isn't exactly the most forthright of men."

"Whatever his failings, his advice regarding the managing of the estate was sound."

So that was it. I had won my freedom but failed to secure the lake. I would forever have Lord Williams to thank for the giant scar marring our landscape and serving as a reminder of our time together. Defeat slumped my shoulders. "I hope it goes well."

"No fight? No tantrum about how it shouldn't be done?"

"I've grown weary of fighting."

"Father told me what happened. Well, not all of it. He doesn't know what happened exactly at the end."

"It doesn't matter."

"If it didn't matter, why have you not smiled since your return?"

"What have I had to smile about? Alice's illness?"

"My engagement to Louisa."

He was correct. I should be smiling about it. I forced my lips to curve. "Yes. You are right. I am very happy for you."

He shook his head. "You are not happy at all."

The corners of my lips fell back down. "I'm working on it."

Daniel settled a hand on my shoulder before I could leave. "I'm sorry for what occurred. Truly I am. Which is why I came to forewarn you: Lord Williams will be here tomorrow. He has agreed to oversee the project."

What? "You invited him, after everything?"

"I wrote to thank him for sending the doctor from London and —"

"He sent the doctor?"

Daniel's brows drew together. "Didn't you know?"

"I thought it was Father's doing."

"Does Father know a doctor in London?"

I shrugged.

"Anyway, I wrote to thank Lord Williams and informed him I was moving forward with his idea. He insisted on attending. He felt it was his responsibility, since he was the one who proposed the project in the first place."

Business. He was coming on business, to see a project through. Perhaps he didn't want it to end up a failure since it would have his name associated with it. Sending for the doctor was probably merely business as well, a way to clear his name in case the worst should have happened. "I understand."

"I hope you'll still come." Daniel squeezed my shoulder with affection and reentered the drawing room.

■ ■ ■ ■

The next morning I hurried down the path to the lake, anxious to watch the morning rays sparkle off its surface one last time. A breeze blew through the trees, the soft rustle of their leaves a background murmur to the twitter of birdsong. But the lake still stood stagnant and brown.

My time at Lord Williams's had darkened everything I used to love; no matter how I tried to focus on the way the light danced off the water, I could not dismiss how my senses seemed more aware of the mucky marshland around the lake's edge and the putrid stink that assaulted me with every breeze. The lake had all the appearance of life, but just beneath the surface all that really existed was death.

How long would it take for the path to disappear completely when no one walked it? How long before the scars of something I loved disappeared once it was drained? I reached up to tear a leaf from a tree, then let my hand drop away empty. It was better just to leave it be and move on.

When I reached the rocky shore, a spot of white on the boulder caught my attention. A white rose about to bloom lay alone in the sun. I glanced around, but there was no one near. Retrieving it, I brought it to my nose, smelling its freshness and life. Perhaps Daniel had left it for Louisa.

She wouldn't find it. She was busy planning a ball and a wedding and wouldn't have time for a morning walk. I determined to take it back to him, so he could give it to her properly.

I climbed onto the boulder and walked to the edge. The lake's surface was unusually still even with the breeze. Did it know it was about to disappear? Did a lake sense its own death?

Lying on my stomach, I reached down and brushed the surface with my finger, sending ripples off across the water. When the surface calmed enough for my reflection to stare back at me, I thought of all the time I had spent out here, all the memories this place held. I even allowed myself to remember Lord Williams in the water, asking me to help him out of his coat. And now I had to go face him, one last time.

For the last time, I sat up and stared across the lake, surveying the scene around me, soaking up as much of it as I could, knowing it would forever be altered and I was powerless to stop it.

Men's voices sounded in the distance.

It was time.

I could be strong one last time.

My steps slowed as I neared the place Daniel had said to meet him. Tenants were already at work, digging away at a piece of the shoreline. Daniel stood nearby, watching. And next to him, his back to me, stood Lord Williams.

He was wearing a blue coat. Did he know it was his best color? Had he worn it to purposefully torment me?

If I didn't look at him, I wouldn't be tormented. I shouldn't be tormented anyway. I was business. A wager.

I stepped to Daniel's other side. "How goes the work?"

Lord Williams glanced at me, but I focused on the men digging.

"Right on schedule," Daniel answered. "Once they breach the shore, the water will flow down that trench until the whole lake is drained."

Lord Williams hadn't moved, his gaze still resting on me. It took everything I had not to glance up at him. "Won't that take some time?" The trench was tiny, only two feet across and maybe three feet deep.

"Days, probably," Gregory said, his voice soft and low, and I realized it was foolish to call him anything but Gregory. He would

431

always be Gregory to me. "The breaching won't be long now." There was a pause. "Will you stay to watch it?"

"For a while. Daniel, Louisa won't find this. You should give it to her directly." I held out the rose.

"That isn't mine."

"You didn't leave a rose for Louisa on the rock?"

He frowned. "Why would I do that?"

"Because it's what you're supposed to do. Flowers, gifts —" I stopped myself, but the unsaid word hung in the air. *Kisses.*

Daniel shook his head. "What are you talking about?"

It didn't matter. "Maybe she left it for you." I thrust it at him. He took it uncertainly. "What will happen when the water is fully gone?" I asked.

Again Gregory answered. "This land should be quite fertile." Did he know how his voice called to me, how my body wanted to respond by moving closer?

"Yes," Daniel said. "Once it's dry, we'll plow it under. Come spring, it should be covered with green shoots."

Another place to farm. Another spot of land from which our tenants could live. "I hope it yields well."

One of the men gave a shout. Water

streamed and glistened along the trench, charging toward us, then dashing past us. I turned to the lake. It looked the same. There was no indicator that its very essence was draining away. Yet the water raced along, gurgling as though with joy at finally being freed.

"What do you think?" Daniel asked me.

"I think it is going to take a long time to drain the lake with only that tiny outlet."

"It will," Gregory agreed. "But there is no reason to rush it." I loved the sound of his voice. It made everything, even the draining of my lake, feel like all would be well.

"We don't want the water to overflow the trenches and flood the fields," Daniel explained. "It would undo all our hard work. This way the ground can soak it in and we are able to ensure all our irrigation works."

I would rather it burst all at once and be done with it. This process seemed too slow, too painful. Like being bled to death. Or like standing feet from Gregory and not being able to touch him. "It isn't very satisfying."

"No," Gregory agreed. "But it is the better way."

"Is it?" It was foolish to linger. Foolish to have come in the first place. "I suppose it must be true." I turned. I had to get away from him. "Good day."

I'd taken no more than a few steps when he was beside me. "Wait. Please." I stopped but didn't turn to him. "I am glad your sister is recovering." His voice was low, coaxing me to look at him, to lean into him, to be drawn in.

As he had for the wager. Hadn't I known that first night at the Hickmores'? Hadn't I been warned by his smile that I wouldn't be able to resist him?

Now he was here, but not as a suitor. Not even as someone trying to win a wager. Solely on a matter of business, attempting to ensure a project went properly.

Business. Nothing more. "Yes," I replied quietly. "Though it will still be some time before she regains her full health. I understand we have you to thank for the doctor from London?"

"I —" He hesitated, then shifted closer. Or had I shifted closer to him? "I cannot express how sorry I am."

There was the proper apology. Now he was done. He could leave with a clear conscience. "Neither can I." My voice was barely a whisper. He was so close I could reach out and brush his hand with almost no effort. Perhaps I could even make it look like an accident. "Thank you for coming, for assisting Daniel." My fingers twitched toward him. Was he feeling the same pull, the same desire to forget there'd ever been a wager or a rushed engagement or a Mr. Northam and to just be together, he and I?

I glanced up. His expression wasn't severe, but he was frowning. Just like at the first. Just as though nothing had occurred between us.

He didn't feel it. He hadn't come for me, or for any other purpose than seeing a project through.

It was time to sever the magic with which he held me bound. "Please, excuse me. I should be returning to her."

"Of course. Good day, Miss Brinton." He stepped back. My bonds broke. So did something inside.

I made it back to the path before stopping. Before turning around for just one more glimpse of him.

Gregory had returned to Daniel's side, pointing at something downstream. Back to his business of which I was no longer a part.

Unlike the excited shouts at the breaching of the lake, only a muffled sob paid evidence to the tears sliding down my cheeks. Turning, I walked away, away from my lake, away from Gregory. Yet no matter how far I walked, I was unable to walk away from the

435

pain of loving things that were now forever lost to me.

FORTY-ONE

Two days later, Mary entered Alice's room as I was reading to her. "Miss Margaret? These've just arrived."

I looked up to find Mary holding a small vase of exquisite wildflower blooms with a white rose at the center.

"Oh," Alice exclaimed lifelessly, still too weak to leave her bed. "Who are they from?"

"The man didn't say."

"A man delivered them?" They were beautiful flowers. And the vase looked quite expensive. "Who?"

"I don't know."

"When did the man come?"

"Some ten minutes ago."

I set the book down, walked to the window, and looked out. No one was about. "What did he look like?"

"John answered the door. I didn't see him."

"Is there a card?" No one had ever deliv-

437

ered flowers to us before. It was the thing to do in London, of course. But here in the country?

"Yes. There it is." Mary held the flowers out, card facing me. In a fine, flowing script was written only one word: *Flowers.*

"Flowers?" I glanced between Mary and Alice. "Perhaps this is some sort of joke. Or a mistake. Are you certain they aren't meant for Daniel? Louisa was leaving flowers for him down by the lake." I had to stop thinking of that area as the lake. It had already drained lower than it had ever been during a dry season. "Or maybe someone sent them for Alice, as a sort of get-well token?"

"Oh." Mary glanced down at the flowers in confusion. "That could be. The man said it was for the miss of the house. I just assumed. . . ."

"It's all right, Mary. Alice, why don't we set them right here where you'll be able to see them without too much effort? They really do brighten up the room, don't they?"

"They're lovely," Alice responded in a tired voice. "Who would have sent them?"

"I don't know." I picked the book back up. "Perhaps Mr. Johnson? He is still in awe of your recovery. Or . . ." I leaned over. "Perhaps you have a secret admirer."

She coughed. "Now you are teasing me."

"I am not teasing you. You are a young woman of intelligence, beauty. . . ." *A certain disregard for modern sensibilities. . . .* I shook my head. I couldn't seem to silence the sound of Gregory's voice. "Any man of sense would be won over by you. Perhaps he'll introduce himself at the wedding."

Alice smiled. "Maybe you'll dance with him at the ball."

I smoothed the hair off her forehead. "If I do, I'll be sure to act the perfect lady."

Alice shook her head. "Don't be like Louisa. Be yourself."

I leaned over and kissed her head. "Deal. Now should we get back to this story?"

There was a package next to my plate at breakfast the following morning. "What is this?"

Daniel shrugged. "It was there when I sat down."

I untied the ribbon and unfolded the paper.

"What is it?" he asked.

"A book." I opened it.

"Who gave you that?"

It wasn't just any book. It was the companion to my favorite book of poetry. I flipped through the pages and the book opened to a poem near the center. A piece of paper had been stuck between the pages. I tilted the book to read it. *Gifts.*

I frowned. Gifts?

Flowers. Gifts. *Kisses.*

I stood. "Where is he?"

"Who?"

"Where is Lord Williams?"

Daniel shrugged again. "He left after we'd ensured the trenches worked according to plan. There was no reason for him to stay around."

"But is he in town? Is he coming back? Surely the project needs checking on a second time."

Daniel shook his head. "It's been three days. The project is just fine." He regarded the book as he raised a cup to his lips. "Is that who the book is from?"

"It has to be."

Daniel set his glass down without drinking. "Now, Margaret. Don't go getting your hopes up. I admit I had wondered if his coming for the draining might have brought you two back together. But he seemed wholly focused on the project. Didn't even ask after you. I'd hate to have you hurt again."

I wouldn't be hurt again. This was from Gregory.

Our father walked in. "Father," Daniel

said, "did you order a book?"

"What book?"

"The one in Margaret's hands."

I held up the book.

"What is it?"

I tilted it so he could see the spine. "It's the companion to that book of poetry."

"Oh. Yes. I hadn't known it had arrived. It came rather quickly. I'll have to send my thanks."

I lowered the book. "You ordered this?"

Father took his seat. "Yes. It seemed a shame we didn't have a copy, don't you think? Though they must have had one already on its way to town. I didn't expect it for another week or two."

Opening the book again, I stared at the word. *Gifts.*

Sinking into my seat, I removed the note and held the book out to my father. "Here."

"Oh, no," he said, lifting his hand as though to block me from giving it to him. "I ordered it for you. You liked the other one so much." He paused. "I hope it helps ease all that's happened."

I frowned. This couldn't be a coincidence. If the book wasn't from Gregory, why was the note in there?

That night, Alice and I finished the book

we'd been reading together.

"What will we read now?" She'd eaten a few bites of dinner, and it showed in her voice — still weak, but with a promise of growing stronger.

I stood and adjusted a bit of the bedcovers. "What would you like to read?"

"Daniel said father gave you a new book today. Should we read that one?"

"If you'd like." I had brought it in with me in case she fell asleep before Mary came. Mother still insisted someone be with Alice through the night as a precaution.

I opened it, intending to begin at the first, but instead turned to the page marked with the paper.

"Who knows not hope, that light eternal
    showing
The lake from which churns true love's
    fire aflowing?
It is that which makes all past mistakes
    begone.
This, the one true note, of Love's eternal
    song."

I sat back in silence. It was a poem about lakes and rivers and music. About hope and forgiveness and love. How did someone else's words fit my feelings about Gregory

442

so perfectly?

Silently, I read over the poem again. Hope truly was the eternal light. It just wouldn't die. Even when I wanted it to.

"I'm sorry I stayed out in the rain," Alice said, fingering her lace handkerchief, and I realized I'd been quiet for some minutes.

Reaching over, I placed my hand on hers. "I think, between the two of us, I have much more reason to apologize."

"Do you miss him?" Her expression was honest and a little sad.

There was no reason to hide the truth. "Yes."

"What will you do now?"

I didn't know. I had no prospects and no plans of discovering any. I would become what my family had feared — a liability for Daniel and Louisa. "I will go to the ball tomorrow and see if I can't find someone interesting. And then I will come home and relay all the details to you and let you be the judge of his worth."

Alice's tired smile was a grayed version of her former brightness. The delight that used to light her entire being seemed smothered by exhaustion.

I set the book aside. "You should rest, Alice."

She nodded and allowed me to assist in

making her comfortable. As I added wood to the fire, she said, "I have something for you. For tomorrow."

Surprised, I watched as she pulled a blue ribbon from under her pillow. "I asked Mary to pick it up for me."

I sat on the bed next to her and took the ribbon. It was the perfect shade to compliment the embroidery on my ball gown. The shade of Gregory's eyes. "Thank you, Alice. This is a wonderful gift."

"Will you wear it?"

I placed my hand over hers. "Of course I will."

FORTY-TWO

The lake was nearly gone. No more than a trickle ran down the stream the men had cut into the hill, its grooves now so deep from the draining that the shadowed water didn't even sparkle in the afternoon light.

There was really nothing left but a giant, muddy hole. No more reflection of the sky and the trees on its surface, no more promise of peace. Even the sound of the birds had dimmed.

I turned and slowly strolled back to the house. Where should I take my walks from now on? Through the fields? Into the trees? Neither idea seemed appealing.

It was a problem to be figured out later, after I survived Mary's fussing over my hairstyle for the ball. I decided to take my book upstairs to distract me so I didn't become antsy while she worked.

Retreating to the study, I had just located my new book when my mother's raised voice drew me toward the front. "Margaret, what is the meaning of this?"

She stood before the open front door, blocking the entrance of a gray and white donkey, its rather large ears stuck out from a newspaper hat.

"It's a donkey. Wearing a hat," I said lamely, knowing that if I removed the hat and added a few more folds, I could make a boat.

"Yes. I am well aware it is a donkey. What I wish to know is why there is a donkey on the front porch."

"I don't know," I replied in all honesty, though that conversation with Gregory and Mr. Lundall about winning the good opinion of someone you cared for, of winning hearts, popped into my mind.

She glanced at me. "Are you certain you have no idea why there is a donkey on our porch?"

I might have had *some* idea as to why the donkey was here, and it filled me with hope. "Why do you assume it has anything to do with me?"

Her brows rose. "Do you really need to ask that question?" Her exasperated expression asked if anything unusual ever happened around our house that didn't have something to do with me.

I tilted my head in acknowledgment of her reasoning, set my book on a nearby table, and slid past her. "I promise I had nothing to do with this. I'll take him to the stable and —"

The donkey brayed at me, long and loud. I stepped back. "I don't think he likes me."

"Oh, where is John!" My mother sighed. "Take him. Be quick, though. You need to be getting ready for this evening. I don't want to be late." She shut the door.

I stepped forward. "Come on, then, donkey." A rope hung loosely around its neck. I reached for it and the donkey backed away. I reached for it again, and the donkey turned, blocking me.

This was the most nonsensical situation. "Now, see here. I have a ball to go to tonight that I'm not looking forward to, a mother who will be furious if I'm not ready early, and . . . and I guess it's just those two things. So, let's get you settled so I can go be miserable."

The donkey's ears twitched back and forth. I took that as a good sign. "I promise to find the best stall in the stable for you until we can figure out who you belong to." The donkey nodded its head, though I doubted it was in agreement to my plan. Perhaps it was laughing at me. I think I would be laughing at me, had our places been reversed.

"I'm just going to reach forward and take a hold of this rope, though it doesn't really look long enough for much. . . ." I slowly extended my hand. The donkey's ears twitched again but the beast didn't move. My fingers closed around the rope and I stepped back.

"There, now. You're a good donkey, aren't you? Let's just go —"

The donkey jerked back, tugging the rope from my hands.

I didn't have time for this. Mary would be frantic about not having enough time for some new twist she'd just thought up. "This is ridiculous. Wait here. I'll go find John and he can deal with you." I started walking across the grass toward the barn, but stopped when the *clip-clip-clip* of hooves followed. I turned slowly. The donkey was a few steps behind me. I walked a few more steps and peeked back — the donkey was now right behind me, so close I could touch its nose.

"Well, an extra bucket of oats for you, I guess. Donkeys eat oats, right?" We padded in a single-file line to the barn, where the door stood open. "John! Are you here?"

No one answered. I pushed the door open

further and strode inside. The horses stuck their noses over their doors and the donkey bumped me, as though wanting to stay close. I patted its nose. "All right. No need to worry. Even if they are four times your size. There's an empty stall there. Let's get you settled." The door was partially ajar, and when I opened it, it appeared as though fresh bedding had been laid and fresh hay stuck out of the feeder. "Well, see? There's a nice little spot all ready —"

A white rose with a long stem lay on top of a folded letter between the stall's wooden bars. I withdrew the rose and letter. *Miss Brinton* was scrawled along the front in the same superb handwriting as the other small notes.

My fingers trembled with hope and anticipation as I broke the seal.

My dearest Miss Brinton,

It was from him. It was from Gregory. I glanced around the barn. Where was he? Why wasn't he here?

There was no noise but the stirring of the horses. Aside from me, no one was here. I turned back to the letter.

I will never forgive myself the part I played in your sister's illness, nor in the hurt I have caused you and your family. I have acted with all the selfishness and arrogance you once

449

accused me of. Yet seeing you again —

The donkey shoved at me. Startled, I fell back a step and the donkey made its way into the stall, turned a couple of times, then settled in the bedding.

Huh. Perhaps donkeys were as intelligent as people claimed.

I shut and latched the door.

Yet seeing you again has made me more determined than ever to secure your affections, if it is not already too late.

You once said you found something disagreeable only when it gave you no other choice. I know that I have given you no other choice. Yet if this poor donkey, of which I have it on good authority you have such a strong dislike, can possibly find a place in your affections, then perhaps there is reason to hope that I can, too.

Forever yours, Gregory

They were from Gregory. The flowers, the book, the donkey. Though the donkey was a little much.

I peeked back in at the animal. It lifted his head and almost purred at me. Perhaps I could get used to donkeys. Or at least this one. Maybe I'd name him Gregory. Lady Williams would be amused.

I glanced back down at the letter and the rose.

The rose. The one that had been at the lake. He'd left it for me? He must have known I would walk there one last time.

I closed my eyes and breathed in the fresh scent that reminded me of the arbor in his garden.

Perhaps Gregory would be at the ball. Surely Daniel would have invited him, after Gregory had come all this way to ensure the lake project ran smoothly. It must be why he didn't want me to see the guest list — he wanted it to be a surprise.

Tonight I would see Gregory. Tonight we would dance.

I shook my head. I shouldn't want to dance with him. I'd been a wager.

But he'd confessed his feelings had changed from what they'd been at first. He was out to secure my affections.

Foolish man. They were already his.

With a smile so large I knew I looked ridiculous, I walked back to the house, rereading the note and twirling the rose between my fingers.

FORTY-THREE

My hair was pinned up, a curl cascading over my shoulder, the white rose from the barn worked into my chignon as the only adornment. My white gown with blue embroidery was buttoned and pinned tight enough to be modest, loose enough to allow movement. My new blue ribbon from Alice was secured around the raised waistline, accenting the embroidery just as Alice must have known it would. A dab of perfume scented my wrists and neck. I was ready.

A knock at my door announced my mother's entrance. "The carriage is waiting."

I grabbed the thin blue silk wrap off my bed, its color matching my dress and Alice's ribbon perfectly, and made to leave.

My mother, looking exquisite in her own ivory gown with silver embroidered flowers sprinkled along its bodice, skirt, and hems, placed a hand on my shoulder. "James Johnson showed a great deal of interest in you the last time he visited. Perhaps tonight you might show him some deference?"

James? "Mother, he has no more interest in me than I do in him. I promise you."

"Still, a ball is a wonderful place to change opinions."

"Because that's how you and father met?"

"Many couples meet at a ball." Her gaze drifted to a place behind me. "I'll never forget when your father asked me to dance. I had no desire to dance with him. There was another man I had my eyes on. But since refusing your father meant sitting out the rest of the dances, and the evening had just begun, I accepted. I don't remember ever struggling so hard not to laugh as I did during that set. Your father kept up such a relentless conversation of witty jokes, I was afraid of snorting right in the middle of the ballroom." She smiled to herself, then at me. "You look beautiful. Let's just hope James notices."

It was not for James that I'd taken such care with my appearance. For while my mother may have met her love at a ball, my heart had been sealed in a ballroom to the north, with mirrors lining the walls and where the promise of a waltz lay unfulfilled.

We bid goodbye to Alice and joined Daniel and my father in the carriage. When we

453

descended at the Rosthorns', it was to the glow of dancing flames lighting the drive and stairway. Daniel offered me his arm and we followed our parents in to where Sir Edward and Lady Rosthorn awaited us in the hall.

Every wall sconce in the house seemed to be lit, for there was hardly a shadow to be seen. The polished floor sparkled and the wood of the staircase gleamed. I glanced at Daniel to find him anxiously glancing upstairs, his own eyes a reflection of the dancing flames along the walls.

"Louisa has not yet descended," Lady Rosthorn said by way of greeting.

"May I go up?" I asked. "She asked me to attend her."

Daniel's expression turned to a poorly-constructed mask of unconcern that did nothing to hide his jealousy.

"Of course," Lady Rosthorn said. "She would be delighted."

"My dear," Sir Edward said in a hushed warning. He indicated the stairs with a few nods of the head.

I glanced up, but there was nothing there. Had Louisa expressed a desire for me not to join her?

Ridiculous. I smiled and climbed the stairs, turning at the last moment to blow

Daniel a kiss. Louisa would soon be his, and this was perhaps that last time I could goad him where she was concerned.

As I rounded a corner, I almost slammed into a man. I took a quick step back before realizing the man before me was Edward. His hair was darker than it used to be and his eyes seemed a little more tired, but otherwise he had not changed.

It seemed obvious he would be here. Why had I not expected him?

This must have been why Daniel had flipped over the guest list. So I wouldn't see Edward's name on it.

Had he thought I wouldn't come if I had known?

Did that mean there was a chance Gregory wasn't invited after all?

"Margaret." Edward inclined his head.

It wasn't worth the effort to request he call me Miss Brinton. It would only have made him laugh and handed him a tool with which to rile me. "Mr. Rosthorn." I dropped a quick curtsy.

"I was wondering if we would see you this evening."

Surely he didn't think I still pined for him, that I would stay away because he was in attendance. "I believe it is customary for the sister of the groom to attend the betrothal ball."

He smiled. "I see you have not changed. I am glad of it."

Seeing his smile and the casual way he assumed that his being glad I hadn't changed would somehow please me made me realize just how little I cared for him now, no matter how much I had fancied myself in love with him in the past. Relief seeped through me, and also a twinge of pain — I missed Gregory. "Please excuse me. I am here for Louisa."

"Certainly, though you really needn't bother. Evelina is with her."

And he'd brought his wife, too. How awkward it would be to interrupt Louisa and her sister-in-law.

Edward offered me his arm. "Allow me to escort you back downstairs."

No. I would not take his arm. I was Louisa's friend and soon-to-be sister-in-law. She had asked me to come. I wanted to be with her. "No, thank you."

I made to step past him, but he blocked my path. "I don't believe you ever had the opportunity to meet Evelina. Shall I introduce you?"

How had I ever cared for him? How had I not seen the shallowness of his person, the calculation of his every move? "I am certain

I can manage." I stepped around him, knocked on Louisa's door, and entered without waiting for a reply.

"Louisa, I hope you don't mind," I said, closing the door, "but I —"

She stood, and every word I had meant to utter fled. Her hair hung in perfect golden ringlets around her face. Her dress gathered at the bodice and then fell in sweeping lines to the ground. The slim sleeves, slightly longer than those of most ball gowns, added the most enchanting touch, especially with her face flushed with color and her eyes sparkling with excitement.

"You look beautiful," I whispered.

"Thank you."

A lady rose from the chair next to Louisa. She had large, brown eyes and full lips, and she was much shorter than I had expected.

"Evelina, I do not believe you have yet met my friend Margaret."

Evelina — Mrs. Rosthorn — curtsied. "It is a great pleasure to meet you."

I liked the quiet sound of her voice, the small but friendly smile, the slight hesitation in her eyes, as though she was uncertain how she would be received. I returned the curtsy. "The pleasure is all mine."

Louisa grinned. Retrieving a necklace off the table behind her, she held it out to me.

"Margaret, would you help me with this?"

"Of course." I moved next to her and took the gold chain. She turned so I could clasp it at the back of her neck.

"I hope you'll go down first," I murmured. "I want to watch Daniel's expression when he sees you."

Louisa giggled.

"Don't forget this, Louisa." Mrs. Rosthorn held a white and gold fan out to her.

Once the fan was hanging around her wrist, Louisa took a deep breath and smiled. "I am ready."

She led us out the door. Mrs. Rosthorn and I hung back to allow the focus to be upon Louisa as she descended. Daniel's sharp intake of breath was audible all the way to where we stood. He dashed up the stairs, meeting Louisa halfway to offer his arm. His gallant and doting behavior was so different from how he had acted before, and as the former Lady Swenson and I followed her down the stairs, I wondered if Louisa had understood the potential within him when I had not.

Since the Rosthorns did not have a ball-room, they'd had the carpets in the drawing room rolled and removed, the settees, tables, and chairs pushed against the walls. Candelabras shimmered around the perimeter, and a giant chandelier had been installed for the occasion. Within an hour, the room was full of people mingling, waiting for the dancing to begin. I stood to the side, watching the entrance, as family after couple after family entered, all looking about them in anticipation of an evening of pleasure. But Gregory didn't appear.

When the opening strands of a minuet were played, Daniel and Louisa took their place at the head of the line.

My father appeared next to me. "May I have this dance?"

I forced my gaze away from the door. "With pleasure."

As we stood across from each other in our lines, my father asked, "How are you faring?"

I raised my brows and received a knowing look in return. Placing my hand in his, I curtsied to the front of the room with the rest of the women in the line. "Father, I am perfectly content."

"I did not know they invited Edward. I am sorry. If I had known they were thinking of it —"

"It makes no difference. Truly, Father. He means nothing to me beyond his being Louisa's brother." I dropped his hand and danced to my new position on the opposite side of the woman next to me.

My father didn't speak until we joined hands again. "I only ever wished for you to be happy."

"And I am. I will be." But as Daniel and Louisa flashed into view, I realized the small twinge of pain I'd felt earlier was no longer small.

I was aching with loneliness for Gregory. Where was he?

FORTY-FOUR

James Johnson claimed my hand for the next dance.

"You look quite lovely tonight, Miss Brinton."

"Thank you."

"We are all relieved to hear of your sister's recovery."

"Yes," I said, dropping his hand to turn. "Thank you. We are —" I glimpsed his sister Catherine along the wall, speaking with a brown-haired gentleman whose back was to me. But I knew those shoulders, the tilt of the head. My breath caught and I stumbled.

James grasped my hand, steadying me. "Are you all right?"

"Yes," I replied. I searched the wall, but neither Catherine nor the man was visible any longer. Perhaps, in my current state, I had mistaken someone else for Gregory.

We stepped away then stepped back together. "I believe we were speaking of your sister," he prompted.

"Oh, um, Alice. We are quite relieved about Alice."

"Will she be recovered enough to attend the wedding?"

We turned to dance back down the room. "I believe so."

"Your brother and Miss Rosthorn look very happy."

I followed his gaze to the head of the line, where Daniel and Louisa smiled at each other, seemingly unaware of the rest of the town's presence. "It has been a long time coming. Which reminds me, by asking me to dance you have played quite into my mother's expectations."

The dance required we shift partners. When James and I rejoined each other, he smiled. "And you still believe my feelings for you have not changed?"

I lifted my brow. "Are you going to pretend they have?"

He laughed. "No, you are quite right."

I caught sight of Catherine again. She was dancing with a man who was definitely not Gregory. "My mother will be very disappointed."

"Disappointing mothers seems to be my lot in life," James replied.

"Mine, too."

Once the set finished, I allowed James to walk me to the side of the floor, but it wasn't long before another man claimed my hand. I twirled and clapped and forced myself to smile through dance after dance. But eventually the searching and the waiting became too much. I had seen numerous men who resembled Gregory in some way, each time my heart lurching with hope and anxiety until I recognized them for who they were. Or, rather, who they were not. Gregory wasn't here. It was well past the time for people to arrive. Which meant he wasn't coming.

I slipped out the open side doors onto the terrace. There were only two more dances until supper, but I wasn't up to tolerating the crush of people, perfumes, and body odor that plagued the room. Though I wore long gloves, the night was chilly without my wrap. I inhaled the fresh air with relish, then immediately began rubbing my arms with my hands, walking until I reached the banister at the far side of the terrace, where no one would notice me if anyone also decided to enjoy a break from the festivities. I leaned on the railing and looked out over the dark lawn.

The ball was a success. Everyone was commenting on how they had never seen a couple so happy. Daniel had left Louisa's side only to fetch her a drink. The musicians were superb, the punch divine, and all the guests seemed content to spend the entire night in celebration.

I tried to ignore the emptiness inside me by studying the stars and the outlines of the trees, but the ache wouldn't go away.

I had been so certain Gregory would come.

"Margaret?"

I turned away from the balcony. "Daniel, I'm here."

He walked over and followed my example of leaning against the railing. "Louisa sent me to find you. How are you?"

"She did? I didn't think she knew anyone was in the room aside from you."

He chuckled.

"Of course, if Louisa had come out here I would have said the same about you." I poked him gently in his ribs.

"We're not that bad."

I lifted my brows high and looked down my nose at him.

"Well, maybe we are." His large, toothy grin indicated that he was not in the least apologetic about it.

"You are," I stated with decisiveness.

His smile faded. "How are you? Edward

and Mrs. Rosthorn mentioned they had seen you."

"I don't understand why everyone is so concerned with how it would be with Edward."

I turned to study the darkness over the lawns.

He placed a hand over mine. "It's all right. I understand."

I didn't understand. Gregory hadn't come. He'd given me all the signs. There was a donkey in my barn, for goodness sake. And, yet —

What if Mr. Northam had sent those things as a joke?

Was I that much of a fool? "What if I never marry, Daniel?"

He hesitated. "You are still young. I would hardly suggest putting yourself on the shelf yet."

"Twice engaged and never married."

"You will always have a home with Louisa and me."

I faced him. "A place as the unwanted burden, you mean. An expense you will never be rid of, who will never bring in income, who will only be a drain on you and your family. That is what you mean, for that is what I will become. Though I would make a good governess to your children."

Daniel suddenly straightened, his brow furrowing. "I doubt you will have to stoop so low. Know that I wish for you to be as happy as I am." He reached forward and awkwardly patted my arm, then turned and strode across the terrace to the party.

I frowned, astonished at his abrupt departure. Had my summation of what he stood to lose just become real to him? Had he only now realized the burden I would be? He had not even asked me to return inside with him. Perhaps this was his way of uninviting me to the ball.

The clearing of a throat behind me chased all thoughts of Daniel from my head. I spun, afraid of being cornered on the balcony at night.

Even in the poor light I recognized my companion instantly. *Gregory.*

He'd come! He stood only a few paces from me, his dark coat blending in with the night. I wanted to leap into his arms, be held against him, tell him how much I'd missed him.

No. I would keep control of myself. Everything I said and did would be polite. Formal. Proper.

I opened my mouth to bid him a good evening, but instead asked, "What are you doing here?" My question was no more than a strangled whisper, so faint I wondered if I had actually spoken.

He took a hesitant step toward me. "I received an invitation. Well, two, actually."

"You received two invitations?"

"Yes. One from your father and one from your brother."

My father and my brother? Daniel's actions just now — he had seen Gregory behind me. My father's words earlier — had he known Gregory would come?

"And, I believe you dropped this." Gregory held out his hand, the blue ribbon Alice had given me resting comfortably in it.

I glanced down at my dress. How had I not realized it had fallen? How embarrassing. "Thank you."

Reaching for it, I indulged myself by brushing my fingers against his hand, the thinness of my glove allowing me to feel the lines in his palm. My whole body seemed attuned to his nearness, to his chest rising and falling with each breath — did his breath hitch when I touched his hand? — to the muscles of his shoulder keeping his palm stretched before me — was it offered a fraction longer than necessary? — to the way it would take only a step to put him close enough to kiss me — did he want to kiss me? My stomach clenched while my lips tingled.

He was here. And I was still in love with him.

I placed a hand on the banister for balance. "I didn't think you would come."

"I wasn't sure how I'd be received."

"I had hoped —" I stopped.

He shifted closer. "You had hoped . . . ?"

I nodded. I had hoped. Foolish eternal hope.

Except he was here. "There were the flowers. And the book. Those were from you, were they not?"

He placed his hand on the banister next to mine. "Is there someone else they could be from?"

"We thought at first the flowers were for Alice. And my father ordered the same book. But the notes . . . Only, your cousin — it could be a mean joke. But then the donkey came. How would he know of the donkey?"

Gregory nodded. "His name is Oscar."

I shook my head. "Gregory."

"Yes?" He sounded confused.

I bit back a smile. "The donkey's name is Gregory."

Gregory stilled. "You didn't. You wouldn't."

"I did. Your mother would approve." I

468

lifted my gaze. His hair, though styled, still curled above the ear. And his face — how had I ever thought him less than the most handsome man I had ever beheld? And his eyes —

His eyes met mine, and I never wanted to move again. I wanted to stay forever with him looking at me just like that, hunger and hope and slight exasperation openly displayed in his eyes.

How I'd missed him.

"I believe my mother would approve of a great number of things that ought not be approved of, Miss Brinton. What happened to poor Oscar?"

"*Gregory* is quite content in a stall. Well, I believe he is content. I probably should have removed his hat."

"You left the poor animal with that hat on?"

"I didn't want to be late for the ball. In case...." I slid my hand closer to his.

His fingers touched mine. "In case what?"

I brushed my fingers against his. "In case there was someone here I was supposed to meet."

His hand crept over mine. "Was there?"

The tips of our thumbs touched and I grazed mine against his in a playful motion. "My mother did instruct me to pay special attention to James Johnson."

Gregory tensed. "Did she?"

"Yes. She said she wanted to see me as happily settled as Daniel and Louisa."

"And she believes Mr. Johnson would make you happy?"

"He has a strong constitution to withstand my opinions," I said, recounting Gregory's counsel to me from when we'd discussed ending the engagement. "And I believe he has enough sense to support me comfortably."

"But will he give you flowers?"

My body tingled. "Probably."

"And gifts?"

My heart began to pound. "Oh, yes. I believe Mr. Johnson would give very good gifts."

Gregory shifted nearer. I probably moved toward him as well. It didn't matter who had moved anymore. I adjusted my weight forward, awaiting his next question. *Kisses.*

"And . . . donkeys?"

I paused, letting the disappointment soak in before settling back down onto my heels. "Oh. Probably not. Which is a shame. I guess he wouldn't suit after all."

His hand clasped mine. "Perhaps there is someone else out there for you."

"Hope's eternal flame," I murmured.

"Your hand is cold."

"Is it?"

His thumb ran over the back of my hand in a gentle caress. "As a gentleman, I should insist you return inside."

"Are you not a gentleman, then?" I would never tire of looking at him, of searching his face for his thoughts, of waiting for his teasing replies.

The corners of his mouth twitched. "I believe arrogant aristocrat describes me better."

"In which case, even if you insisted, I would probably refuse to give heed."

"I suppose it then becomes my duty to warm this poor hand, does it not?" He lifted my hand to his lips. The kiss was as soft as a dream and turned my heart to liquid.

"You cannot believe," he said quietly, "that my intentions toward you were ever solely based on winning a wager."

He clasped my other hand and raised it to his lips. "From the moment Mrs. Hickmore introduced us, I was drawn to you."

"And I to you," I confessed. "That was the problem."

I reveled in the feel of my hands in his. Having him near felt so right. I wanted this. I wanted him. I needed him. I would always need him. Admitting it sent a shiver racing through me.

He dropped my hands, shrugged out of his coat, and draped it across my shoulders. The smell of him surrounded me. Every empty place within me filled to overflowing. It was too much. I swallowed, but it didn't keep the tear from slipping down my cheek.

His hand raised, hesitated, then rested on my cheek, his thumb slowly wiping my tear away in an achingly tender arch. "I never meant to hurt you."

I leaned into his hand, thirsty for the feel of him, unwilling to deny myself a moment of his touch. "You never promised you wouldn't."

"But I did promise to try not to. And I thought — I thought I could make you care for me. I thought I could make you love me."

His gaze was so full of tenderness and desire it was hard to breathe. "You did."

He lowered his head until he was staring straight into my eyes. "I love you, Margaret. I'm not sure if it happened when you looked me in the face and boldly declared, quite truthfully, that I had never been in love, or when you fell off that wall while spying upon your own family. I knew I would do anything to keep you when you showed me that letter."

"The one from Louisa?"

He nodded. "Although, come to think of it, I believe I realized I was falling for you when you couldn't keep your eyes off me after dumping me into the lake."

"I distinctly remember *not* looking at you," I protested. Unlike now, when I couldn't take my eyes off him.

He smiled. "Perhaps we'll have to agree to disagree?"

"Is that even possible?"

His hand slid under my chin, lifting it. "With you, anything is possible. Marry me. Please. This last week has been agony. I do not think I can bear to pass another moment without you in my life."

His whispered words dissolved any remaining hesitation; all my silly promises swept away. A weightless sensation steadily filled my chest, dispelling the misery that had lodged there for too long. "My lord —"

He let out a long sigh. "Are you ever going to call me Gregory on a consistent basis?"

The corners of my lips twitched as I struggled to keep a straight face. "You would prefer I call you the name of a donkey?"

"Margaret!"

His low sigh of exasperation made me

smile. I raised a hand to his chest, my fingers curling around one of his lapels. "Yes, Gregory."

My response surprised both of us. "Yes?" His voice was breathless with hope.

"Yes." Because even if there was pain in my future, or betrayal, or heartache, the promise of being with him was something I wanted more. Something I was willing to risk all of my safety for.

We stared at each other. The cold of the night disappeared. The darkness lightened. Time stopped. And then I became conscious of the sound drifting from the open door. A strain of music in three-quarter time floated to us from inside.

Gregory's lips curved. "A waltz, my lady."

I could scarcely speak. "I believe you owe me a dance."

He took my hand and slowly raised it to his shoulder. "There are numerous positions for the waltz." His voice was as gentle as his touch. He lifted my other hand to his other shoulder before his fingers slid down my arms, coming to a stop on my own shoulders. "This is one."

Then they slid down my back, encircling my waist and pulling me closer to him. I gasped.

His voice held a trace of laughter as he

said, "This is another."

"This is not a dance position. This is an embrace!"

"Not yet, it isn't." He grinned before his gaze fell to my lips and all amusement vanished. He pulled me closer and a hand slid up my back in an agonizingly slow path to my neck. His fingers slid into my hair.

"Is this another position for the waltz?" I asked, breathless.

He froze, then started to pull his fingers from my hair.

"Because," I said, curling my own hand into his hair, "I believe you owe me much more than a dance."

His smile grew deliciously wicked. "I believe you are correct."

His arms tightened, his head lowered. I lifted onto my toes.

Our lips touched, softly, as though neither of us could believe it had finally happened.

I pulled away.

Gregory lifted his head in surprise, his expression quickly turning to concern.

"That was for the wager," I said quietly. "You should have won."

He quirked a brow. "Then this is for everything else."

He lowered his head and our lips met again. His lips were warm and tender, almost hesitant. I didn't pull away. I pressed against them. I never wanted to be apart from him again.

His kiss turned insistent, possessive, as though he felt the same way. His arms wrapped tighter around me and I moved closer, wanting more, needing more, needing him, and was gratified to hear a strained murmur of my name escape him.

A throat cleared behind us. Suddenly recalling where we were, I jerked away, but Gregory tightened his arm around my waist so the most I could do was turn my head. "Why are we always interrupted?" he groaned quietly.

My father stood not far from us. "This is not quite the scene I expected to find."

My cheeks flamed with embarrassment and the lingering warmth of Gregory's lips. "Father, I. . . ." There was nothing to say, no excuse to make. Except that I couldn't be sorry.

Gregory relaxed his grip, one of his hands sliding down my arm to my hand. "Mr. Brinton, I have asked your daughter to marry me. She has consented."

My father murmured something that sounded suspiciously like, "Finally."

"Father!"

He chuckled, then stretched out his hand

to shake Gregory's. "I offer you my congratulations."

"Thank you, sir," Gregory replied, a wide smile on his face.

"Shall we return inside?" my father asked. "I believe the company is about ready for supper."

I glanced up at Gregory, who smiled down at me. "Yes."

He brought my hand up to his lips and kissed it again, then wrapped it around his arm. We paused just outside the door and he assisted me with Alice's ribbon. As he tied the bow, he leaned toward me and whispered, "It appears I need to teach you the waltz in private, to ensure we are not interrupted again." He moved back to my side and again placed my hand on his arm, his smile curving suggestively.

Excitement shivered through me. "I believe that is a very good idea."

FORTY-FIVE

18 Months Later
"Are you ready?"

The warmth of Gregory's whisper brushed my ear, sending chills of pleasure down my back.

I glanced behind us to where the back of Gregory's house — our house — stood like the backdrop to a play. The morning sun threw most of the garden in shadows, but the parts of the river that showed through the trees sparkled like mirrors reflecting the light.

Turning back, I took in the lake stretching before us, the white of the stone gazebo on the tiny island at its center barely visible through the light mist rising from the water. Low black clouds threatened in the distance, plunging the land beneath them into darkness.

He had built it for me. My family had come for the ground-breaking, including

Louisa, who was now at home for her lying-in. Alice, fully recovered in health but not quite in spirit, had stayed to watch the progress. We were all hoping that a change of scenery would bring back the excitement and easy laughter that had disappeared with her illness. She would join us for the formal ceremonies celebrating the completion of the lake this afternoon — if it didn't rain.

But this morning it was just me and Gregory.

"I'm ready."

He stepped into the boat, took my hand, and helped me in. I settled on the seat across from him as he untied the rope.

The boat jerked when he pushed off the dock, then eased into a slow, rocking movement. I leaned back to admire the way his coat bulged as he strained at the oars.

"It's going to rain," I said.

He looked over my head into the distance. "The storm is some way off yet."

Tilting my face to the rising sun, I closed my eyes.

"You're going to end up with freckles," he said.

I opened one eye and squinted at him. A breeze ruffled his hair. His tanned skin made his blue eyes even more stunning than normal, and his smile revealed a small crease — not quite a dimple — in his cheek. My heart began to race.

I shrugged, knowing it would do nothing to hide the way he affected me but hoping to convey indifference all the same. "I've already caught a man. He's bound to me, freckles or no."

Gregory frowned. "Poor chap."

Dipping my hand in the water, I brought it up quickly and splashed him.

"That wasn't very wise, Margaret, considering I'm the one with the oars."

I lifted a brow, straining for unconcern even as a smile tugged at my lips. Dipping my hand in the water again with the intent of getting him really wet, I was thrown off balance when the boat lurched to the side. Gregory yanked my hand out of the water and flicked it so the water landed on me.

"Gregory!" But I was laughing too hard to resist him.

"Looks like I'll have to distract you until we arrive at the island."

I smiled when his lips found mine.

By the time Gregory's rowing sent the boat butting against the small dock near the gazebo, the clouds were overhead, blocking the sun. I held on to the dock while Gregory secured the boat.

We made it only two steps up the hill

when the clouds let loose. The warm spring rain streamed down, soaking us in seconds. I grabbed Gregory's hand and we raced toward the gazebo.

Once out of the rain, he stood behind me and wrapped his arms around my shoulders. I leaned into him, the rise and fall of his chest at my back warming me better than any blanket as we watched the confusion of ripples dancing across the water.

"I told you it would rain," I murmured.

"Are you worried about getting back?"

I shook my head. With his arms around me, his chin resting on my head, and the rain plinking on the roof above us, I felt more safe and comfortable than I ever had before.

On an impulse, I slipped from his arms and walked into the downpour.

"Margaret, what are you doing?"

I tossed him a smile, lifted my head to the sky, stretched out my arms, and welcomed the rain.

ACKNOWLEDGMENTS

Creating a book full of characters and conflict and love involves a weird combination of daydreams, hard work, and a slew of good people. My thanks go out to so many for their support of my writing and for their guiding hands in the creation of me as a writer: Sabrina, Erin, Julie, Heidi, and Allison, for reading romance when it wasn't their thing. To Lisa Davis, for telling me I'd written a good book; Lisa Hyde, who introduced me to the world of Jane Austen fandom; and Stephanie and Julie, who unknowingly started me down this path. To my readers Kristy, Stephanie, Ellisa, Tristan, Chris, Tiffany, Jennifer, Melanie, and countless others for the invaluable feedback and cheerleading. To my Coco Ladies, for the years of support; you can finally read it, hooray. To Samantha, for the professional thumbs-up and for answering so many publishing questions, and to Jennifer, Josi, and Sarah, for the time spent mentoring me.

So many thanks go to my agent Sharon Pelletier, for taking me on and working tirelessly on the contract; to Shadow Mountain, for accepting this book that I wrote specifically for them; to Lisa Mangum, Heidi Gordon, and Tracy Keck for their help.

And, for those who not only help me write but help me to live, a special thanks. To Deb and Natalee, for the daily writing chatter and life encouragement — you two ladies kept me writing and keep me sane; thank you. To my family, Matt, Hillary, Courtney, Tijan, Craig, and my Garriott in-laws — no matter the distance, families have a special bond, and I'm grateful I share it with you. To my mother Kathryn and my grandmother Ruth, for our numerous conversations about books and for always having stacks of the best literature at hand — thank you for your examples, for who you are and who you help me to be. To my husband David, who managed while I spent hours chasing this dream and who has willingly been inducted into the world of romance — I love you. To my kids, William, Joshua, and Elizabeth, who keep asking to read my books and keep trying to write their own — ninjas and blood are coming, I promise; dragons may be a little more difficult to work in. And to

my God, for accompanying me down paths
I willingly traveled and paths I traveled
more reluctantly — thank you for your guid-
ance.

ABOUT THE AUTHOR

Though she earned degrees in math and statistics, **Leah Garriott** lives for a good love story. She has resided in Hawaii and Italy, has walked the countryside of England, and owns every mainstream movie version of *Pride and Prejudice*. She's currently living her own happily ever after in Utah with her husband and three kids. Leah is represented by Sharon Pelletier at Dystel, Goderich, and Bourret. You can visit Leah at www.leahgarriott.com.

The employees of Thorndike Press hope you have enjoyed this Large Print book. All our Thorndike, Wheeler, and Kennebec Large Print titles are designed for easy reading, and all our books are made to last. Other Thorndike Press Large Print books are available at your library, through selected bookstores, or directly from us.

For information about titles, please call:
(800) 223-1244

or visit our website at:
gale.com/thorndike

To share your comments, please write:
Publisher
Thorndike Press
10 Water St., Suite 310
Waterville, ME 04901